VAMPIRES OF MOSCOW

BLOOD WEB CHRONICLES BOOK ONE

CAEDIS KNIGHT

VAMPIRES OF MOSCOW

Blood Web Chronicles Book One

By Caedis Knight

Copyright © 2020,
Caedis Knight.
All Rights Reserved.

The right of Caedis Knight to be identified as the author of this work has been asserted by her in accordance with the copyright, designs and patents act 1988.

No part of this book may be reproduced or transmitted in any form or by any means, electronic or mechanical, including photocopying, recording or by any information storage and retrieval system, without written permission from the author.

This is a work of fiction. Any names or characters, businesses or places, events or incidents, are fictitious. Any resemblance to actual persons, living or dead, or actual events is purely coincidental.

To all the men I've banged before

(none of these sex scenes are based on you)

CHAPTER ONE

My editor is going to kill me. I don't mean rip out my throat and eat my heart whole, or whatever the hell Shifters like him do on weekend getaways in Jersey City. I mean, like, normal human *kill* me. Or fire me - which is infinitely worse.

I speed up and step right into a puddle gathering at the corner of 57th and 8th Avenue.

"Fuck!" I curse at my suede boots. These were an amazing Salvation Army find, vintage Chloe boots for twenty dollars and now they're ruined.

Just like my day.

Just like my life.

I sigh and trudge on to the head office of The Blood Web Chronicle, my soon-to-be-former place of employment. To the naked eye, it looks like a mid-level insurance firm - grey carpeted hallways, IKEA-esque cubicles, the smell of cheap coffee wafting from a too-plain kitchen, and yogurts with people's names on them. But under the generic disguise, it houses the Blood Web's most widely read news source for the international English-speaking Paranormal community.

Ten million unique hits a month. That's how many Paras read my work.

But I'm not going to get a big head about it, mainly because it's hard to feel smug when you can barely pay your rent. The second reason is that no one knows who I am. My investigation pieces on The Blood Web Chronicle are anonymous, like everything else on there. The Blood Web, our little Para corner of the human dark web, is where my kind goes to fill their day-to-day needs - from female Werewolves looking for someone to share their litter with, to Vamps searching for custom blends of blood, or Fae seeking to buy ancient artefacts.

It's also where you go to buy Para sex toys. But that's beside the point.

As a reporter I fill the Para curiosity need. The desire to know what's happening in our underworld; what the truly wicked Paras are up to and how to stay the fuck away from them. So, if like me, you expose murderous clawed, winged, and fanged monsters for a living, then anonymity is key.

As I walk toward Midtown, I play my usual game to make me relax. A little game I like to call - *What's he lying about?*

That man nursing a six-dollar latte and chatting to his girlfriend at the cafe is lying. *But what's he lying about?* Probably about where he was last night. Or about how he feels about her sister.

I pass a hot dog cart owner lying to his customer. *What's he lying about?* Probably the freshness of his buns. Or maybe, like his makeshift sign, he's lying about having the best dogs in town.

I pass a man lying to his child and hear the last bit of his sentence. "The zoo if we have time..." *Liar!* He has no intention of passing by the zoo even if they do have the time.

I play a couple more times but it's all boring run of the mill stuff. The game has worked though, I'm feeling a little calmer. Thoughts of who might murder me because of my job have all but escaped me.

You see, I get this *ping* feeling when someone is lying. This tiny, insignificant ability makes me a *Verity* - the lowest type of Witch. That's not my self-esteem talking, I'm literally ranked as a low Witch. Witches usually make money from their special gifts, but all I can do is conduct lie detector tests (not hugely useful seeing as human law enforcement doesn't know us Witches exist). In theory, I can tell people if their partners are cheating, or if their employee is scamming them, but none of that is going to pay a regular salary.

Which is why this investigative reporting gig is a lifeline - something interesting to do with my gifts that pays the bills. And, of course, I did with it what I've done with all my lifelines.

I cut it.

The Blood Web Chronicle head office isn't hard to find if you know what you're looking for.

1. Cross the 20's midtown marble lobby.

2. Ride up to the 32nd floor.

3. Walk down the hall to Smith, Burley and Browne Accounting.

4. Waltz in, because the buzzer doesn't work on purpose.

5. Sign in with our receptionist Joan, who will do everything in her power to deter you from using our accounting services.

But, if you're as curious and persistent as a man named Garth, who a few years ago made it all the way past our receptionist on his search for an accountant, you might end up sitting across from Jackson Pardus. Jackson is my editor, and on his desk, he has a fake name plaque and fake business cards to match. He will be your last hurdle as he will straight up tell you that we are fully booked for a year and send you away.

The only problem with using Jackson as a final deterrent is that you *will* want him to do your taxes. You'll look at all six feet of dark Shifter muscle peppered with conceptual tattoos and you'll think, *"Fuck it, do my taxes a year late. What do I care?"*

I'm thinking about this, five minutes later, as Jackson contemplates me across the table. He's frowning at me. When he's this mad a vein in his neck always pops up. It reminds me of the dick vein on a Snickers bar.

Great. Now I'm hungry *and* horny.

"What the hell are you smiling about, Saskia?"

God, I love his English accent. This isn't helping. I wipe the involuntary smirk off my face and my editor's frown deepens.

"I sent you to investigate an unregistered Paranormal brothel in Queens and you did *what?*"

I'm definitely not smiling anymore. I can feel the scorch of his glare on my skin, the heat of what I did. Stabs of stupidity and self-hate start a picnic in my brain.

"But there were Shifter girls there," I say. "Locked up. Scared. They were young."

He looks back at me with a flicker of empathy. His brown eyes are speckled copper when he's happy, but they glow yellow when he's not. Like right now. Jackson's never told me what kind of Shifter he is, but I'm pretty sure he's a panther, maybe, or a cheetah. Whatever, something feline and powerful. I have a little notebook at home where I keep a running tally of what I think he might be based on different titbits of information he let slip. Which is next to nothing, because for a man who founded the largest whistle-blowing platform in the Para world, my boss is ridiculously private.

I'm guessing there's a good reason for that. But I doubt I'll ever know it.

Jackson's eyes are still shining gold against his dark skin, and I find myself leaning in closer.

But his empathy drains a second later.

"You're meant to *write* about traffickers, Saskia. You expose them. You don't burn their headquarters down."

"Right, because when rich criminals get exposed by the media they are immediately stopped." I roll my eyes.

"We are not law enforcement. You have a job to do."

"The victims were *your* people," I murmur, trying to fish that empathy back up. I'm telling the truth. There were Shifters there, of all ages, imprisoned and sold to god-knows-who. It's disgusting how many sick people like to keep young Shifter girls as pets. Write it up and walk away? Nope. I waited until the sun was a promise in the sky, until the place was nearly empty save for the owner, and I burned it to the fucking ground.

Yeah, it cost me a pretty penny to have the place evacuated just in time by some Shifter cronies I paid off. Thus, furthering my inability to pay rent. But it was fucking worth it.

I shrug. "They deserved it."

"*You don't get involved*," Jackson growls. "You report on it."

"And what good would reporting on it do?"

"That's an odd thing for a reporter to say." He pauses and rights his fake name plaque. "What do you want to do, Saskia? Call the police?"

I breathe loudly through my nose. Police are for humans, they don't know about our world – and those who do work for us.

"I wish the Paranormal world had a governing body," I mumble, not for the first time.

Jackson laughs. "Yeah, OK. I'd like to see that. Witches have their Mage Association and Wolves have their pack hierarchy, but beyond that everyone is free to do whatever the fuck they want. You think anyone or anything is powerful enough to tell a Vamp what to do?"

I shrug. He's right. There's no democracy in the Paranormal world. Everyone is out for themselves.

"This is why *we* exist, Saskia," Jackson continues. "To shed light on situations where Paras get out of hand. We are not vigilantes – but our reports will direct those who are to those who deserve punishment."

I bite my tongue. I know I'm in the wrong, but surely my boss can see the justice here. Surely, he understands why I acted knowing no one else would.

"Saskia, this isn't the first assignment you've fucked up on. I know I hired you because of what happened in LA with the Sirens, you're ballsy, but that doesn't mean you need to destroy *everything* you touch."

Ouch.

"They all deserved it," I mumble.

Jackson sighs heavily, and it makes me feel like a child.

"Look, I probably shouldn't have put you on this assignment, considering what happened with your sister. I get it. Missing girls are a trigger for you."

He's musing out loud, but what he's really doing is ripping my heart out through my mouth.

"Don't bring Mikayla into this!" I shout, my voice hoarse.

Jackson's face twists in regret and I look down. Shit. I'm really not doing myself any favors today.

My pregnant sister disappeared eighteen months ago and no one has been able to find her – not me or Jackson with all of his Blood Web connections. Not even my mother and her powerful network at the Mage Association. Jackson's right - places where people are held against their will, unknown to the world and tucked away in the darkness, are very triggering for me.

How many of those Shifters disappeared one day?

Is that why I burned it down?

No, I burned it down because they deserved it. That's what I tell myself.

With every report and every cry for help I hear on my missions; my first thought is always that it's linked to Mikayla going missing. That today I'll find my sister.

Jackson breaks the silence.

"Look, Saskia, you're one of our most talented reporters."

Ping. He's lying.

"I want to keep you on, I really do. But I can't."

This time it's the truth.

"No," my voice is still a croak. I steady it. "Please Jackson, I *need* this job. Just give me one more chance. *Please*. One last chance."

I need the pay. I need the resources. I need The Chronicle if I'm ever going to find Mikayla.

"Your last mission *was* your last chance," he reminds me.

"Just one more. Please, pleeeeeease." I beg and pout, doing my best impression of a gender-bent sexually mature Oliver Twist. "PLEASE."

Jackson frowns and reclines in his seat, giving me his famous James Bond stare. "Saskia." He sighs. "I have to prove to my superiors that you can come through on a big story."

Even though Jackson founded The Blood Web Chronicle he still has superiors. He needed the money to get the stories out, so a large part of the newspaper belongs to wealthy Paras who have added it to their investment portfolio. Though Jackson has never told us who they are.

"I can do this, Jackson. I promise not to let you down. Give me any story. I'm on it like white on rice."

What the fuck am I talking about?

He sighs again and pulls a photo out of his drawer, sliding it toward me. Two men – one dark-haired, one blonde, and beside them a larger than life brute clad entirely in a white Adidas tracksuit.

Who the fuck are *these* guys?

I pick up the photo.

"What's the deal?" I ask.

"I got a tipoff about a Vampire crime ring run by these two brothers."

I point at the huge guy. "I'm assuming Mr. Adidas is their security?"

Jackson nods. "The brothers have fostered a mini-empire, no surprises there, but their workers keep disappearing or dropping dead. It's your job to find out why. Preferably without burning anything down."

Vampires. That's a new one – but I'm sure I can handle them. "Sounds simple enough. Where do they live?"

Jackson swallows, making that sexy neck vein throb again. "Russia."

This time *I'm* the one who swallows hard. I knew I was in the doghouse, but *this*? Russia is beautiful, sure, but it's also a cozy hub of Paranormal lawlessness. The stories you hear coming out of Moscow make the New York and London Para communities look like the Amish.

I don't know any of my newspaper colleagues, except our receptionist Joan who is the closest thing I have to a friend. Chronicle journos stay secret even from one another, but that doesn't stop me trying to palm the mission off on them.

"Why don't the other reporters want it?"

"*Why?* Because it's in RUSSIA, Saskia. A Paranormal community with little regulation, high crime rates, arctic temperatures…"

"You sure I'm the right woman for the job?"

"No, but no one else wants it. It's this or the door. You'll need to pack something warm."

His eyes catch on my black leather mini skirt. Another

Salvation Army win. I uncross my legs and bite down on my bottom lip.

"Oh, Jackson," I purr, "Don't look at me like I'm a fresh can of big cat food."

He rolls his eyes. "Please. You know Witches' blood tastes like piss to my kind."

That's true. My blood is poison to Vamps, Werewolves and Shifters.

"I didn't say it was my *blood* you wanted to taste," I say with a grin.

Jackson clears his throat. Flirting with him is kind of a hobby of mine, but only because I know nothing will ever come of it. As usual, my editor brings it back to business.

"Saskia, this assignment is your last chance and my last offer. Take it or it's over."

"OK. No problem. I can do it, Chief."

He smiles. "You can, because you're also the only reporter we have who speaks Russian."

"I speak *every* language. It's one of the reasons you hired me. That and my pretty face."

He rolls his eyes. Only Jackson and my direct family know about my lie-detecting skills and linguistic abilities. My truth-seeing abilities also somehow translate to me "seeing" the truth in each language, and therefore understanding and speaking them all. This is the only thing that sets me apart from most other Verity Witches. Although a lot of the time I stick to speaking English and just listen. Playing dumb is the quickest way to the truth. You learn a lot more when people think you're not listening.

Jackson slides a file over to me along with a thick envelope.

"Most of the intel is here, and all your documents are inside. Everything else you need to know is encrypted on your Chronicle account. I'll get you on a flight to Moscow tomorrow."

As I grab the file I bite back a smile. Jackson is always one step ahead, knowing full well I'd take this job. I head to the door.

"And Saskia," he calls out. "Don't worry about anything, you'll be fine. We'll keep you safe."

I feel the *ping* of a lie but I smile anyway.

"I'm sure you will," I lie back as the door shuts firmly behind me.

CHAPTER TWO

ucking Moscow?! I hate the cold. If Jackson wanted to punish me he could have just bent me over the desk and given me a spanking like a normal person. Not sent me into Slavic perma-frost. I snort-laugh at my own wit and consider sending him a text saying that, but I stop myself just in time.

There's flirting at work, and then there's sexual harassment. It's me doing stupid shit like that which had him nearly firing me today.

I march home, my legs wobbling on boots with heels that weren't meant for walking and zip up my coat higher. New York in January is cold, and once again I question my life choices as the bitter wind blows under my short skirt and penetrates my tights.

I could have based myself in Hawaii, but no. Never mind, Hawaii has too many Siren nests for my liking. I cringe. Fucking Sirens.

Guess I better get used to vaginal frostbite, because a Moscow winter is going to be a lot worse than a New York one. My phone vibrates in my pocket and a knot squeezes my guts. Maybe Jackson changed his mind about giving me one last chance?

Don't let it be Jackson. Don't let it be Jackson.

It's starting to rain and I take shelter under the awning of a hipster cafe.

It's not my boss texting me, it's my mum being annoying as ever. I scan her message and sigh.

A new MA leader will be in New York next week, so I've set up tea at the Ritz for you both. Her name is Luisa. Tuesday 2pm. She's a good contact to have. Wear something appropriate.

Yup, sounds just like mama dearest. No *'hello, how are you?'* No *'what time are you free?'* No, *'are you free to meet with a bitchy MA rep who will try and guilt you into joining us during an awkward tea at the too-swanky Ritz that you can't afford?'* And that last bit - *'wear something appropriate'* is basically code for 'don't wear one of your usual peasant outfits.'

There are no questions with Mom. No consideration. Just stage directions and bids to get me to join her institution. Her power-hungry cult. It was the same way before my prodigal sister disappeared, and it's only gotten worse since.

"Can't. Don't have time. Busy with work."

I text back. She doesn't actually know what I do (it's better that way). She thinks I'm an accountant.

Her reply is near-instant.

"Make time."

When she gets her teeth into something, she's worse than a coyote with a cadaver. Jeez, who died and crowned her queen of the Witch-bitches? Actually, only one person would have to die for her to be the literal reigning queen of the MA, so maybe that's where she gets her infernal bossiness from. Or maybe it's from the fact that she's a super powerful Witch. I roll my eyes and put the phone back in my pocket before braving the rain. I try to forget about my mother as I zig-zag expertly around puddles and hop on the train to Queens, but she is a constant nagging presence in my brain.

Join the MA. Stop wasting your life. Wear something appropriate.

My mom's not the same type of Witch as me. I'm just a no one with nothing to offer but boring truth-seeing powers. But my mom, she sits on the board of the Mage Association in Barcelona, which means traveling the world giving talks to other top Witch covens and being in the Paranormal spotlight. The MA is the biggest, most powerful, collection of Witches in the world. They are also the governing body of the Witch world via ancestral rights. Some would disagree with their outdated matriarchal governance, but it's hard to argue with a rich organization armed to the teeth with some of the world's strongest Witches. Those who argue don't get far. Witches outside of the MA, like myself, usually try to keep a low profile. Not that it stops them from hounding me - they can afford to hound me for the rest of my life.

Well, Mom can stand in line, because the queue of people waiting for me to get back to them is longer than my tab at the Irish pub down the street.

I get off the train, suddenly feeling determined and unshakeable. There's only one place I need to be Tuesday at 2pm, and that's in a snowy underworld full of Vamps!

I reach my apartment block, a brownstone that's not as shabby as most buildings in Queens, but where a broom closet will still cost you as much as a Mormon compound in Ohio. I falter as I spot an unpleasantly familiar silhouette through the frosted glass pane of the main door.

Seriously? Is this day out to finish me off or what?

"Saskia!"

I try and walk past him like I haven't heard his booming voice, but he steps in front of me.

"Number-thirteen! You deaf or something?"

I roll my eyes. At this rate they're going to fall right out of my head. "I'm your tenant, Giovanni, not a prisoner."

Giovanni D'Angelo is an Italian mafia wannabe, except he looks like an aging extra from Grease. He has slicked-back hair, wears tight white t-shirts, and always keeps a cigarette tucked behind his left ear. He smells like Axe body spray.

He's also my landlord.

"Where's the rent, *Saskia-from-number-thirteen*. I'm getting tired of your shit, *porca miseria!*"

He does that – curses in Italian even though the idiot has never left New York. I've met his parents, they're third generation Italian and none of them speak the language, but he thinks it makes him sound tough.

"Tomorrow, Giovanni. I promise."

This time *he* rolls his eyes and lets out a big puff of air. I'm normally a pretty good liar, but this time it doesn't work. Figures, since I've been using the same line for two months now.

"I told you, call me Gio," he says. I can see the wad of gum in his slimy mouth, rolling around like a dead white slug. "You got until tomorrow or I'm putting your shit out on the street, *capeesh?*"

He wipes his hands on his jeans. That's another thing he does. I don't know if his hands are sweaty or dirty or if he just likes rubbing himself. I don't want to know.

I shift my purse to my other shoulder. It's heavy and contains a thick jiffy bag stuffed with documents. I haven't looked inside yet but going by past jobs it will contain a fake ID and a stack of one-hundred-dollar bills.

I dip my hand into my purse and into the envelope, flicking through the pile of bills. It feels like enough cash to last me a couple of weeks. I don't plan to stay in Moscow a couple of *days* let alone weeks, so I'm sure I can spare a few bills.

VAMPIRES OF MOSCOW

"You're going to leave my things alone," I tell Giovanni, giving him my sweetest smile and handing him three bills. "Here, a down payment."

My landlord screws up his nose, his dark unkempt eyebrows meeting in the middle.

"Three hundred dollars? You fucking kidding me, kid? This doesn't even cover a week's rent."

He's getting on my last nerve. I have so much shit to do before flying to Moscow – it's time to work my magic.

"Maria at number nineteen doesn't pay *any* rent, Gio."

His face goes a couple of shades lighter and he wipes his hands on his jeans.

"Of course, she does. Everyone in the block does."

Ping! Lie.

"And she's a relation of yours?"

"Yeah, Maria's my Italian cousin." More hand wiping. More lies.

Two months ago, when he brought the young woman to the block, all big eyes, long limbs and beautiful long hair, he told everyone she was from his *Nonna's* village near Naples. Maria doesn't speak English, but she's not Italian either, she's Brazilian. My ability to understand every language comes in handy when I need to know what the hell my neighbors are arguing about.

She also has a big juicy bun in the oven.

"You're going to take my money, *Gio*, and you're going to wait until I get back from my vacation for the rest. Otherwise I'm going to tell your wife you've got a *bambino* on the way with a beautiful non-paying Brazilian tenant on the top floor. *Capeesh?*"

"That's bullshit! You wouldn't dare." Except it's the truth and he knows I *would* dare. Plus, he's just confirmed my suspicions and given me at least another month to fix my finances. My powers may not be great, but they're pretty damn useful when it comes to pinning down cheaters. I pat him on the shoulder, give him a wink and head on down the hall.

My apartment is small, messy, and smells of old lavender candles and last night's pizza that's still in its box on the coffee table. It's a hovel most of the time, but it's *my* hovel and I love it.

I grab a slice of cold pizza and munch on it as I look under a pile of Salvation Army finds for my laptop. I really need to get my shit together and pack but that will have to wait, it's time to look into the Volkov brothers.

Sitting at my desk by the window I access the Blood Web. Our hidden corner of the dark web makes the human section look about as scary as a Harry Potter subreddit. Near impossible to find unless you know exactly where you're going, the Blood Web is where we share our news and how we connect. And the Paranormal community's favorite news source just happens to be us, the Blood Web Chronicle.

Every day the Blood Web Chronicle is translated into twenty-seven languages with millions of readers worldwide. Ha! Suck on that, New York Times. Although I won't get to stay so cocky if I don't get to the bottom of this Russian crime lords thing quickly. If I get fired I might have to go work for a Paranormal gossip mag. I'm really not interested in writing about how Paul Rudd might be a Vampire because he hasn't aged a lick since *Clueless*.

Need to focus. I can't fail again.

Two clicks and my screen's full with the faces of Russian brothers Konstantin and Lukka Volkov. I let out a low whistle as I read a bunch of articles about them dating back five years. Jackson was right, they're not to be messed with. They have lots of sticky fingers in lots of questionable pies. Konstantin owns a number of businesses, and his brother just looks like the definition of shady.

But what Jackson *didn't* tell me is that they're pretty easy on the eye too.

Konstantin is the oldest. He's not what I expected. Sharp suit, neat hair, lean frame – he looks more like a well-groomed art dealer than a neck muncher. Everything I read only describes what he's done since being turned, I have no idea who he was back when he was human. Looking at him I'm guessing he was already important.

His brother though, he's a different story. I zoom in and laugh out loud. Lukka's hair is messy with bleach-blonde tips, he has tattoos up both arms that go right up to his neck, and in one photo he's standing bare-chested in front of a bright yellow Lamborghini, wearing baggy purple Supreme trousers and an empty purple gun holster. *A fucking gun holster!*

If I wasn't so desperate to keep my job, I'd swerve these two like a New Yorker swerves wide-eyed tourists – but actually, I'm getting kind of excited. Nerves and excitement feel the same, right? It's only your brain that decides what to run away from and what to run towards. Maybe, if I keep telling myself that, I'll begin to believe it.

I delve a bit deeper, clicking through the links which get darker and more mysterious the more I find out. They're definitely not short of a Russian ruble or two. Between them they own a huge construction company, five bars, a restaurant, shares in a small shipping line, and…top of the cliché board…they run Moscow's most elite Paranormal strip club. The Black Rabbit. Classy.

I try to find the club's location and fail.

A yellow stripe flashes at the bottom of my screen. Jackson has sent me an email. It's the link to my plane ticket and information about where I'm staying.

I zoom in on the booking info. Cheap motherfucker has got me a one-way ticket. Clearly, he's not going to splash out on a return until he knows I've survived the mission. That's probably not his actual reasoning. Jackson cares, but he only books a return when the story is complete or when a reporter needs immediate removal. According to him it's so that he doesn't need to keep changing them, but us Blood Web reporters go missing a lot - so he's not stupid either.

It's time to prepare myself.

I reach for my purse, pull out the fat envelope and empty it onto my desk. Jackson may be a pain in the ass boss with a ripped body too fine to waste behind a desk all day, but he *does* think of everything.

I take each item out one by one. Money, about two-thousand dollars in cash, paperwork to get me into Russia and a passport. As far as fakes go this passport is not the best, but Jackson has all of our fake documents bewitched so that not a single border person would ever deny us entry. The Chronicle has a Witch for hire and she can do things like that, not that I've ever met her. Like everything else in his life Jackson keeps his special employees and their information to himself.

That arrogant pussycat! He must have known I'd say yes before I did and has been planning my mission for days. I'm not sure if to be flattered or insulted.

I flick through my fake passport and my somber face stares back at me. Apparently, according to my boss, I have a 'nondescript' face which helps when I'm under-cover. With my bland brown hair, average height and weight I could be from any western country, aged anywhere between eighteen to thirty. It's useful to be so normal looking, because not being a head-turner gets you into more places than a pretty face and a perky butt. Sometimes I dye my hair or change my blue eyes to a different color with contact lenses, depending on the mission, but I don't have time now. The Vamp brothers will have to take me as I am.

Then I notice the name on the passport. Brenda? Jackson has called me fucking *Brenda*? I guess that's part of my punishment for pissing him off earlier.

I stomp into my bedroom, pull the suitcase off the top of the closet and start throwing clothes into it. I have nothing appropriate to wear in the snow. Last time I wrapped up warm was four years ago when I went skiing in Vermont with my mom and sister. Yeah, it snows in New York, but that doesn't mean I own any snow boots.

A heavy stone drops into my gut at the thought of Mikayla.

Her photo is displayed by the side of my bed and I bite my lips together as I pick it up. I'm not going to cry; I've done enough of that over the past year. Mikayla was everything I'm not - beautiful, a powerful Witch, smart and loved by everyone. *IS everything I'm not*! I have to stop thinking about her in the past tense. She's missing, not dead.

My sister is the reason I became a journalist, and why I spend every night on the Blood Web trying to figure out where the hell she is. I doubt the answer is in Moscow, but I feel that with every bad guy I take down I get a little closer to finding her and figuring out who took her.

I throw her photo into my bag, along with all my jeans, jumpers and boots, and go pour myself a vodka. I don't know much about Russians, but I *do* know how to drink like one.

CHAPTER THREE

Moscow's second-largest airport, Domodedovo International, is emptier than I would have expected, save for the grumpy immigration officers that pepper the wide halls drinking coffee from their own mugs and earning their keep with scolding glares. There are no vending machines, no cafes, no posters. The immigration line itself is a nightmare and I thank the Witch gods for JFK being my home hub and not this hell hole. When I finish with the thirty-five-minute immigration wait I find myself staring through the thumb-printed glass box at a blond girl in a swamp green uniform with gold military epaulets.

The stoic immigration officer glares at me. I read her name tag - *Svetlana*.

Svetlana would be pretty if she wasn't scowling so deeply, and if her uniform wasn't a military shade of puke.

She doesn't look up from my fake passport when she speaks. "Reason for your visit?"

Investigating a couple of Vampire brothers for the world's most prominent Paranormal publication.

"Tourism," I quip. "I want to see those Easter egg church tops everyone talks about. Oh, and the Red Square!"

Talk fast, talk a lot. That's the trick. Then they think you're dumb and have nothing to hide. Not that I have to convince her because Jackson's bewitched visa-less passports work every time.

She says a couple of sentences to her booth mate, Stepa. He laughs. They're making fun of me. Specifically, my enthusiasm. It reminds me of getting a pedicure at the Vietnamese salon down the street from my Queens apartment – not that I ever let them know that I know what they're saying about me. Knowledge is power and all that. Plus, they give the best gel manicures, I'm not about to ruin that just because they think my outfits are ugly.

The officer stamps my passport reluctantly.

"I hope you enjoy your trip."

I feel the *ping* of a lie as I make my way through the revolving bars and out to baggage claim.

Mercifully, my bag is intact. I go through customs and am instantly assaulted by a throng of men yelling in various languages about their taxi services. I ignore them and order an Uber outside by the parking lot. That's how Jackson trained me - *trust companies, not people.*

The Uber driver is nice. He offers me gum and water. He also lies a lot - about his history, about not being married, about having been born in Moscow. The *ping* of his lies breaks up the monotonous techno pulsing from his stereo. I ignore all of it because I'm too busy watching the strange city flash by. The streets are huge, spanning six-car lanes. The traffic is thick. There are Christmas lights everywhere, even though it's January. Giant opulent Christmas trees preside over giant roundabouts. The driver explains to me that Christmas is celebrated in January in Russia.

It's snowing lightly, and when it hits the traffic it turns to smog-kissed mush beneath the wheels. It's not exactly pretty, but it is enchanting.

It takes nearly two hours to arrive at Strogino, an area 20 minutes outside the city center. The buildings are massive soviet blocks, derelict and covered in too much smog to be able to identify what color they were originally meant to be.

My Uber driver asks for my phone number. I smile sweetly and tell him I don't have one, hoping all Russians are going to be this easy to lie to.

I put in the code for the building, which Jackson included in my file, and I cross the pissed-stained stone lobby. The tiny elevator takes me up to the eleventh floor as I curse Jackson's cheapness. My Airbnb host is already waiting for me at the door as if I were an inconvenience.

Regina is a stout woman in her eighties, with a scowl that could rival any immigration officers. Her grey hair is back-combed and hair sprayed so hard it looks like a helmet, and she's wearing a cable knit cardigan tightly buttoned over a thick woolen dress.

"No party, no men, no business," she says, showing me around the tiny carpet-covered apartment.

I'm pretty sure she just told me I can't hook out of her flat. That or I can't run a business here. I imagine running a start-up from this shithole and giggle at the thought.

She shoots me a "no giggle" look.

I glance around the shabby accommodation. Christ, even the walls are covered in carpet. I guess it helps with insulation but it's like I've rented an abandoned carpet section of an Ikea. In the corner, there's a small kitchen with an encapsulated balcony. I glance out, the sheltered balcony is covered in jars of pickles and tomatoes. A few Soviet-looking Christmas decorations dot the apartment - a wooden cut out of a blue Santa, a glass astronaut bauble, a bowl of dusty tinsel. It's shabby, but considering I didn't even bother decorating my own apartment this Christmas it's kind of nice.

"When move out, clean up, make fridge empty too," she barks in broken English, before waddling away from me towards the stack of sheets by the single bed. "I clean everything before you come."

Ping. Liar, liar, babushka scarf on fire.

I nod along. "Is there a restaurant nearby? Or maybe a shop?" I ask.

The Aeroflot meal wasn't enough to keep me full. I can feel my stomach rumbling with displeasure.

"No," she says simply. Then she gives me the keys, puts on a coat that at least six animals had to die for, and leaves.

I unpack my suitcase and decide to venture out.

The cold truly is biting. It's like an invisible force, licking its way up my body in search of any exposed flesh. I feel the frost in the spaces between my gloves and coat, the cold whipping across my chin, and stinging my eyeballs like a balaclava made of ice.

The *pelmeni* meat dumplings I find at a chain restaurant down the road don't taste too bad, and I chase them down with a shot of cranberry *nastoyka*- homemade vodka. It stings worse than the cold, but I need liquid courage for what I'm about to do next.

After a quick Google maps search, I find the darkest courtyard in between the compound-like buildings of Strogino. I light a menthol. I'm not a smoker but I've learned on assignment that a lit cigarette disarms people and makes you more approachable. I take a seat on a rickety bench, pretending to sway drunkenly side to side. My head *is* swimming a bit from tonight's choice of beverage, but I don't feel as bad as I make myself look.

It's not long before someone finds me. The first guy is a drunken slob who tries to hit on me, but I flash him the knife tucked in my boot and he walks off spewing a stack of Russian profanities. The second man is a construction worker who asks me if I'm OK.

The third man to find me is tall with a sickly pallor. And he's exactly who I've been waiting for.

I pull out another cigarette and he lights it for me. From the outside, he might look like a regular guy trying to pick up a girl on a park bench, but I know what to look for. The glint in his eye is too sharp, his movements too fluid, his lips too pale.

"You speak English?" I coo, pouting seductively. "I'm lost. My hotel is somewhere around here." I giggle like an idiot for emphasis.

"What is the name of your hotel, beautiful girl?"

Vom, vom, vom.

"It's called hotel *Stolichniy*," I lie.

He smiles. "I know it!"

Ping.

"Come," he offers his arm. "I will take you there."

Ping.

I sway again for emphasis, then take his arm, pretending to stumble drunkenly as he leads me to a nearby underpass. He doesn't even wait until we are fully submerged in the shadows before whipping me around and slamming me into a brick wall.

Ouch...and rude!

His fangs flash white in the moonlight before they sink into me.

I've always wondered what this would feel like and why humans fantasize about being fang food. The stranger begins to drink fully and greedily and I flinch at the sweet sting. I wonder if he can taste the cranberry *nastoyka* in my blood.

Less than a minute has passed and I'm wondering whether my clever idea was actually a really fucking stupid one. Nothing is happening except the fact I'm beginning to feel really faint. Then, with a grunt, the creep pulls away heaving and spewing. I smile and straighten up as the Vampire spits the last of my blood onto the pavement, then starts coughing violently. He falls to his knees, clutching his stomach, looking up at me in shock and revulsion.

Maybe I'm not so stupid after all.

I take my sweet time regaining my senses before looming over him.

"Witch blood," I smile. "Otherwise known as Vampire poison."

My blood gurgles at his throat as I push him down with my heel, his cheek grazing the sidewalk.

"It's lethal to your kind, especially since this greedy little piggy drank about a gallon of it."

The Vamp writhes and clutches his stomach, managing a few Russian curses.

I dig my heel deeper into his sinewy chest, fetching a small vial from my back pocket and holding it out to the Vamp. Jackson isn't the only one who thinks ahead.

As the daughter of a top-ranking Witch I've learned a few things in my time. The main lesson being 'don't talk to strangers', and if you do - always be prepared. In this case I brought with me a potion that only the MA knows exists.

I shake the glass tube in his face. "Without this antidote, my blood will kill you."

He reaches for it but he's weak. My shoe dirties his white shirt as I press harder against his chest. "I need information. I'm looking for a Paranormal strip club called the Black Rabbit. You're going to tell me where it is."

He mutters more profanities while reaching out for the vial.

"*Now!*" I growl.

"You fucking bitch. I've never heard of this club," he grunts.

Ping.

Silly little liar.

"Fine. Enjoy dying." I take a few steps before he calls out to me.

"In Dedovsk," he coughs. "There's an abandoned church. It's there!"

I wait for the ping. It doesn't come. *Bingo!*

I set the vial down in the snow twenty feet away and glare at him.

"Crawl to it."

Then I turn and run. I don't know how long it will take him to get to the antidote, but I'm not about to wait and find out.

After five minutes of running around the grey jungle of high-rise blocks and abandoned squares I hide in the shadows and order another Uber.

"Dedovsk?" the driver says, staring at the address that just popped up on his phone.

"There's an abandoned church there."

He gives me a look like I'm high. Then shrugs and starts the engine.

Money is money.

The church looms against the charcoal black sky and I stare at it through the car window. Even though I was being facetious when I told the immigration officer that I was here to see the Easter egg-style church tops, they really are a magnificent sight. This one is shining iridescent gold, like a bunch of Christmas baubles sparkling in the night.

I get out of the cab and the driver shakes his head at me as I stand there, gaping at the old building like a tourist that really does want to see it all.

"Stupid girl," he mutters before taking off.

From this angle the church certainly looks empty and abandoned, just like the Vampire said, but there's so much more lurking in the dark corners. I can practically smell the Paranormal activity in the bitter winter air. As quietly as I can, I make my way through the bushes and snow to the back of the church, peering at the locked doors and high fences. Then I spot what I'm looking for. A stairway leads down to an underground hall and at the bottom is a doorway blocked by a large man. A bouncer. I instantly recognize him as Mr. Adidas from Jackson's intel folder. I must be in the right place.

I walk down the steps towards the bouncer. With muscle mass *this* unreal he has to be a Shifter. Perhaps a bear. And I'm ninety-nine per cent certain that this bear bouncer is guarding the entrance to the Black Rabbit.

As I step up to him his hand shoots out in front of me like a massive log, making the thick gold chains at his wrists clink together.

"No," he says in a voice colder than the night air.

"I'm just trying to have some fun," I reply innocently in English.

"No," he says again.

What is it with Russian people and the word no?

There are voices behind me. Two businessmen walk right past me and enter the club.

"Hey! How come *they* can go in?" I whine.

The bouncer ignores my question, and it suddenly dawns on me. He's waiting for a bribe!

I reach into my purse and pull out the equivalent of a hundred bucks in rubles, pushing the money into his hand. That should be enough to treat himself to the latest Adidas tracksuit.

He takes it then laughs at me. Actually laughs.

I laugh along and try to walk around him but his hand remains an iron bar blocking my entrance, the promise of violence in his eyes. Black eyes, just like that of a bear.

I take a step back.

"Only clients and dancers," he says in broken English.

"I'm a client," I say.

"No female clients."

"Well that's not very gender forward."

His gaze shifts and he looks angrier now. I don't think I'll be winning him over with my jokes. Or my looks.

A faint growl escapes his throat. "Go, or I hurt you."

He's not lying, plus I'm smart enough to walk away. Vamps and Shifters might find our blood poisonous to consume, but that doesn't mean this Shifter can't bear-claw me to ribbons just for fun. I'm not willing to risk it. Tomorrow is another day.

I look back at the church.

If I'm getting into that club, I'm going to have to do it undercover. And something tells me I'll be much more convincing as a stripper than a businessman.

CHAPTER FOUR

Finding sleazy lingerie in Strogino is proving to be harder than expected. I don't know much about strippers, but I *do* know I can't fake being a pole dancer wearing my ratty pink underwear from Target. Neither will I get passed the bouncer looking like I did yesterday.

I have a great ability to detect lies, but I also have a sixth sense when it comes to finding sleaze. By late afternoon I give up looking for a lingerie shop and eventually track down a sex shop instead, where I find a cute pink wig, a burner phone with Russian SIM (amazing what you can find in sex shops out here) and an outfit that looks more like a complicated puzzle of black straps than underwear. I struggle into it, do my hair and make-up as dark as I can, and strap on a pair of skyscraper glass-looking heels.

It's showtime!

"You can't come in," the bouncer grunts in Russian, three lines appearing across his thick cratered nose as he screws it up in disgust at my wig. Either that or he doesn't like my perfume. Maybe I should have scented my neck with manuka honey instead.

If he recognizes me from the night before he doesn't let on.

"I'm a dancer," I reply in English, knowing full-well he understands me.

"For audition?"

Auditions?

"Yes," I say, giving him my biggest smile and a wink for good measure. He sneers again – although this time he lifts up his arm and lets me through. *Yes!* I finally get to check out the club and do some digging.

"No," he barks at my back. Ah, Russia's favorite word again. He points to a door at the side of the club marked 'STAFF ENTRANCE' in Russian. "That way."

Fuck! I didn't actually intend to audition. I was hoping I could slip past him into the main club, walk around for a bit, blend in with the other dancers, and ask a few questions.

The door to the staff quarters is heavy and creaks loudly as I peer inside. It's a long dark hallway lined with doors. Each door has a number on it, and through their glass windows I can see girls moving against poles. No, not moving.

Dancing. Gliding. Flipping like stripper gazelles.

This is where retired Russian gymnasts go to die, once they are over sixteen and too old for the Olympics but can still make money bending their beautiful bodies into impossible shapes. Also, the outfits they are wearing are more *Agent Provocateur* and less back alley sex shop. I adjust my cheap wig and swallow down the panic rising in my chest, watching them through the windows. *Shit!* Whatever these women are doing I can't move my body that way. I have to get out of here and into the club.

I look for an exit but grind to a halt as a woman appears out of nowhere.

"You." She's so beautiful I'd have assumed she's one of the dancers, except her elegant fingers are wrapped around an iPad. She hands me a form written in Russian. "Go to room nine and start dancing. We will be watching through the window. If you get picked you fill this in."

I nod, doing my best impression of looking like I'm not completely terrified. Not only am I going to have to dance, but I'm getting judged too. Great.

The room is at the end of the corridor and I'm guessing it's where the private dances happen. I think they call them champagne rooms, but maybe in Russia they're vodka rooms.

I take a deep breath and take off my coat.

You're on your own, I tell myself as I pull the straps of my ridiculous outfit into place. I didn't expect to actually have to dance in it. The thick strap has been riding up my lady garden the whole way here.

Just remember the dance classes you took, I tell myself. *It's like riding a bike. Channel your inner Jennifer Lopez.*

Mikayla bought me pole dancing lessons for my eighteenth birthday five years ago. It was all the rage back then, all about working on your balance and core muscles – although it's a lot easier pulling yourself up a metal pole wearing sweatpants than a leotard made of tight fabric strips cutting into every inch of your body.

I step up onto the tiny stage, wobbling on my stupid shoes. There are mirrors above each pole, but I try not to look at myself. I'm not as skinny as the other girls, and my breasts are real so they actually bounce, but if I can somehow balance on these heels and look sexy without falling on my ass, I might just get away with it.

The pole is freezing. The whole room is. I blow into my hands and rub them together, but it doesn't help. Despite the cold, my hands are wet with sweat. So sexy. I attempt a simple run up pirouette and slip.

I try again, this time swinging around and twisting, managing to flip upside down. Not bad. I still have it. I shimmy around the pole and do a dip and slow rise while trying not to think too hard.

Channel Jennifer Lopez, Saskia! Channel Jennifer Lawrence, Jennifer Garner, Jennifer Love Hewitt. Hell, any Jennifer will do, just stop looking like a damn caterpillar trying to hump a twig.

I do another pirouette because it is the least embarrassing thing I've done so far.

"One more time!" a voice bellows from the corner of the room.

With a gasp, I lose my grip and drop to the floor. My pink wig has slipped, obscuring my view. I hadn't heard anyone enter the room. Whoever it is spoke in English, but with a strong guttural accent. How did he know I speak English? I adjust my wig, scramble to my feet, and repeat the pirouette. The man steps out of the shadows, sits down on the red plush sofa surrounding the mini stage, and lets out a low laugh.

I know that face. Lukka. The younger of the two Volkov brothers.

Well, that was easy. I thought I'd have to look for him but now he's right here, right in front of me. Be careful what you wish for, because sometimes the Witch gods throw it straight into your lap. Or in this case, your lap dance.

Back on my feet, I lean against the pole, hands above my head, trying to act nonchalant. Although in my brain I'm still screaming CHANNEL A JENNIFER.

"Keep going," he urges.

I move my hips slowly from side to side, buying some time so I can take a proper look at him. I'm not ready. I thought I had at least a few more days to snoop about before I had to confront the bosses.

Up close, Lukka's different from what I imagined. When I looked at photos of him on the Blood Web I thought he was a clown, the clueless younger brother of Konstantin, who is clearly the real brains behind the organization. But Lukka is no clown, he's more like The Joker. Foolish, but somehow frightening in his foolishness.

A terrifying joke.

I watch him as he watches me. The man is never still, his lips twitching into a half-smile then falling again into a murderous expression, revealing a glint of metal on his teeth. His painted fingertips keep moving like they're looking for something to grab hold of. He's wearing a hockey shirt and sweats, with an empty gun holster strapped over his shoulders like a backpack.

What the fuck?

His fingers are laced with tattoos that look like a child's doodles and his arms are lined with them right up to his neck. There's even a tattoo on the side of his left eye and at his temples.

His hair is shaved all the way around the sides leaving a spiky blonde mop at the top and he's wearing sunglasses - even though it's close to midnight and we're inside.

Suddenly he stops smiling and his whole-body stills.

"Keep dancing," he commands.

He pulls down his glasses to stare at me and I gasp. His eyes are white, as in *all* white, except for two tiny pinpricks in the center like splashes of blood on a hotel bed sheet.

My mouth is dry, making it difficult to swallow, but I can't look scared. Nothing turns a Vamp on more than fear. If I can't get into the club by sneaking around then I need this job. I need to make Lukka my new boss if I'm going to get to the bottom of this investigation and out of this fucking country before winter ends.

I give him a slow smile and what I hope looks like a coquettish nod of my head, then wrap my hands around the icy pole. With another swing I hoist myself up and flip my legs over my head, facing down so my nose is inches from the floor.

"Nice," he says.

No smile. He pulls a dark bottle out of his pocket and takes a swig.

Who the fuck has bottles tucked into their sweats?

He wipes away a faint dribble of red from his full lips, and I count at least seven gold rings on his fingers. I wonder how far down his sweats the tattoos travel.

"Name?"

I've memorized my fake ID and my back story.

"It's Bren...Brandy. You can call me Brandy."

Well I can't exactly use Brenda anymore. Brenda is *not* a stripper name.

"You're American," he says. It's not a question.

"Yes, how did you know? From my accent?"

"The shoes."

I'm still upside down, my vision getting blurry as I hold my stance. It's hard enough throwing yourself around a pole, but it's even harder when there's no music and a Vampire is watching you like you're a rotisserie chicken in a kebab shop window. What's wrong with my shoes? I flip myself over and try to memorize every part of him – from his face and body to his clothes and tics.

"I only accept best dancers at Black Rabbit and you..." he rubs the tip of his tongue against his left incisor. "You can't dance."

No ping, he's not playing. I'm fucked, but I don't say

anything. I've learned the hard way that the less you say the less bad things happen to you.

Straightening up he steps closer to me. Then he leans forward, so his forearms are resting on the stage.

"Where you from?" he asks in broken English.

"New York."

"Why Moscow? You like cold?"

He looks at my chest as he says that. My nipples are already hard from this freezing room, but his snow-white stare is making them go even harder. Lukka's weird marble-white eyes travel to mine and lock in place like he knows what I'm thinking.

"Sit," he murmurs. "Let's have conversation."

I sit on the mirrored floor, my legs splayed out behind me like a frog, then I crawl forward so we're face to face. I may not be able to dance, but there are other things I can do to get guys like him on my side.

"I'm running away," I say under my breath, making him inch closer. "It's so much easier to be who you really want when you're far away from home."

It's all part of my act, but then I realize with a jolt I also kind of mean it. I think of my mom who's always nagging at me, and Jackson giving me this one last chance, and my sister who I miss like a severed limb, and I realize running away is exactly what I do at The Chronicle. I like the Blood Web, I like the anonymity and constant travel. Because I like to forget. And tonight, tonight I get to be a pole dancer in Moscow called Brandy, and Brandy doesn't have a painful backstory. She just has a story to chase. And a white-eyed lead.

My lead licks the corner of his mouth, sending a flutter of fear across my chest, past the lace at my stomach, and straight down to where the strap is cutting into me.

"Who you want to be, Brandy?" he asks, running a finger

across my forehead and brushing strands of neon pink hair out of my eyes. He's so close I can feel his breath on my cheek. It smells of champagne and blood.

"I just want to have fun," I say. He strikes me as the kind of man who likes fun. And I'm right, because he's giving me a lopsided smile which feels like ice cubes being dragged down my spine.

I lean closer and then, faster than humanly possible, he takes my face in one hand, my chin grasped between his thumb and fingers, and gazes at me.

Normally I would pull away, of course I would, but I have to see where this leads. I have to gain his trust. He traces his finger down my neck, his face coming closer to mine. His lips look soft and maybe it wouldn't be so terrible if I…

I yelp out in pain as I feel a light scratch across my neck and jerk away from the sting. His bone-white eyes snap to mine as he touches the scratch and pulls his finger away, bloodied. Slowly, like he's daring me to stop him, he puts his finger to his mouth and sucks up the drop of my blood like he's sampling fine whisky. Immediately he spits it out, screwing up his face in revulsion.

"Hello, little Witch," he coos.

Fuck, he knows what I am! I'm so screwed.

I scramble backward but Lukka grabs my ankles and pulls me towards him until my legs are dangling off the stage.

He smiles, his fangs shining in the murky light of the room. Then he pulls off my wig and throws it aside.

I do everything I can to keep my breath steady. Does it matter that he knows I'm a Witch? It's not like he also knows I'm a reporter. Then again, he might really hate Witches.

"Why are you at the Black Rabbit, Brandy?" His voice is stone on stone, his face still.

I don't answer. He shakes me. "Who sent you?"

I improvise.

"You, Lukka. I wanted to meet you. I've heard a lot about you."

I aim right for his vanity. If that doesn't work I'll have to get the knife from my coat and aim for something else. He pulls a strap on my outfit and lets it snap back into place.

"Flattering. And your skills?"

"My what?"

His face is inches from mine, his gold chains cold against my chest. I'm vaguely aware that he's between my legs.

"Don't play dumb American. What Witch powers you have?" he whispers in my ear.

"I'm a Verity Witch. I can tell when someone is lying."

He steps back and I stumble forward as if he's just released me from his snare.

"That is all?" he asks.

Even though the room is freezing cold I feel my cheeks burn with the same humiliation I've had to endure all my life. Saskia, daughter of one of the world's most powerful Witches, but all she can do is detect untruths. Pathetic.

He seems to be losing interest in me by the second and I can't let that happen.

"I also speak a lot of languages, including Russian," I add hesitantly.

"We go meet my brother," he says, picking up the bottle of what I'm now sure is some poor bastard's blood, and holds it up in the air.

"*Na zdorovie*," he cries, wishing me good health before taking another swig. "Kostya might be interested in your services."

Konstantin? "As a dancer?" I stutter.

Lukka tips his head to the ceiling and laughs, long and hard.

"Alright! I get the point," I snap.

"Sorry, but you dance like shit, little Witch. Like old drunk babushka on moving bus."

He cackles. The look in his ghostly white eyes is positively crazy. Then just as quickly his face turns serious, contemplating me with a tilt of his head.

"But Kostya will not like you like this. No. Kostya likes everything fine and perfect. Your wig is cheap." He picks it up off the stage floor and throws it behind him. Then he snaps another one of my straps into place. "Your lingerie is cheap too," he says.

I roll my eyes. "At least I don't look like the Russian version of Vanilla Ice."

What? I'm supposed to sit here half-naked while he insults my dancing *and* clothing?

He takes off one of his thick gold chains and loops it over my head, muttering *"ice ice baby,"* as he twists it round and round until it forms a noose around my neck. Then he pulls at it, gently yanking my head towards his, and kisses my cheek, staining it with the blood he was drinking.

He leans back and looks at me for a long time.

"There. Much better!" he beams madly. "Let's go. I have better lingerie in my car."

Lukka heads for the door and reluctantly I follow.

Better lingerie in the car?!

CHAPTER FIVE

Lukka leads me into the basement beneath the church. I haven't seen the club yet, but the basement is modern and bright. A stark contrast to the dilapidated church exterior. There's a large neon-lit parking lot full of expensive cars with tinted windows, and three holding cells in the corner that turn my legs to Jell-O. I tell myself the brothers probably keep them down here for the kinky folk or the drunken brawlers - but I have a feeling that's not the case.

Lukka unlocks his car, a Lamborghini so sleek and flat you wouldn't think anyone could fit inside it. I don't bother suppressing my snort.

"I've never seen a car like this before," I say, stifling a laugh. What is that expression about money not being able to buy you taste?

"My cars are my pride and joy," he replies in Russian. "I don't let anyone near them."

I make a face, but he's enjoying the subject matter so he keeps talking. In my line of work keeping people talking is key.

"I have surveillance on them twenty-four-seven," he explains. "High tech nanny cams for my precious babies. If anyone so much as breathes on my cars I get a phone alert and I kill them. Easy."

I don't know if to laugh or shudder, so I tease him instead. "But a *yellow Lambo*, Lukka? Is that so you can blend in?"

He grins and I can see his fangs.

"Big and yellow," he says. "Reminds me of the sun I never get to see."

The unexpected poetry of his words catches me off guard and I stop teasing him. It's no secret that Vamps don't get to see the sun. They don't burst into flames or start to sparkle like in the movies, they just get really sun sick and die a long and painful death. For them the sun is like cancer, it gets inside their veins and slowly eats them up from the inside out. I guess Hollywood Paranormals decided that sun cancer wouldn't look as pretty on the silver screen as teenagers dipped in glitter.

I slide into the passenger seat, hyper-aware of my exposed flesh catching on the black leather. The rope-like lingerie cuts into my skin and I can already feel welts forming on the inside of my thighs. Dressed like this inside such a ridiculous car I look like I'm about to film a high-budget porno.

The garage door opens and I'm suddenly pushed back into my seat by the violent speed of Lukka's driving as he swerves out of the lot and flies out onto the icy road. Minutes later we've merged into the traffic. Lukka is swerving in and out of spots, cutting cars off and cackling at their honking as he races across the highway.

"Isn't someone going to stop you if you drive like this?"

Lukka smiles. "I don't have plates."

He takes a sharp right onto an exit ramp and speeds down

it. I say a silent goodbye to everyone I've ever loved and dig my nails into the side door as if that would stop me from flying right through the front glass on impact.

He catches the sight of my fingers, paling against the car door, and slows down a bit. Traffic lights reflect in his ghostly stare like Christmas lights.

"Do you wear contacts?" I ask.

"No."

"How come your eyes are like that? I've not seen eyes like that on a Vamp before."

"Once upon a time I asked a little Witch to curse me so that I would see the world less clearly."

My mouth drops open and I shut it quickly. "Why would you want to see the world less clearly."

He thinks for a moment then accelerates, making my heart drop into my lacy underwear.

"Like you, little Witch, I've seen a lot of the truth. Too much." He smiles, revealing pearly-white fangs laced with gold. "The lie is always sweeter."

I don't know if he's spouting poetry or pure bullshit, but I haven't heard the *ping* of a lie. In fact, I haven't heard a single *ping* since I met him, which must be some kind of record for any man - Paranormal or not.

The car jerks to a stop.

"We're here," he says.

I look up and gasp. We're outside an exquisite building, eight up-lit columns supporting an ornate triangular roof like something a Roman emperor would live in. This has to be the famous Bolshoi theatre.

Lukka is out of the car like a flash. I swivel round and watch him pop his trunk and fetch something from it. Then he opens my door and dumps a corset on my lap, a leather skirt, and a fox fur coat.

Are we going inside the theatre? I sigh. And *this* is his idea of appropriate attire?

Practically having to dislocate my limbs I try my best to slip the clothes over my lingerie with dignity. Not an easy feat in the small front seat of a Lamborghini. If Lukka's brother likes his girls classy, like he said he did, then Konstantin's not going to be any more impressed by this outfit than my stripper number. Personally, I'd kill for some yoga trousers and a jumper right now.

My spindly heels wobble as I follow Lukka into the theatre. The security guards nod at him as we pass indicating that they know him. We walk up red velvet-lined steps and I stare up at the golden frescos on the vaulted ceiling. Why are we here? I thought I was on my way to meet his bigshot older Vamp brother. Surely Lukka doesn't think Konstantin meeting me is so important we need to interrupt his night out at the theatre.

We walk down a long, gilded hall, away from what looks like the main entrance to the theatre, and stop by a door. There's the dull tone of gentle piano music coming from the other side. Lukka knocks but doesn't wait for an answer, pushing open the door quietly. We're in a dance studio, and my ridiculous outfit is staring back at me from a multitude of floor to ceiling mirrors. I feel myself turning red.

At the far end of the giant room, twelve dancers are at the barre practicing. Impossibly slim women with long necks and pointed toes and a few male dancers scattered among them. I had no idea dancers trained this late in the evening.

Then I see him and my breath hitches.

Konstantin is one of the male dancers – shirtless and wearing nothing but tight beige leggings and ballet shoes. Even from this distance, I can see the muscles rippling over his broad back.

Lukka laces his hands around my waist and pulls me

towards the far corner of the room where there's a bench. Nobody stops for us. The dancers continue to stretch and take turns to dance one by one as we watch, the pianist striking each gentle note on a white piano the color of clean bones. But all I can do is stare at Konstantin.

I'll be dammed. A ballet dancing Vamp. Wait until I tell the guys at The Chronicle about this.

It's time for Konstantin's solo and he breaks away from the group, jumping through the air as elegant and light as a sparrow. His muscles pulsate, contracting like corded knots across his stomach and chest as he twists into impossible positions.

If someone had told me last week I'd be watching a Russian crime lord ballet dance I would have laughed. But there's nothing funny about the way Konstantin moves. It's extraordinary.

Fingers extended, toes pointed, he takes a giant leap and with one twist goes from sparrow to prowling lion. The sheer force of his body, the power rippling beneath the surface of his skin, is intimidating. I feel Lukka's milky gaze brush over me, judging my reaction. Does he want me to be scared? Impressed? Or uninterested?

I should stop staring, I want to, but I can't.

Konstantin's solo dies down and the spell is broken by the applause of the other dancers. He remains humble and gives a small bow, waiving their praise away. With a tinker of chatter the other dancers grab their towels and bags and make their way out of the studio. As they leave, they pay us little mind. I assume they've seen Lukka and his girls before - or maybe they know better than to look over at the white-eyed crazy younger brother.

We are now the only ones left in the studio. Just me and Moscow's most infamous Vampire brothers.

Lukka rises to greet Konstantin as I follow awkwardly,

the sound of my cheap stripper heels invading the silence of the studio as they click nastily against the polished wooden floor.

Konstantin wipes his brow with a towel. "What are you doing here, brother?" he says to Lukka in Russian, pushing his wet brown hair back. His tone is civil and dry.

Konstantin's cheekbones are sharp, his eyes chocolate brown like his hair. My eyes dart from him to Lukka. You would never think they were brothers - not in a million years.

Lukka gestures at me. "I found a little Witch at our club. She was trying to dance."

Trying to dance? Rude!

Konstantin turns to me for the first time then back to his brother. "And that's worth interrupting my practice?" It's clear he doesn't expect an answer.

Lukka's fingers loop around his empty gun holster like it's a comfort blanket.

"She has truth-seeing abilities. I thought she could help us get to the bottom of the missing cargo with Varlam."

This earns me another look from the ballet dancer, more interested than the first. The way Konstantin holds himself, his stillness, the power of his presence renders me silent. I find myself with nothing to say.

"I will tell you three truths and one lie," Konstantin says to me. "You tell me which is which."

I nod.

"I have drained a prima ballerina. I pray sometimes. I miss my mother. I think Lukka is a bad driver."

I gulp. "You don't miss your mother."

Lukka bristles at the driving comment yet seems unsurprised by the rest.

Konstantin looks impressed. "No," he says. "I don't miss that woman one bit."

I don't reply and I try not to think about the drained ballerina, the image of blood on a fluffy tutu. The idea of Konstantin praying is equally disturbing. I've never heard of a Vamp praying, but then again, I've never heard of a ballet dancing Vampire. I wonder how many other surprises he's hiding.

"Lukka is right," Konstantin says. "I may have a little job for you tonight."

Half an hour later we're in a private room at Sakhalin, one of Moscow's most elite restaurants. Sitting across from us is, from what I've gathered, a Georgian crook and his cronies. The waiter's hands shake as he sets a plate of fancy crab before me. I don't blame him for being scared. The Vamps and I look like a criminal sandwich; I'm sitting between the brothers, Konstantin to my left and Lukka to my right. Opposite us is the man who was introduced to me as Varlam. He's covered in so many scars his face looks like a Picasso portrait. Varlam is flanked by men even less pretty which he hasn't bothered introducing to us. They too look like death incarnate.

Konstantin downs an oyster then fixes his attention on Varlam.

"So, our shipment went missing?" he asks, his tone amicable.

"Yes. It's gone," Varlam replies.

He's telling the truth. I've been instructed to squeeze Konstantin's thigh when I sense a lie. Not a plan I'm super comfortable with, but I don't exactly have a choice.

Konstantin keeps his eyes level. "What do you think happened to it?"

"Stolen." Varlam sits back nonchalantly and lights a cigarette. I look around. Are they allowed to smoke in here?

One of Varlam's cronies is looking at me as if he's wondering if I'm also on the menu. I feel so exposed in this fucking outfit. If I ever get back to the safety of my soviet Airbnb I'm going to burn everything I'm wearing.

Konstantin takes a swig of champagne, his movements as elegant now as they were in the dance studio earlier.

"Do you know who stole the shipment, Varlam?"

"Of course not!" the man scoffs, looking offended.

I feel the lie on my skin and squeeze Konstantin's thigh lightly.

His lip curls. "Varlam," he says, his voice a gentle purr. "Did you play an active role in my shipment being stolen?"

Varlam shoots up from his seat indignantly. "How *dare* you! I won't sit here listening to this filth, Konstantin! You insult my honor! I take brotherhood very seriously. You know that."

Konstantin's voice is low. "Answer the question."

The scarred man huffs. "Of course not!"

I squeeze Konstantin's thigh, harder this time, and his hand shoots beneath the table and clasps mine, pulling me closer.

Varlam's voice is rising in front of us with further indignancy, but every word he says is just lie upon lie.

I squeeze Konstantin's hand in mine and he nods at his brother. Only a small nod, one you'd hardly notice if you weren't looking for it. Yet in an inhumanly fast blur Lukka grabs the fish knife beside his plate and jumps up.

Konstantin leans over to me, his lips brushing my ear. I feel the heat of his breath against my cheek.

"Close your eyes, sweetheart," he whispers.

I obey.

My hair whips in my face at a sudden movement beside me. A slashing sound, followed by two more. A grunt, a gurgling sound, and a thump. Something wet and warm sprays across my chest.

I clench my eyes tighter, my breath coming in sharp pulls. Vomit is rising in my throat at the smell of blood and I swallow down the bile. I'm doing everything I can not to move a muscle as I feel Lukka settling back by my side.

My eyes flutter open but I don't look up. I will never look up.

I attempt to steady my breathing and wait for my heart to stop racing. In, out. In, out. A stream of blood trickles slowly across my white plate, like a river of scarlet sauce that's been drizzled over my crab.

"Don't worry, sweetheart." Konstantin's melodious voice pulls me from my trance. "We'll order you another one."

CHAPTER SIX

"You want me back at the club tomorrow night?"

I'm standing outside my soviet apartment complex with Lukka, the sky behind him turning an inky shade of lilac. It won't be long until the sun is up, so technically it's *tonight* I'm working.

Lukka doesn't seem concerned with the imminent sunrise.

"Ten o'clock, tonight and every night after that," Konstantin drawls, leaning out his brother's car window. A light sneer passes like a shadow over his chiseled face as he looks my building up and down. The flicker of displeasure is gone as quickly as it came.

"Every night?" I stare at him. If he thinks he owns me now, he can shove that entitlement right up his tutu.

"You work for us now," he says. "Isn't that why you auditioned? Because you wanted a job?"

"You want me to dance?"

My inner thighs are still smarting from the straps of that ridiculous outfit I've been wearing. Both brothers burst out laughing at my suggestion and I bite my bottom lip to stop myself saying anything else I'll regret.

I look down. There's blood on my hands and I'm itching to wash it away. In fact, I want to wash the *entire* night away. Varlam's gaping mouth, startled in death, flashes before my eyes and I shudder.

I'm vaguely aware of Lukka watching me. He leans back against his sun-bright car, his golden jacket clashing garishly against the paintwork. Not that I can think of any outfit that would look *good* next to his music video prop car.

Konstantin's phone rings and he takes the call as Lukka's white eyes narrow on me. "How are you feeling, little Witch?"

I shrug. "Fine."

"You can tell when people lie, but you're not so good at lying yourself."

He gives me a look that makes my stomach ache with a mix of sadness and fear. His hands are still lined with dark brown streaks of gangster blood drying in the folds of his palms.

I had Lukka pinned as a clown, a fool, a rich spoiled brat who likes blood and bling. Yet tonight I watched him kill three men with a blunt fish knife, then continue to eat his crabs gleefully, cracking their panzers wide open and howling at his own jokes while the fresh blood stained the tablecloth and dripped down to his elbows.

Lukka Volkov is no fool. He's dangerous. Very dangerous. With his poetic lines and whitewashed eyes, it could be easy to forget that.

"Varlam wasn't a good man," Lukka says. "He won't be missed by anyone."

Is he justifying his murder to me? I swear his tone has gone quieter, as if he doesn't want Konstantin to overhear. I shrug, feigning disinterest.

I haven't commented on their murdered business associates. I stayed silent the entire time, picking at my dinner and trying not to vomit up my crab. If that was a test, I think I passed. Varlam's death is not my story. Besides, it's not a secret to anyone that Vamps are murderous, especially crime lord Vamps. My job is to find out why a good chunk of their employees are disappearing, and a select few are showing up drained and dead.

Surely if the brothers were hungry for a human snack they would do it elsewhere, not on their home turf? Konstantin strikes me as the 'don't eat where you shit' type.

As if in answer to my thoughts Konstantin finishes his call and looks at me. His gaze is penetrating and I shift uncomfortably. He doesn't have a speck of blood on his crisp white shirt.

"Wear something nice tonight," he says. "If you have it."

God, my mother would love him. I'm starting to think Konstantin Volkov is a real pain in the ass.

"If I'm not dancing, then what will I be doing?" I ask.

"You will walk around," Lukka says, the night light glinting off the gold on his teeth.

"Walk around?"

Konstantin sighs from the front seat. "Recently we have had problems in the company - missing cargo, theft, other far nastier troubles," he says.

Like employees dropping dead? I don't voice my question, better to keep my cards close to my chest for now. If Konstantin also wants to get to the bottom of the deaths and disappearances in his company then I will get to the truth even faster.

"As far as my staff are concerned you will be the new hostess at the Black Rabbit," he adds.

"And in reality?"

"In reality you spark conversations, listen, find lies and report back to us. It's easy work."

"We pay you, we feed you, you keep your mouth closed and ears open," Lukka adds.

Charming.

"And my legs?" I snap. "Would you prefer I keep them open or closed?"

I'm referring to their bullshit proprietary behavior, but the dig is wasted on them. Konstantin looks at his phone and Lukka winks at me.

"What you do with your legs is of little concern to me, darling," Konstantin says. "As long as you keep them far from my podiums. Black Rabbit clientele has very high standards."

I glare at him wishing I could shove my blood down his throat and watch him struggle like I did with the other Vamp.

"You want the job or not?" he asks calmly.

I swallow and nod. "Fine. I'll be there."

What choice do I have? I need the story and this is the best way to get it.

Lukka pulls something out of his pocket and steps towards me. It takes everything I have not to flinch.

"For you," he says. Something shiny swings between his bloody fingers. A gold necklace with a small charm hanging off it.

He steps behind me and I shiver as he places the chain around my neck, his cold hands brushing against my collarbone. I can smell the blood from here, his iron heady scent mixing with the smell of...watermelon bubble-gum? Seriously?

"Never take it off. These necklaces keep all our girls safe," he whispers into my ear. Bewitched jewelry? So, the Volkovs also employ Witches for hire? I make a note of that.

I can see what the charm is now - a tiny black rabbit with a diamond for a tail. The club's logo.

"Now, little Witch, you are an official black rabbit," Lukka says, his voice low and his breath tickling my ear. "But don't run, little bunny. The bear will always find you in the woods."

Does he always speak in riddles or does he just enjoy being confusing?

I hold my breath. My back feels cold as he returns to the car and gets in the driver's seat. Maybe I should say something. Something smart or funny or brave. Instead I just stand there as Konstantin gives me a nod and winds up the blackened car window without saying goodbye. His brother makes up for it by blaring his horn three times as he screeches out of the courtyard, narrowly avoiding a neon-clad street cleaner.

●

Sleeping during the day has never been easy for me, and after last night my dreams were soaked with blood and crab carcasses. I've only managed to snatch a few hours of rest and I'm in no mood to deal with fucking psychopathic Vamps tonight. I just want to get to the bottom of these murders and go back to New York so I no longer have to sleep on a mattress made entirely of broken springs and unidentifiable stains.

"Only clients or dancers," the bouncer growls as I stomp up to the club entrance.

I hold up the rabbit pendant hanging on a thin chain around my neck. It works faster than any magical charm as the bouncer removes his arm out of my way without looking at me and I step into the old church entrance and into something resembling a foyer. Bubbles like cheap champagne start to pop in the pit of my stomach. Finally! My chance to check out the infamous Black Rabbit club.

OK, *this* wasn't what I was expecting.

Actually, I'm not sure what I was expecting from a church converted into a strip club by two Vampires - but nothing could have prepared me for the unholy glittering space that unfolds before me.

That's the thing about the Paranormal world- the outside never reflects the wickedness within.

CHAPTER SEVEN

Many cities like to make the loud claim that they don't sleep, but when Moscow says it, it's telling the truth. After interrupting a midnight dance rehearsal and dining at three in the morning I'm no longer surprised to find the club merely in its prep phase at 10 pm. Bartenders bustle around and beautiful dancers stretch out their limbs on the podiums; practicing their moves in preparation for the big night ahead. Regretfully, I rip my gaze away from a stunning woman clad in less fabric than you would require for a doily and take in the room.

Actually, it's less of a room and more of a grand church vestibule leading into an ornate hall.

The original architecture of the building is still there - dipping arches, dilapidated columns, and marble flooring, but the interior has been transformed into an over-the-top shrine to all things sin. Where pews once were, there are now clusters of red quilted-velvet booths forming half-moons around small private stages. Each stage is crowned with tall silver poles, jutting out incongruously against the church's flaking crown moldings and blank-eyed statues.

Golden icons, speckled with age, hang on the walls. All of them desecrated with black bunny ears and painted blindfolds where their eyes should be.

I turn a full circle, squinting in the dimness. The stained-glass windows have been boarded up on the outside, but inside they are backlit in vibrant shades of pinks and reds and dark purple. The only other light is from giant mismatching crystal chandeliers hanging over our heads. The church is laid out over three floors, two of them balconied - I guess where the choir once sang. The main level has a bar running along it glowing an electric blue. I can see the shadows of staff setting up for the night.

Although some of the paintwork on the walls is faded and peeling, the ceiling remains gilded in gold with frescoes of golden-haloed saints staring down at the naked dancers.

I watch a girl dance in the corner. I hadn't even noticed the music playing until now. She's slight with small hips and elfin features. Her cheekbones could cut glass and her hair is black and straight, hanging down to her waist. There aren't many clients in the club yet, but Mr. Adidas the bouncer is watching her intently. I don't blame him. She's pretty and delicate, but at the same time quick and strong. As I watch her something flickers just above her hairline, something long and furry. Ears? I blink and they're gone.

Up on one of the smaller balconies is a DJ spinning tunes. She notices me and nods over in time to the music.

My eyes wander to another dancer, a flaming redhead. Her outfit is made up of strips of purple and green lace, her large breasts completely on display. Her stare is locked on a point in the distance as she holds onto the pole behind her head and slowly slides down it, her legs parting as she reaches the bottom then snapping together again quickly. She jumps up and launches herself at the pole. Then, mid graceful flight, she flickers briefly into a shift, and her back arches and blooms with green and purple feathers. Like an iridescent rainbow, her bright plumes become an armor spreading across her skin. A second later she spins around the pole and the feathers disappear.

A parrot Shifter in Moscow? I've heard about them south of the equator but never thought I'd find one here. Parrot Shifters are rare and a desired spectacle in the Paranormal world. Popular with Para millionaires they're employed either as colorful arm candy or for entertainment at luxurious parties. I've never seen one in real life.

I can't tear my eyes away from her and the way she shimmers, her feathers adorning her head like a Mardi-Gras crown. She catches my gaze and I look away, cheeks burning.

Konstantin wasn't lying when he said his club had high standards.

Is everyone here non-human? The bouncer is definitely a Shifter, probably a bear, but surely the dancers aren't *all* Paras? What about the DJ?

"Brandy?"

I jump at the sound of my fake name. Standing behind me, holding a glossy boutique bag in one hand and an iPad in the other, is the woman from yesterday. The one who had directed me to the private rooms for my pathetic excuse of an audition. Her dress is tight and white, and her lips dripping red. She doesn't smile.

"Konstantin said you must wear this," she drawls, handing me the bag. I recognize the designer logo on the side and it feels heavy like there's shoes inside too. I look down at my own outfit, boots, jeans, and a t-shirt. I'll admit I dressed as simple as I possibly could to get Konstantin back for his clothes comment. But it looks like he was already prepared for that.

"Where do I change?" I ask.

The woman sighs and marches ahead, so I follow.

I presumed this grand church entrance was it, the main club, but I was wrong. She pushes through double doors at the back of the main hall and we're in a narrow corridor lined with red strip lights and a carpet so thick I'm practically bouncing as I walk. There are doors on either side like a hotel, each one numbered in gold.

"Private bedrooms," the woman says before I have a chance to ask.

Right. The dancers here do more than just dance.

We head down a set of winding stone stairs, the decor changing from red velvet to black satin as we reach the bottom. There are no windows down here but there's an onyx marble bar, more poles, and another stage. A guy in a suit is drinking a tumbler of whisky at the bar while a blonde woman in a dress so short her ass cheeks are hanging out laughs at something he says. Early arrivals? Friends of Konstantin? I make a mental note of checking them out later.

More hallways, more rooms, more stairs heading down. Does this place ever fucking end? There's no way I would have been able to find the changing room on my own.

We pass the viewing rooms where I first met Lukka and made a fool of myself, that corridor must have two entrances as I'd accessed it from the street, and at the end of the long hallway is a door marked 'private'.

"In there," the woman says, then she's gone. And by gone I don't mean she walks away, I mean she totally disappears. I suppress a shiver. I thought the Volkov brothers were enough of a handful, but I was right - they aren't the only Paranormals filling up this chapel of sin.

I gingerly push open the door and it slams behind with a bang, finding myself in a bright changing room. Nine women in various stages of undress are staring back at me.

"Hi," I say in Russian.

Six of them ignore me and the other three look me up and down like I'm a client who's taken a wrong turn. To be fair, I'm wearing more fabric than all their outfits put together.

Two of the women, presumably dancers, are sitting before a Hollywood-style mirror studded with lights. One's tanned, her thick dark hair covering a pair of breasts that are the size and shape of melons. She turns to the younger girl next to her wearing a black mesh outfit and mutters in Croatian.

"If *she's* a new dancer then Lukka has finally lost his mind," she says. They both laugh.

Rude. But I keep my mouth shut. No one in this room knows I understand anything but Russian. The best thing about being a Verity Witch is getting to eavesdrop as people spill their guts thinking I don't understand them.

The rest of the dancers step out the room in a cloud of perfume, leaving me with the two bitchy girls and a trestle table full of food. *What the fuck?* Why is there a buffet in a stripper's dressing room?

I walk over and check out the selection. Squares of flaky Napoleon cakes, sugar-iced gingerbread loaves, a mountain of mandarins, and stuffed *Pirozhki* of every kind. That I *wasn't* expecting. I presumed the Volkov brothers would not want their prized dancers pigging out on carbs.

One of the dancers gets up and grabs a piece of gingerbread loaf and eats one. Then another one, then a third one.

"Have some," she says her mouth full. "*Pryaniki.* They are amazing, all the food here is. The only reason I ever stop eating is because I have to go on stage." She gives an elegant laugh and it makes the rock-hard abs in her stomach pulsate.

"I don't think I have your metabolism." I smile.

"Oh, that's the best part! Konstantin has everything

specially made low calorie. I've lost weight since I started working here!"

"That might have something to do with the pole acrobatics," I gesture to the door.

"Have some," she says again. "It's Christmas!"

She winks at me, while her friend glares. It feels weird to be told it's Christmas in January but who am I to resist local cultures? I pop a square of *medovik* cake in my mouth. It's creamy and tastes like nuts and wild honey.

With one last swipe of blusher the pair scuttle past back into the club leaving me alone with my mystery bag of clothes. Does Konstantin care enough about his dancers to have a chef make them low-cal Christmas treats? Is it because he's a dancer himself? I sigh. Konstantin is about as easy to understand as Lukka's riddles.

I sit at the dressing table and peer in the bag. Let's see what monstrosity I'm expected to wear tonight. The dress Konstantin has chosen for me is tight, black and very short with a plunging neckline and virtually no back. Understated, elegant and sexy enough to fit in with every other girl in this place. I should have known he'd have better taste than his brother. There are matching shoes too.

A tag is attached to the dress with a message written in a swirling script.

To Saskia. Behave.

Saskia? My stomach twists when I see my real name. I drop the dress. How the fuck does he know who I am?

I pick the dress back up and peel off my jeans, fear spreading over every inch of my body. My real name has never been discovered on assignment before. Should I tell Jackson? No, not before I find out how Konstantin got a hold of my identity.

I startle, doing up my dress quickly as the door to the changing room creaks open and a girl walks in. Another dancer, the one I was watching earlier with the elfin features and crazy cheekbones. I stay quiet as she walks straight past me to the lockers at the back of the room, punches in a number and pulls out a phone. She's talking into it before it hits her ear.

"It's me, Ansel," she says, her voice barely a whisper. It takes me about three seconds to work out what language she's speaking. Kazakh. Ansel means 'Honey' in Kazakh. *Cute.* She sits with her back to me, but I can see in one of the mirrors that she's smiling, her eyes fixed on a thin ring she's twisting round her finger.

"I go on in five minutes," she says. "I miss you, Maxim. When can we meet again?"

There's a pause, then her smooth brow creases.

"Fuck my brother! Arman doesn't own me. So, it's OK for me to work in a place like this but it's not OK for me to date his best friend?"

I pretend to do my make-up so she doesn't realize I'm listening. Although I'm not sure she's even seen me.

"Can you get away at dawn?" she asks the guy on the phone. "I finish work at six. We could have breakfast together. I know a place."

There are footsteps in the hallway. I move away from the door just as it slams open.

"There you are, my little Witch!"

Lukka gives me a demonic grin. Tonight, his six front teeth are capped with a golden grill shaped like fangs. The dancer has hung up and is sitting straight in the chair like a rabbit caught in headlights. Lukka turns his smile to her and she jumps up, fumbling with her phone and stuffing it back in her locker.

"I'll get back to work," she says to Lukka in Russian, popping a grape in her mouth from the trestle table and scampering past him.

Oh, great. The girl's telephone conversation sounded interesting, but she's already been scared away by one of the brothers' Grimm.

"I better do some work too," I say to Lukka.

He shuts the door with his foot and stands in front of it.

"Welcome, Saskia," he says. "Or is it Brandy? Or Brenda? Maybe I will make up my own little name for you. How about *Sabrina the little Witch?*"

"It's called *Sabrina the* Teenage *Witch*," I answer in Russian. "How about I call you DrakLukka the limp-dicked Vampire?"

I intended to be nice and get into his good graces, but I'm clearly failing miserably. I don't know where my attitude problem comes from, blame it on my childhood. Lukka smiles, nearing my face. He doesn't rise to my taunt.

"So, how do you like our little empire?" he says. "I bet you didn't think you'd find Vampires inside a church." Although his eyes are ghostly white they light up at the mention of the club.

"Yeah, it's a nice place," I reply. "But isn't converting a church into a strip club a little...blasphemous?"

"God has forgotten all about us." He waves his hand at the elaborate moldings decorating the changing room ceiling too. "Konstantin stopped believing in God the day we were turned. My brother says us Vampires are the real gods now. The Black Rabbit is where people like us come to worship the things that really matter to them."

"Sex and money?" I say.

He shakes his head. "Power."

"Konstantin didn't properly explain what I have to do tonight," I say. "Is there anyone I should specifically speak to?"

"You walk around and greet customers, you listen to them and you say nothing. That's it. The easiest money you will ever make. You hear anything suspicious you come to us."

I nod, although as soon as I find out anything about the killings I'm going to my editor Jackson.

"No more lies from you and no more surprises, Saskia." His eyes wander down to the pendant nestled in my cleavage. *"Ponyatno?"*

Lukka stares at me for a long time before stepping to one side and letting me pass. As I brush against him I note the sizable outline inside his designer sweats and realize the limp dick quip was probably inaccurate.

There are a lot of stairs leading back up to the nightclub, and I blink to adjust my eyes to the dark red glow of the main area. The converted church is a lot fuller now, dancers everywhere spinning like queens using nothing but their crossed ankles, all the while making eyes at the crowd of eager clients. Swiftly the girl I saw on the phone earlier lands on her knees and pulls one side of her bikini bottoms down, letting the men in suits stuff bills inside.

Standing by a large velvet curtain I scan the rest of the room. The club is beginning to fill with suited men, their pockets heavy with rubles. Looks like there will be plenty here to keep me busy. Time to do some digging.

A shadow shifts in my peripheral, probably a trick of the light. I take a step forward when suddenly something cold and iron-like clamps around my throat.

A scream dies on my tongue as I'm yanked backwards, deep into the velvet darkness.

CHAPTER EIGHT

My feet are no longer touching the floor as I'm slammed against a nearby wall, the heels of my shoes scraping uselessly against the paintwork. The hands at my neck are impossibly strong. Inhumanly so. There's not much light behind the curtain but I can still make out my attacker's eyes, bloodshot and angry.

"You think you can poison me and I won't find you?" says the Strogino Vamp from last night. The one I let bite me so he'd tell me where to find this club. I can tell he's still suffering from the intoxication caused by my blood.

Fuck! I should have known he'd look for me. I basically gave him an address.

His cold hands loosen at my throat as if waiting for a reply.

I cough. "You don't look so good. May I suggest a spa getaway?"

He growls. With one hand, so fast it's a blur, he lets go of my throat and pins both of my wrists above my head. I cry out from the pain, thrashing against him, but my screams are drowned out by the thumping bass.

So much for *Tonight A DJ Saved My Life*.

I scream again but it's pointless, his grip is too tight and the music too loud. My heart is thudding in time to the shitty techno beats. Kicking out, I push against him but he's too strong.

His high-pitched laugh slithers near my ear. "You should never have given me the Witch blood antidote," he says. "Vampires don't forgive or forget. We just fuck and feed."

"God, that's a lot of alliteration. Have you ever thought of self-publishing your poetry?"

Keep him talking. Buy yourself some time.

It's not as if he can bite me again, he wouldn't take that risk, so he can't kill me. Then in answer, he pulls something silver from his coat pocket and runs it cold and sharp along the side of my dress. Oh yeah, there's more than one way for a Vamp to murder someone.

"I brought you a present," he coos.

His rancid breath permeates the space between us as his body presses hard against mine.

There's a dull sting as he traces the knife across my stomach. My body is shaking. I can't breathe. I can't move. I can't scream. There is nothing I can do to stop him gutting me like a piece of fresh game.

"But first I will have some fun with you," he says, his grip on my wrists smarting. I blink at the glare of his pale face, his lips dry and coated in flaking black blood. He's already fed tonight, but I can tell he's still sick. This must be him at his weakest, which is a scary thought.

"I'm going to enjoy cutting you into small pieces while you're still alive," he says. I try for another scream. *Nothing.* His hand is back at my neck and he squeezes it. I can't breathe at all; the edges of my vision go blurry. Darkness ebbs in, spreading like black paint before me. One second the

Vamp's angry vengeful eyes are boring into mine, the next he's pulled away and flung aside.

Konstantin materializes behind him. With a resounding crack, he snaps my assailant's neck as if it were nothing more than a twig of dry birch. The Strogino Vamp slumps forward at my feet.

Konstantin observes him, his face passive and unmoving.

"I will get someone to dispose of the body properly."

I nod shakily. Vamps don't die from a snapped neck, I know that much. They have to be dismembered or burned. I look at my hands and try to quell their manic shake.

Konstantin notices. Suddenly, he scoops me up and all I feel is a gust of wind in my hair as we rush lightning speed through the club until I find myself in his office, slumped in a chair.

I still haven't taken a breath. My hands are trembling and the stench of my Vampire attacker lingers in my nostrils.

"Here." Konstantin pours me a shot of vodka. "For your nerves."

I chug it, my throat aching where the Vampire's fingers had grasped so tightly. He pours me two more and slides them over.

"Again," he says gently. "Drink until you forget."

CHAPTER NINE

Despite the evening's initial excitement, the rest of the night has been slow. My heavily made-up eyes itch with the need to sleep. I thought gathering intel in a busy club would be interesting, but it's been endless boring hours. My legs ache and I've learned nothing - plus my throat is sore and bruised from that Vamp's grip.

Lukka told me to wander around all night and listen, try and pick up any information that may come in useful for them, but the truth is every guy here is either talking business or planning which girl they want to take back to their private room. No one has mentioned the Volkov brothers yet or anything that might give me a clue as to who is killing their workers. The club is so large, on so many levels, the back of my ankles are already stinging with blisters.

I pick up a few empty glasses, anything to make the time pass quicker, and head to the bar.

"You new?" the barman asks in Russian as I hand him the empties.

He's a monkey Shifter and he's mid-shift, using his dexterous langur tail to pour bottles at triple speed. The rest of him is wiry, fidgety, marred with tufts of dark messy hair that stick up all over his head and knuckles. I understand having a Shifter bear at the door, that bouncer is a brute, but what's a monkey Shifter doing in Russia? They normally prefer warmer climates.

I sit down on one of the high leather stools and rest my head on my hands.

"Yeah, I'm the new…" Konstantin didn't give me a proper job title when he offered me this job. "…guest liaison manager?"

Monkey Boy makes a face but doesn't ask questions. I don't imagine anyone that works here asks questions. Except me.

He holds a vodka bottle out. "Want a drink?"

I nod and he pours me a splash in an icy shot glass. It's clear with tiny flecks of gold floating in it. I knock it back in one and shiver as my stomach turns into a pool of lava.

"What time does the club close?" I ask.

"When the last client leaves. Around six, normally."

I grab his hairy wrist and turn it so I can see his watch. There's less than an hour left. The dancers are leaving one by one, picking up bills from around their poles, and stuffing them into their bras. A few have disappeared towards the private rooms, a man trailing behind them, but most are heading back to the changing rooms. In no time at all it's just me, Monkey Boy, and a group of loud Vamps in the corner.

They must have just come in earlier when I was upstairs. Typical Vamps. Only men capable of ripping you apart in one swift move would act so fucking loud and obnoxious. At least no one has flashed their fangs yet, thank god. I've had enough of that for one night.

"Who are they?" I ask the barman.

"Regulars."

He's polishing a glass as he talks to me, which is a bullshit tactic I know bar staff uses to make customers feel less uncomfortable when they're standing there with nothing to do. I wish he'd put the glass down, it's clean enough now. But he doesn't strike me as the kind of man that likes to keep still.

"I know they're Vampires," I say. "But what *kind* are they? 'Stare at you longingly through your bedroom window' Vamps, or '*30 Days of Night* suck Josh Hartnett dry' Vamps?"

He gives me a look that says he doesn't understand either of my movie references. Not my fault I'm a Netflix subscription with legs.

"They're business associates of the Volkov brothers," he says. The 'rich' kind. The 'mean' kind. The 'don't make eye contact with them' kind."

I nod at the vodka bottle and he pours me another shot. This is quickly turning into the kind of job that can't be done sober.

The Vamps are chanting something, and I look at the barman questioningly.

"It's feeding time," he says, glancing at his watch. "Once the dancers have finished for the night, the customers are allowed to eat."

I watch as the club door opens and the huge Shifter bouncer walks in, followed by four girls I recognize from the dance floor wearing identical tight white dresses.

"But they're Shifters," I say. "I thought Vamps preferred human blood."

The barman looks uncomfortable. "Shifters wouldn't normally let Vamps near them. We can stand up for ourselves." He screws up his face. I don't blame him for being disgusted by this arrangement. "But Shifter blood is a delicacy, and Konstantin guarantees the cleanest blood in town."

The cleanest blood in town? What kind of purist bullshit is that?

I recoil. Everything in my body stiffens as I watch the girls approach the Vamps, led like lambs to the slaughter.

"Chill," the barman says. "They're doing it of their own free will. They get paid a lot extra on top of their normal rates."

I forgot monkeys are good at picking up on emotion.

"How does Konstantin keep the blood clean?" I ask. "And what does it matter to the Vamps if blood is clean anyway? What? Do they need Organic Fairtrade blood?"

"The boss keeps these girls on strict diets, drug tests them regularly, and makes sure they are generally healthy."

I wouldn't call honey cakes and *pirozhkis* part of a strict balanced diet.

"The Vamps like it because of the taste" he continues. "It guarantees they don't accidentally come across junkie or Witch blood."

I swallow nervously.

"You know I can smell you, right?" he says.

Damn, it's like being cursed to wear skunk spray for the rest of your life.

I shrug. "Yeah, I know."

The Vamps grow louder, hungrier. A fear from earlier curdles in the pit of my stomach at the sight of their fangs. There's a moment of silence between the monkey and me as we watch the beautiful women smiling invitingly at the braying Vamps, like they're about to hold up numbers and walk around a boxing ring.

"Why are they all in white? Are they all virgins?"

Monkey Boy laughs through his nose, but there's no humor in the sound.

"Konstantin calls them his Blood Bunnies. White fabric helps heighten the experience for his clientele."

So, Konstantin is some kind of fucked-up Vampire sommelier?

"Do the Vamps drain them?" I ask, thinking back to my story for The Chronicle.

The barman shakes his head. "It's not like that. Konstantin keeps the girls safe. Strict rules are in place."

Well, at least there's that. The bear-like bouncer opens a door beside a stage. How many secret hallways are there in this church? Three Vamps stand and follow the Shifters through the doorway. I want to follow too. I need to see what they're up to.

But I can't, not on my first night.

The monkey mixologist looks over at me and raises his eyebrows.

"Believe me, you don't want to see the Blood Bunny room," he says.

"Why not?" says a smooth voice behind me.

I swing around and find myself nose to nose with Konstantin.

"Nothing, Boss. Apologies," the barman mumbles, putting down the glass.

"Mo, you're dismissed," Konstantin drawls.

The Shifter puts down the glass he's been polishing for ten minutes and shuffles away.

"My name is Brandy by the way!" I call after him.

"Oh, is it now," Konstantin smiles lightly as if it's our inside joke. He looks me up and down, smiling at the sight of me in the dress he chose. "I think you may enjoy the Blood Bunny room, Saskia," he adds quietly. It sounds like a threat.

"Where have you and Lukka been all night?"

He doesn't answer me. "Come," he says, then turns around before I have time to say anything. I trot behind him like the good little spy Witch I am.

"Sit," he says, pointing at a chair once we are inside his office.

I do as I'm told, then tug at the hem of my dress as it rises so far up my thighs I'm practically flashing him. Not that Konstantin seems to notice. I look around, expecting his brother to appear, but Lukka isn't here. I should feel relieved I only have one to contend with, not two.

"What have you learned tonight?" he asks, shuffling some papers on his desk without looking at me. Clearly the attack from earlier is old news now, although I'm curious as to what he did with the Vamp whose neck he snapped in two.

I clear my throat.

What have I learned? That this club is full of Paras, but other than crooked Vamps getting cheap thrills, and their questionable idea of dinnertime, I have nothing to go on.

"Those Blood Bunnies..."

His head whips up. "They aren't your business." Konstantin is by my side in a second, the light breeze from his Vamp speed making the papers on his desk flutter to the ground. "I hired you to listen and report," he says, placing a hand on both armrests and looming over me. "Not to have opinions on my business practice. So, what did you hear?"

I take a deep breath but struggle to get any air into my lungs.

"I haven't learned anything, "I stammer. "I listened, I spoke to a few groups, I collected glasses. No one mentioned you or your brother."

He breathes out through his nose and pushes his hair back.

"You should probably know there have been a few...deaths...in my company lately. Bodies, drained of blood, have been appearing on my construction sites. I don't like it. I need you to find out who's behind them."

I pretend to be shocked. But, well, I *am* shocked. I didn't expect him to tell me this. He's not lying either.

"Come back tomorrow. Same time," he says, not waiting for my reaction. "I want you here every night until you discover who's betraying me and who's killing my workers. As soon as the regulars get used to seeing your face they will be less guarded."

Konstantin takes off his jacket, a signal that he's done for the night and business is over. The white button-down beneath clings to the contours of his muscly arms and I think back to him dancing - all lithe limbs and a glistening torso that rippled as he leaped through the air.

The weird thing is I'm a little disappointed I've let him down. As if Konstantin is really my boss and *this* is my real job. I think of Jackson back in New York waiting to hear how I'm getting on.

I make a quick calculation and work out that 6 am Moscow time is 11 pm back home. Jackson is normally in the office by six every morning, so he's probably asleep already. Maybe I'll just text him.

Konstantin is looking at me and I realize I've been standing here for a full minute as if waiting for instructions.

"Shall I wear the same dress tomorrow?" I ask him.

He makes an exasperated face and shakes his head.

"You think our girls wear the same outfit twice? Leave the outfits to me. Just be here tomorrow and get me the information I need."

I nod, tempted to curtsey sarcastically at the megalomaniac. His lips twitch to one side showing a glimpse of his oversized canines as if he's just read my mind.

CHAPTER TEN

No matter how many times I step outside in this country, the cold never ceases to shock me. I exit the club and the icy air hits me like a sledgehammer to the face leaving me with bright red slap marks on my cheeks. I push my hat down over my ears and pull my scarf up to cover my nose. All that's exposed are my eyeballs and they feel like frozen marbles ready to roll right out of my head.

My fingers feel like icicles as I quickly type out a message to Jackson.

Hey boss. Freezing my ass out here for you, you owe me! Got a few leads, nothing concrete yet. Though I think I may have a bad case of vaginal frostbite, so The Chronicle will need to upgrade my insurance. I'll keep you posted about the story (not my vag.)

Jackson texts me back with a screenshot of the dictionary definition of the word 'decorum'.

I contemplate a snarky comment when I hear a shout in the distance. It's three of the Vamps that were in the club earlier, the ones who'd stayed on to live feed. I screw up my nose at the thought of what happened after these Vamps had

had their fill. Where is the rest of the group? Is there a frenzied blood-soaked fuck-fest going on in one of the club's private rooms right now?

One of the suited men is shouting at someone leaving the club. A girl.

I squint into the darkness, trying to make out if it's one of the dancers.

"Why don't you hop on over here?" the guy is shouting out at her.

I slink back into the shadows where he can't see me. This is my job, I tell myself, to watch and report. Not get involved.

The girl ignores him and reaches in her purse for something. I see the orange glow of a cigarette float in the darkness as she brings it up to her lips. The guy's voice is getting closer.

"I saw the way you moved in there," he slurs. "How about we go back and we have some private time?"

"I'm not a Blood Bunny. I'm just a dancer," she says.

"I know what I saw."

There's a scuffle, the sound of someone being pushed against the wall, and a yelp. I'm not sure if it comes from him or her. I move closer. The amber glow of the cigarette is on the ground now and the man is shouting.

"You fucking whore!" he cries. "I'll catch you!"

He's reaching around on the ground, stumbling drunkenly. I can't see the girl anymore and I can't tell what he's looking for so low down on the ground - then something warm and soft brushes against my legs. A rabbit. What the hell is a rabbit doing outside a church in Moscow at the crack of dawn?

I scoop down, pick it up, and walk as quietly as I can away from the church and down a side road.

"Leave the stupid bitch!" one of the men is shouting at the

drunk Vamp. "The sun's about to come up. She's not worth the risk."

I cradle the rabbit closer to my chest and in the light of a doorway I hold the animal so we're nose to nose.

"What have we got here?" I ask in Russian. "Are you someone's pet?"

Then I remember the first dancer I saw, the one with the soft dark ears that flickered for a second above her head. I switch to Kazakh. "Or maybe you're a very talented dancer who also happens to be a Shifter bunny?"

The rabbit's back legs start to pound furiously against my chest. I place her carefully on the pavement, expecting her to scamper off, but she doesn't. She huddles close to the corner of the doorway and slowly starts to grow and morph.

I know plenty about Shifters. The daughter of any Witch is taught about them as part of her studies, and with my mother on the board of the Mage Association I've seen a lot of strange things growing up. I mean, I even had a fight with a lizard Shifter in Venice Beach once. But I've only seen a full shift a handful of times. The change is fast and silent, and what always surprises me is that the clothes and shoes return too.

I was right.

"Hi Ansel," I beam at her. It's the same girl who was on her phone back in the club's changing rooms. The one named after honey.

She fumbles into her purse with a shaking hand and pulls out a cigarette. She doesn't say a word until she's lit it and taken three deep drags.

"Thank you," she says in Kazakh. "That Vamp has been after me for days. I was distracted at the pole today, so he must have seen my ears. Should have known that would have excited the creep."

I raise my eyebrows but don't reply.

"You don't look like you're from Kazakhstan," she says.

"I'm not. I'm from the US," I reply. "But I speak a little."

Not a complete lie.

She nods. "Cold night, isn't it?"

When the fuck isn't it, in this snow globe of a city?

I'm glad to see she's wearing sneakers and jeans under her thick coat. She reaches inside her purse again and pulls out a bunch of sweaty crumpled rubles. Some bills are green and purple, others of higher denominations are blue and dark orange.

"I owe you," she adds. "For helping me. You work at the club, right?"

She's pointing at the rabbit pendant around my neck. She's wearing an identical one.

"Yeah, I'm new," I say, stifling a yawn. I really need to get to bed, but at the same time this is my real job. Talking to people. Finding stuff out. "I meet and greet customers."

She grimaces, as if my job sounds way worse than hers, and then she links her arm through mine.

"Come on. Let me buy you breakfast. I was meant to meet my boyfriend but...long story. This place I know does amazing *syrniki*."

My stomach grumbles at the mention of cottage cheese pancakes. When was the last time I ate?

She pulls a bobble hat out of her coat pocket and pulls it over her head. It has a pink pompom on the top which wobbles as we walk. She's nothing like the girl I saw in the club, twirling regally around a pole. She looks timid and soft.

I smile at her, and she smiles back at me.

The twenty-four-hour cafe is brightly lit, warm and kitschy, with labeled clocks all around the room showing you that it's always breakfast time somewhere in the world. We head to a table in the corner.

"Your name is Ansel, right?" I say. "I heard you talking to your boyfriend earlier."

The mention of her boyfriend lights up her whole face. Looks like I've found my conversation starter.

"I thought you were meeting your boyfriend for breakfast?"

She shrugs. "He canceled. He works in construction and had to go to work early."

I let out a whistle. "Before six in the morning?!"

"Yup," she nods. "The site is open the same number of hours as this cafe." She laughs softly. "If the Volkovs could add an extra hour to the day they would. They work their staff like horses."

So, the boy she was talking to also works for Vamps. I wonder if he knows.

"Does your brother work for the Volkovs too?"

"Yes. My boyfriend Maxim, and my brother Arman, are both employed by KLV Constructions."

I've done my research on all of the Volkov's businesses. The brothers founded KLV four years ago, just after they turned, and it's one of Moscow's fastest-growing construction companies. The site nearest to the club is also where the latest drained body was found.

"KLV is why we came to Moscow," Ansel adds. "Their company is famous in my village because they take workers without papers. I wanted to come but my brother didn't want me to. Then I found out on the Blood Web that the Black Rabbit takes care of Shifters."

"Is your whole family Shifter?" I ask.

She shakes her head.

"No. Just me. Maxim doesn't even know I'm not human. He has no idea he works for Paras."

"The three of you came together? You, your brother and Maxim?"

She nods and looks down, scanning the menu on the table.

"Our mother is old and sick. She needs treatment. We were desperate for money to send her. KLV pay cash in hand, they are always hiring, so we knew it would be worth the risk."

A sour-faced waitress is waiting to take our order and I let Ansel order for me. The food arrives and Ansel's face relaxes as she explains what the best dishes are. I delve into the *syrniki* covered in sour cream and blackberry jam.

"What does your brother think of the Volkovs?" I ask, my cheeks bulging with food. I hope I sound casual.

She swallows.

"Aside from the hours, they're good employers," she says. "They are always feeding the men, making sure they never go hungry."

I wait. No *ping*.

"Maxim and my brother are very happy there."

There's the ping. The lie. Interesting.

I push a bit harder, leaning in close and dropping my voice to a whisper. "I heard one of the clients in the Black Rabbit say that a construction worker had been found dead the other day."

Ansel's forkful of pancake stops halfway up to her mouth.

"You didn't know?" I add.

She takes a while to answer, chewing her breakfast slowly.

"Maxim, my boyfriend, mentioned something."

I sit up, struggling not to look too eager. This is the first time I've gathered any kind of information for my story.

"What did he mention?" I ask.

Ansel looks down. "It's probably nothing. He said not to tell anyone, but…" She absentmindedly moves her food around her plate with her fork. "A few of Maxim's colleagues have disappeared lately. I know it's normal for us immigrants to go back and forth, some of us even end up in jail, but these were his friends. They wouldn't have left without saying goodbye." She shrugs. "I told him not to worry, but it has put Maxim and my brother on edge."

This is the most she has spoken since we left the club.

"On edge, how so?"

Ansel shrugs. "He keeps trying to snoop around and find out more. I told him he needs to chill, mind his own business."

Ping.

That's the first lie. But it's not a very significant one. She probably hasn't told him to chill and is lying to backtrack. Or maybe she doesn't want me telling our bosses she doesn't trust them.

"I've been wondering... What are *you* doing at the Black Rabbit?" she asks. "You don't dance or work behind the bar."

She picks up the carafe and pours milk over a small bowl of buckwheat. *Weird.*

"I needed a job and Konstantin gave me one. I needed to... umm... get away from my life back home."

"I know what that's like." She smiles at me, cradling her drink, her hands tightening around her tea glass holder which I've noticed is embossed with Soviet astronauts.

"Sorry if this sounds a bit rude, but you smell kind of strange," she says. "It's my Shifter senses. You know, scent is a big deal to us."

God, again with the smell! Shifters never get tired of talking about our scent, they'd probably sniff each other's butts if it wasn't deemed socially unacceptable. I swear I've seen Jackson take a secret whiff of my hair and recoil.

"Not in a bad way!" she adds, looking mortified at my silence. "Your smell is good. Like apple juice and cinnamon. I was just wondering why."

Oh. I've never had anyone describe my scent nicely before. It certainly doesn't align with what Paranormals have said to me in the past. She's probably just being kind.

"I'm a Witch," I tell her. What's the point in hiding it when I work in a club full of Paras?

Ansel looks excited.

"Oh my god! What are your powers?"

Here we go. "I can tell lies from the truth," I say reluctantly, waiting for the disappointment that usually floods people's faces when I tell them about my meager abilities.

Ansel, however, looks even more excited than before. "That's so cool! You'd be a hit in my village. We had one local who called herself a Brew Witch, but I think she was a fake. Her concoctions never helped the local girls grow prettier."

I laugh. "Were you the only Para in your village?"

"My grandad was like me before he died, but I don't know of any others."

Ansel tells me more about her grandparents and her small village in Kazakhstan. She tells me she hates the Russian cold and can't wait until her and Maxim have made enough money to move back and get an apartment.

We've nearly finished our breakfast when my new friend checks her phone.

"I have to go. Sorry. But don't rush on my behalf. Stay and finish your breakfast."

She leaves money on the table and walks off before I have a chance to ask her anything else, but as she pulls the door open she turns and waves at me.

"See you tonight!" Her smile is infectious.

"See you!"

A flurry of snow has started outside. I watch her walk away, hands cradling my own honeyed sea buckthorn tea. It's kind of nice to have a friend - it's been a long time since I gossiped with another girl. I tell myself it's just for my story, that Ansel isn't a *real* friend, except it feels real.

I smile at my reflection in the frosty glass and polish off the last of the *syrniki*. I have a lead. I have a friend.

And just like that, I've finally found some warmth in the cold.

CHAPTER ELEVEN

"Are you enjoying yourself?" Lukka asks, spinning around on a barstool beside me.

I've been working at the club for four days now. Every evening I report back to Konstantin, and while hardly looking at me he tells me I'm not trying hard enough and to get back out there. All I've discovered so far is that his so-called business associates are creepy as hell, and as nice as they seem to the brothers' faces the Volkov's aren't trusted by anyone. When I tell Konstantin that he smiles and nods, as if upsetting people is his favorite hobby.

I planned to ask Ansel some more questions too, but she's not returned to the club since we had breakfast together. The other dancers say she's had stomach flu.

More lies.

I turn to Lukka. He's positioned himself so he's sitting with his back against the bar, a leg either side of me. I've not seen him since my first day here and I'd forgotten how different he is to his brother.

"Yes, I love working here," I lie.

His pale eyes travel up my thigh, gliding over yet another

VAMPIRES OF MOSCOW

outfit his brother picked out for me. This one is red, tight, and strapless.

"Your dress is boring," he says. "Maybe next time I choose something for you."

Dear God, no. Tonight he's wearing jeans slung so low I can see his hip bones and a tight top that keeps riding up his middle. And, as always, his empty purple gun holster is strapped across his shoulders like a backpack.

He smiles. No gold-capped fangs this time, just a diamond skewered through the tip of his tongue which he runs between his teeth. He leans back, his arms spread along the length of the bar. I notice the other working girls look up from the men they're talking to and check him out. Lukka has a reputation in this place. Not because they've all had him - but because they all want him.

I grin to myself at the thought that I'm currently standing between the legs of the toy everyone wants to play with.

"Where's Ansel?" I ask him.

Lukka looks confused.

"She's not here? Why?"

This is strange. "Did you know her boyfriend works for your construction company?" I ask.

He sits up quickly, his knees clasping shut around my legs.

"And what do you know about KLV?"

His thighs hold me still, then slowly and ever so lightly, he begins to stroke the back of my knees. I clear my throat to hide the gasp I just made.

"Your brother said some of your workers are going missing," I manage to say.

He shrugs and leans back, but he still doesn't let me go.

"The workers come and go. I don't have much to do with it. Kostya deals with the businesses."

"So, what do you do then?" I say quietly, enjoying the fact the other girls are no longer hiding their stares.

"I look pretty," he says, wiggling his tongue through his teeth again.

"Lukka." Konstantin's voice rings out and I swear even the clients make themselves look busy. Not Lukka though, he couldn't be more languid as he sits up and tips his head to one side, staring at his brother with those white vacant eyes of his.

He tips his chin up as if to say 'what?' and Konstantin sighs impatiently.

"I need to talk to you about a new shipment we have coming in. Saskia?" I jump to attention as he takes a long stride towards me. "I have some special guests arriving soon. I need you to look after them."

I look at my watch. "It's 5.35 am," I say. "Aren't we closing soon?"

Konstantin raises his eyebrows and a light smile plays at his lips. "You were curious about the Blood Bunnies, right? Well, now you get to watch. It's nearly feeding time."

It's not easy trying to keep my face from showing the panic I'm feeling.

"Who are these special clients?" I ask.

"They work with Boris, my business partner. In fact, I should probably introduce you to him soon. I flew these men in from Switzerland this evening. Make sure they have a good time."

"How come I get to meet them?" I ask. "Don't you trust them?"

"I don't trust anyone," Konstantin says.

I walk from the upstairs bar back down to the main club, through a collection of winding corridors, and find a group of men waiting with the bouncer outside a set of ornate doors.

The bouncer glances at me with disdain. A club this big yet I keep seeing the same muscle. He's the bear Shifter who wouldn't let me in the day I came to audition...and he still hates me.

"Welcome to the Black Rabbit, gentlemen," I say in English. Konstantin mentioned they were Swiss, but they don't need to know I understand their language. In fact, I'm banking on it. "Can I get you anything to drink?"

There are three of them. All young, fair and handsome.

"I plan to drink my fill when I get inside," says one of them to the group in French. He's younger than the others.

They all laugh and I put on a dumb face, as if I have no idea what he just said.

"Champagne," he says to me with a thick accent. "Make the Bunnies bring it." His mouth opens a fraction and his canines wink in the dull red light as they grow a little in anticipation. Unlike the movies, real Vampires don't have huge fangs, they just grow a little and sharpen up whenever they sense blood. I've noticed some fangs are bigger than others - clearly length and girth matter in the Para world too.

The men are restless with excitement and I wonder if it's because Konstantin's blood is special, pure like Mo told me. Or because it's a feast of *Shifter* blood they're about to enjoy.

The bouncer opens the double doors with a flourish and gestures for the three men to take a seat. It's a small room made up of large white plastic couches, white glossy walls and a white tiled floor. It looks clinical, so different from the rest of the club, then I spot a coiled hose discreetly tucked away in the corner of the room.

Of course. The blood.

Konstantin has created a whole user-centered experience. Never mind that the room looks like the inside of a spaceship holding cell, the Vamps want to see the contrast of the red blood against the white. Pools of it on the floor and splatters against the wall. I don't know if I'm more disturbed by this visual, or the fact Konstantin has so meticulously customized the Vampire feeding experience.

I walk back to collect the champagne glasses, spotting three Blood Bunnies striding across the empty dance floor. I'm not one to judge how people make a living, but I can still feel that nasty Vamp's hands around my neck and the sting of his fangs sinking into my flesh. I'm scared for the Bunnies. No amount of money is going to make this pleasant for them.

I make a mental note to call Jackson when I get back to my shitty apartment and tell him about the Blood Bunnies. I know he'll want to cover this exposé too. Even though it's probably a human-interest piece for The Chronicle's leisure section at most. I'm here for a much bloodier story.

I hand each girl a champagne bucket and they follow me as I grab six glasses and lead them back along the corridor to the room. The bouncer is outside guarding the entrance and lets us in, slamming the door shut behind us.

Then everything happens in fast forward.

In a super-speed flash of black suits, the three Vamps whisk the girls away, sending bottles of champagne smashing to the ground. When I look over at the couch one of the men already has a Shifter lying across his lap while he sucks hungrily at her neck. Silvery scales flicker across her skin and I realize she's some form of reptile Shifter. Blood mixes into the Vampire's beard and dribbles down one of her scaly shoulders, staining her white dress in rose blooms over her breasts. I'm surprised when she whimpers in delight. It certainly didn't feel good when the Vamp attacked me in Strogino.

Who knows? Maybe being fed on *can* be pleasurable

when it doesn't kill the biter. I wouldn't know. Witches despise inter-Para relations so much I was brought up to hate any kind of interaction. I've spent my life in complete ignorance that some Paras actually enjoy having their blood drunk.

I watch as the Vamp cradles the Shifter in his arms, groaning into her collarbone as she pushes his hand beneath her skirt. Yep, everything can be enjoyable when there's consent.

On the other side of the room one of his colleagues, the oldest looking of the three, has clamped his teeth into a Shifter's back. She moans in response to the feral act. This is all so intimate I feel like a peeping Tom - but at the same time, it's hard not to watch.

I look around for the younger guy and find him on the ground. His Blood Bunny is on her back, her tight white dress pulled up over her thighs to her waist. The vamp has pulled her underwear to one side and is sucking on her femoral vein. She's writhing beneath him, pushing his head deeper between her legs, as blood shoots into the air. The tiled floor and plastic couches make sense now. The room stinks like an abattoir and the couples are sliding around in the blood, the Vamps' hands and faces stained red.

Is it like this every night? How much feeding can one Shifter take? The girls' eyes are fluttering shut and their bodies are growing limp, but they are still asking for more. I can't help thinking of the drained bodies that keep turning up at the construction site. Is this what happened to them? Were they a feed gone wrong?

Unlikely. None of them were pretty young girls, most were men.

I want to intervene, tell the Vamps they've had enough, when I notice the blinking of a red light in the corner of the room. Security cameras. So that's why Konstantin sent me in here. It can't just have been to listen in on their conversation - it's hard to talk when you have a mouth full of throbbing jugular. The bastard is testing me and my loyalties.

"Konstantin was telling the truth," the Vamp with the goatee shouts out to his friend. "It's the best quality blood I've ever tried." He drops his girl onto the couch with a squelch and sits back, straightening his tie. "But if he wants our help it won't come cheap."

The Vamp on the floor gets to his feet and licks the blood off his fingers one by one. "He needs our facilities. He's still small-time."

Is he planning on franchising his Blood Bunny service? God, that's disturbing.

"He might have a small operation, but look at what he's built. I say we charge the asshole triple," says the other Vamp.

His Blood Bunny is groaning on the ground, a puddle of blood between her legs.

I inch back against the wall. What exactly am I meant to do? I didn't think to ask Konstantin at what point I'm allowed to leave. Am I meant to get the girls back to the changing rooms safely? Not that anyone has looked in my direction since I stepped into the room.

"He can afford it," the Vamp with the goatee says.

"It's his crazy brother I worry about. He might cause problems," he says moving on to champagne.

"Did you hear what happened to Varlam and the Georgians?" goatee Vamp replies. "Lukka is unpredictable. Konstantin says he has him under control, but I doubt it."

My heart is beating so fast I'm sure they can hear it.

Luckily at that point the Blood Bunny on the floor groans and the young Vamp bites his wrist. He leans over her and she sucks his blood hungrily, holding on to his arm like he's an ice cream on a hot day. He seems to be enjoying her rapture.

"Take your fill, beautiful. I need you to have energy later," he says in English. "I'm still horny," he adds. "You!"

I look up. Is he speaking to me? I walk over to him, careful to avoid slipping on the puddles of blood on the floor. I hope I don't look as scared as I feel.

"Would you like me to fetch more champagne?" I ask in English.

"No. You smell interesting. What kind of Shifter are you?"

With lightning speed, he grabs my behind and pushes me towards him, laughing as I struggle against him.

"I'm not a Blood Bunny," I say. "I'm not on the fucking menu."

He's pulling down the strap of my dress, pushing his face into my neck. "I don't care," he says.

He bites me, then instantly starts to cough. I stumble as he lets go of me and falls back against the couch, his hands grasping at his throat. Bubbles of spit are foaming at the sides of his mouth, his eyes bulging in shock and pain as his friends look on confused. I try and step back but he's grabbed my arm, his strong fingers pressing into my flesh.

Suddenly there's a slam behind me and a rush of wind. Lukka has already knocked him to the ground, and with one clear crack breaks his hand.

"Ask first, bite later," he says with a cackle.

"What the fuck!" shouts the other Vamp. "Why do you have a Witch as a Bunny?"

"Dinner is over." Lukka picks up a jacket and chucks it at him. "Get the fuck out of my club."

CHAPTER TWELVE

"You don't kick out clients," Konstantin growls. Lukka doesn't look up. He's sitting opposite Konstantin's fancy desk reading GQ magazine.

"You," his attention snaps to me. "What did you learn."

"They were considering doing business with you."

"And?"

"And they wanted to charge you triple their rates because they know you can afford it." I don't mention what they said about Lukka. He saved my ass, now I'm saving his.

Behind Konstantin there's a beautiful map of Moscow blinking in different colors - red, green, blue. It's bewitched. I wonder briefly where he got it and what the dots signify. I stare at that instead of the thunderous face of my Vamp boss.

"Triple," Konstantin repeats dryly. There's murder in his voice.

I didn't think it would be possible, but now I feel bad for the Vamps planning to rip him off.

The next day I'm a bit earlier than normal and the nightclub's changing room is packed with girls. I edge my way to the lockers and pick up the outfit that's always waiting for me. A quick peek inside confirms it's another short but tasteful number. Thankfully Lukka hasn't had his way yet and chosen my dress for the night. Right now, I'm grateful for the smallest of mercies.

I've gotten into the habit of putting the right underwear on at home and coming prepared. I slip the dress on and try to bat away my frustration at how little information I've managed to garner for my story so far. All I know is that everyone hates the Volkov brothers and no one knows who's killing the construction workers. Basically, I know exactly what I already knew on the plane over here nearly a week ago.

I go to sit down and stumble. Jeez, I'm tired. Seeing those Blood Bunnies get devoured last night shook me up so bad I couldn't sleep or eat anything all day.

"Are there any energy drinks?" I ask one of the dancers. I think she's American. Her name is Kristy or Kirsten or Kristen.

She shakes her head. "They don't even give us coffee here. But eat something. The food is really delicious and it always gives me plenty of energy," she says, nodding at the table full of food.

I've been too busy to have my fill of the gorgeous buffet table, and Konstantin's dress choices don't allow for binging, but tonight I'm so tired I don't care. I grab a plate and pile it high with raisin cheesecake, bauble-shaped donuts, smoked string cheese, and some blinis with orange caviar, then sit down on a swivel chair at the dressing table.

I'm halfway through my lap picnic when I hear Lukka's unmistakable voice. I've never seen Konstantin in the changing rooms, but Lukka is here all the time.

"How are my pretty birds this evening?" he shouts.

A few of the dancers flock around him and he laughs as the parrot Shifter tickles him with one of her feathers. But it's me he's looking at.

I stuff the last of the blinis in my mouth and chew quickly as he walks over.

"How are you feeling?" he asks, sitting on a chair in front of me. "After last night?"

Has he come here specifically to check up on me? The other dancers return to their mirrors or head for the dancefloor, but I can see them all glancing over at us.

"I'm fine," I lie. "Just a bit tired. I feel better after having eaten though."

I feel more than better, I feel like a million bucks. Lukka glances at the food table, a shadow passing over his face. "My brother insists that his workers eat well."

"That's kind of him."

"My brother isn't kind."

"Are you?"

Lukka looks me up and down slowly, as if he's never been asked that question. He drops his hands on my knees, slips them behind my legs, and quickly draws me closer, my wheeled chair gliding across the floor. His misty white eyes freak me out but I can't look away. He swallows hard and the swirling tattoos on his Adam's apple contract.

"You've seen me murder, Saskia, yet you still ask if I'm kind?"

"Well, do you enjoy the killing? Or you do it because you *have* to?"

This strikes a nerve. He lets his grip on my knee slip and slides his palms slowly higher up my legs. His thumbs press on the inside of my thighs, his painted nails catching on my stockings and stopping just short of their lace trim.

"You do other things," I say, crossing my arms. I can feel the chill of his touch through the nylon. "Good things."

I think back to last night when he pulled me away from those blood-thirsty animals, and how he always has time to talk to the dancers. When he's apart from his brother he's a lot less scary.

The wicked look on his face slips for a moment. He stands. The conversation is over.

"Maybe you look too hard."

He leaves the room without another word and I stand, smoothing down tonight's outfit - an electric blue dress much like the others. Konstantin's elegance never waivers.

The door opens and I look up expecting Lukka again, but it's Ansel. My stomach flips with excitement. God, I feel like I've had ten coffees. Is it the food that's woken me up, or the strange exchange I just had with Lukka?

I smile over at Ansel but she doesn't look at me, in fact, she keeps her face turned away from us all and sits on the other side of the room. I've been meaning to delve deeper and ask her more questions since we had breakfast together, except I'm not normally buzzing this much to speak to a lead.

The rest of the girls carry on their chattering in a mix of Russian and English, most of them talking about Lukka, but I keep my gaze fixed directly on Ansel. She's applying concealer under her left eye.

I sit at the mirror beside hers and she flinches.

"Hey, I've not seen you around," I say as cheerily as possible.

She gives me a faint smile but doesn't raise her head. When you're a reporter you see a lot of shit, and when you're a Verity Witch you know when someone is hiding something from you. Just as I suspect Ansel has a bruised eye and a light cut on her forehead. The bruise has started to fade into shades of green and yellow, which explains why she's been avoiding the club the last few days.

"Who did this to you?" I say, louder than I mean to.

She doesn't reply as she dusts her forehead with more powder.

I pull her chair and swing it around to face me. She yelps.

"Ansel! Who hit you?"

"No one," she says.

Ping. Although I don't need to be a walking talking lie detector to have worked that one out.

I give her a look and she sighs.

"I changed, and in my animal form I was hit by a car."

Another *ping*.

I lower my voice. "Tell me the truth, Ansel. Who hit you?"

She sniffs and dabs under her eyes with a tissue.

"Maxim. He got jealous about my dancing. He hasn't been himself lately, he's been really jittery. Probably working too hard."

I place my hand on her shoulder but I don't say anything.

"Please don't tell anyone at work," Ansel says, her dark eyes looking up at me beseechingly. "Especially not Dimitri. The bouncer? He's very protective. He's had a crush on me for a long time. He'll kill Maxim if he finds out it's him who hurt me."

"This isn't right," I say, understatement of the century. "You can't stay with a man who treats you like that."

Ansel dabs makeup under her eyes which are swimming with tears. "I know. It's the first time it's happened, it's not like Maxim to be aggressive. He was so ashamed of himself he left. I want to talk to him, but now I can't find him," she says so quietly I have to lean in to hear her. "He's missing."

She applies some bright red lipstick but I can see her hand is shaking.

"Missing?"

"My brother said he didn't turn up to work yesterday. He's never done that before."

All the other girls have left the room and it's just the two of us. A faint thud of techno music vibrates from the club, but other than that all is silent.

Ansel takes a deep breath and blinks rapidly, attempting to keep tears from smudging her eye make-up, briefly her rabbit ears flicker. "He'll come back. He's not a bad man, he's just had a lot on his mind lately. Things at work have been...difficult."

"Like what?" I ask. Although I already know the answer.

"Maxim's bunkmate was found dead last week, and it's not the first death."

I play dumb. "Dead?"

"And Maxim has all these crazy theories. When he's not working, he's staying awake looking into it. I told him to stop, that it's dangerous, and now he's..." She dabs at her eyes and I place my hand on her shoulder again.

"Who does Maxim think killed his friend?"

She wipes her nose with the back of her hand. "At first he was convinced it was the police, they are brutal towards immigrants, but my brother Arman thinks it's just local thugs who want bribes."

"And they don't suspect the people they work for?" I ask.

Ansel's chin quivers and she bites her lip. "Vampires? They don't even know they exist, let alone that they're our bosses. I could never tell them the truth. My brother barely tolerates my shifts."

I raise my eyebrows at the last comment.

"Do *you* think someone at KLV Construction is killing their workers?"

Konstantin must be thinking the same thing if he has me listening out for leads in his club. Yet, wouldn't it make more sense for me to be talking to people on his site than here? Maybe I'll ask him.

Ansel mumbles "I have no idea," and with a final sweep of blusher heads for the door. I follow. I should at least look like I'm doing my job. She holds the door open.

"Thank you," she says.

"What for?"

"For helping me the other day, and for listening." My stomach dips with guilt. "Let's do breakfast again," she says.

I smile and we head up the stairs to the club.

It's a quiet night. It's my first Wednesday and I guess it's the quietest night of the week. So much for Hump Day.

I collect a few glasses to keep myself busy and take them over to the bar. Monkey Boy is there tonight. He's there every night. Don't workers get a day off around here? He's chatting to the bear bouncer, clad in his usual XXXL blue Adidas tracksuit. The hairs on the back of my hair stand on end. I don't like that guy, and I don't trust the monkey either.

"Quiet night," the barman says to me as I hand him two champagne flutes.

I nod.

He glances at the bouncer then back at me. "I hear Konstantin wasn't very happy with you last night."

"What did Mr. Volkov say?" I ask.

"That you did not ensure the Swiss had a good time."

Would Konstantin have said something so crude? Mo looks gleeful. Typical gossip-loving monkey.

"Who told you that?"

He glances in the direction of the bear. So, the bouncer is spreading rumors about me. What a piece of shit.

"I was there to serve drinks, not myself," I say.

"I heard you had to be rescued."

"Listen..." I call out loudly so that the bear can hear me too. "If you and *Masha and the Bear* want to gossip, that's up to you, but from where I'm standing you two look like nothing more than a couple of Desperate Housewives of National Geographic."

With that I march to the boss' office, not wanting to hang around long enough to see the bear's murderous glare.

I knock on Konstantin's door but there's no answer. The door is slightly ajar so I push it open slowly. He isn't here.

Shall I wait for him?

I take a seat. Then get up. Then look at the strange bewitched map on the wall. Then sit back down again. Jesus, how did I go from utter exhaustion to this weird restless energy?

I shut the door quietly and walk over to his desk. It's covered in paperwork. I didn't have Konstantin down as messy with admin. It all looks boring, though, nothing but extensive contracts and a litter of invoices. I move on to his laptop where his inbox is open. With a quick glance at the door, I swipe the mousepad and scan through hundreds of Russian emails, waiting for something to catch my eye. More contracts, shipping updates, negotiations - more boring stuff. I head to archived emails. Then I spot them, two emails from two different PI's, and a report from a hacker. I click on the attachments. Interesting. All documents focus on Konstantin's business partner, Boris - his routines and locations, as well as what the hacker found in his Blood Web inboxes and computer files. Wasn't Boris the man Konstantin mentioned last night? The one linked to the Swiss Vamps?

I shouldn't be shocked. Of course, Konstantin would have

PI's and hackers in his employ, and of course, he'd have them looking into his colleagues and employees' business. Why the fuck not? It's no wonder he found out my real name. All he'd need was a hacker to cross-reference my photograph with US security docs and he'd easily find my real passport.

But, I remind myself, it doesn't mean he knows I work for The Chronicle. Thanks to Jackson, that information is far harder to find than my birth name.

I keep scrolling through Konstantin's inbox. Most of his emails are linked to the Black Rabbit, but then I spot a KLV email. With another glance at the door, I search the word KLV and scan through all the construction-related emails until I find something of interest. This one looks different from the rest. It was sent last week and it's from a doctor who works with KLV. In the attachments, there are printouts and hospital-type graphs detailing patient heart rates and BMI, and next to each result is a name and a photo. I flick through them. It's all young men, some of them wearing safety helmets with the KLV logo on. Ansel said the Volkov brothers really look after their construction staff, but extensive medical reports? Why?

I zoom into the pdf to take a closer look when the rattle of the door handle alerts me someone is entering the room. *Shit!* I snap the laptop shut in such a hurry I knock a vase of flowers over. *For fuck's sake, I'm a bundle of nervous energy tonight!* I drop to the ground to pick up the glass and that's how Lukka finds me, on all fours, my bright blue dress riding up my backside.

"I'm very happy to see you too, Saskia," he says, coming closer. He smells of soap and his bleach blonde hair is wet and combed back.

I scramble to my feet and find myself practically nose to nose with him.

"Is that how you always wait for my brother?" he asks.

I pull down my dress. "I forgot to tell him what those Swiss men said about Boris last night and I... I knocked the vase over." I push the broken glass into a pile with my foot. "All good now. Have you seen your brother?"

"He's at KLV tonight. He's there more and more lately."

I think back to the PDF on Konstantin's laptop. What the fuck was that about?

"Your builders work at night?"

"All our workers work day and night," he says. "How do you think we got so rich so fast?"

"But you hire humans."

Lukka laughs. "Of course, we hire humans. You think a Para would work so hard for such low wages? It's different at the club, here we pay well because our clients like the variation of our dancers, and our dancers have fun too. Because we all know when it comes to sex us Paras do it better." He smiles at me when he says that and my guts twist. "But onsite we need our men working without complaint, day and night, rain and shine."

"Is that why you give them physicals?" I ask.

Lukka's forehead wrinkles and I could seriously punch myself in the face. What did I have to open my big mouth for?

"I don't know anything about physicals," he says.

He's telling the truth.

"My mistake. Ansel said her brother works for you and that his bosses look after him. I'm just being American. You know, presuming you offer healthcare and all that."

I roll my eyes and Lukka laughs. "Maybe I can talk to Konstantin at the construction site," I say. "You know, if he's there right now?"

Lukka shakes his head. "He doesn't like visitors on the site. Talk to him tomorrow. Actually, have the night off." I raise my eyebrows and he smiles. "It's quiet and you look tired. Get some sleep and I'll see you tomorrow night."

I nod in agreement. I am going to need my beauty sleep, not because I'm tired but because Lukka has just confirmed exactly where I need to be tomorrow.

Time to do some daylight digging at KLV construction.

CHAPTER THIRTEEN

The *stroika*, as the driver refers to it, is a wide icy lot. I had no idea what to expect from a Russian building site. Manhattan is over-populated and our construction sites are narrow and tall, peppered with men in neon hard hats who eat sandwiches in rows and whistle at you when you walk by. There are a lot of men on this construction site too, but almost none of them in hardhats. As I make my way through the center of the lot, I catch fragments of languages - Kazakh, Tajik, Korean...

I can see the start of an ugly cream-colored building. They've built the parking lot first, it's unfinished and hollowed out in patterns like a honeycomb. Men go in and out slowly, like bees suffering from the cold. How can people work in these freezing conditions?

The edges of the lot have trailers on them. There's one bulky guy at the edge of the site yelling out orders in Russian. I stay away, observing for about ten minutes, but the cold is relentless. I swear my spine is beginning to freeze despite my bulky coat. I opted for sneakers instead of stripper heels today, but it turns out you can feel the cold snow more through sneakers than through heels. Go figure.

I watch the workers, attempting to pick out an anomaly, strange behavior, something important or valuable. I get nothing, they just look like a normal group of workers. I look back over to where the man was barking orders, but he must have disappeared into one of the warm trailers. Fuck it. I'm out of options. I walk up to the largest trailer and knock. The barking man opens the door and stares down at me with surprise. I don't think he's used to seeing women at his job.

"*Angliskii?*" I ask, highly doubting that this man speaks English, but it will give me added credibility. I peer past him to see who else I need to fool, but there's no one there. Inside is nothing but a boxy TV playing…porn. Hah! This will be useful.

He shakes his head at my English request.

"My name is Jennifer Laverne," I continue in perfect Russian. I clear my throat, buying myself some thinking time. "I represent Mr. Bloomberg, an American investor backing this development. Did Konstantin Volkov not tell you I was coming?"

He fidgets uncomfortably. "Ugh, *nyet*."

I make a show of peering past him again, this time more noticeably. I arch a brow and he follows my gaze, finally realizing he's left his cheap porn playing on the TV.

"You're supposed to show me around the site so that I can tell my superior, Konstantin's investor, how the project is going. But if you're busy I can reschedule with him."

I watch as fear flashes across his pig-like features. I've got him. He's not going to risk his boss getting a call about this.

"Of course," he says, putting on a coat and switching the TV off. "Tea or coffee?" he grunts, pointing at his stash of brown plastic cups, a pot of instant coffee, and some stale-looking Christmas chocolates.

"No thanks. Just the tour."

He shuts the door to his trailer behind us and we head over to the other trailers, entering one full of security monitors.

"This is where the night watch sleeps," he explains. I nod along and take photos, pretending to annotate them on my phone. He doesn't look enthralled by the fact that I'm taking photos, but what's he going to do? I have the porn card *and* the 'I'm on a first-name basis with your boss' card. I briefly imagine that these might be the pictures used for my news article and I feel a little pride that I've gotten this far. One week in and my leads are finally getting hotter.

The man points at the different video feeds and explains the development layout to me.

"Where are the blood test reports?" I ask, thinking back to the PDF on Konstantin's laptop.

Mr. Pig-face screws up his tiny eyes and sticks out his lower lip like he has no idea what I'm talking about. Lukka doesn't know, and the man before me doesn't know, but I wasn't imagining it - I definitely saw medical records of the workers.

OK. I need to wing this. "My employer cannot afford a public scandal," I say importantly, hoping the man doesn't realize I haven't a clue what I'm talking about. "I have to make sure this project is low risk, you understand? A breakout of disease, or leaked information on dire working conditions, would interest the press and could cost your investor dearly. Is there anything...unusual...I need to know in advance?"

I let the bait hang there, hoping he takes it. He doesn't.

"There's nothing wrong here."

Ping.

"Fine," I concede. "Then show me around the rest of the site."

I try to tune out the snooze-fest that is Mr. Pig-face mansplaining to me how cement is made, what the different machines are for, and how they will finish the building work. The whole tour lasts fifteen minutes and I'm so cold I'm scared to move my fingers in case they snap off.

"What are your employee working hours?" I ask.

"Eighteen-hour shifts, seven days a week."

What the fuck! One hundred and twenty-six hours a week and no day off? That's impossible. No human can manage that!

"My boss told me you're having problems with the workforce," I venture.

"What kind of problems?"

"That some of them are disappearing." I keep my tone neutral. "Did that affect the timeline for completion?"

He looks me over, as if he's only just noticed I'm a young woman. His beady eyes pause, then scan me from head to toe and finally settle on my sneakers.

"No one has disappeared here. Every worker is accounted for."

Ping. Ping.

I don't have time to question him over his lies. He's looked me over and made assumptions, and the assumption is that I shouldn't be there.

"Tour over," he says coldly, then turns and walks back to the trailer.

Shit. Shit. Shit.

I shouldn't have worn these shoes. Dead giveaway. No one who represents a foreign billionaire wears cheap sneakers. I start to make my way out of the lot, but a sound stops me in my tracks.

"Arman!" someone yells.

I turn and see one of the workers shouting over to his colleague. A man turns and I catch his face. There's something familiar about him, not just the name but the shape of his warm eyes and smile. That *has* to be Ansel's brother. He dumps a load of equipment he's carrying then heads over to the colleague calling him.

I plant myself in his way.

"Hey there. I'm a friend of your sister's. From the club," I say.

His eyes widen as he takes me in, but then his expression grows somber.

"Don't call it a club," he says, "That place is a whore house. But I know my sister is a good girl."

I have half a mind to lecture this dude on feminism and terminology, but that's not what I'm here for.

"She's upset about your friend disappearing. Maxim?"

He's a little taken back, then he looks even more miserable.

"I'm sure he's just taking a break. He'll be back," he says.

"A break? Because of how hard they work you here?"

He looks over at the foreman. He's stepped out of his trailer and is staring over at us. "It's not that bad. We are lucky to have such kind employers."

"But eighteen-hour shifts? That's crazy!"

He shrugs. "I don't feel tired, none of us do. Also, the food is very good. Things could be worse."

I falter. I have nothing left to say that won't raise suspicion. The same colleague that called him over tells him to go back to work.

"I have to go. Say hello to my sister, tell her... tell her I miss her," he says sadly before walking away.

Tell her yourself, I want to say. But then I remember his crazy work shifts and I'm flooded with guilt.

I need to get out of here. The icy ground cracks beneath my sneakers as I hurry away from the building site, my steps quickening, my breath forming foggy puffs. I thought it was a good idea to come here in the day when I could be safe from Vamps, but it's early afternoon now and it being winter the light is already fading. I have an hour until it's dark, max.

Suddenly, I feel someone behind me, their steps crunching on the dry mud. Is it Mr. Porno Pig-man? Has he figured out I was lying to him? I don't want to turn around and look guilty, so I keep walking faster, the steps behind me speeding up to match mine.

Fuck it! I'd prefer to look guilty than die!

This lot is huge, but I can see the exit in the distance. I take a freezing breath and break into a run, thankful I've worn sneakers. I bank left, then sprint all the way out of the lot to the main road. It's busy with cars out here, which means I'm no longer alone, so I dare to look over my shoulder. But whoever was behind me has gone.

I bend at the waist, hands resting on my knees, and attempt to catch my breath. My frozen fingers fumble on the touchscreen of my phone as I struggle to order an Uber. *Come on!* The darker it gets, the less safe I am.

I glance behind me again at the entrance to the lot and my breath hitches. There's a silhouette of someone watching me – someone tall, slim and muscular. Definitely not Pig-man.

My ride pulls up beside me and I throw myself into the back of the car.

CHAPTER FOURTEEN

I thought I'd warm up as soon as I got into my shitty apartment, but it's just as cold inside as out. It started to snow heavily after I got into the cab, and in the twenty seconds it took to walk from the car to my apartment door and find my keys I'm already soaked through and my bones ache with cold. All I want to do is have a bath. My rented apartment may be disgusting, but at least there's hot water.

I go to peel my wet clothes off my clammy skin, then stop. The buildings are so close together around here that I'm basically about to give my neighbors a free peep show. I switch off the lights and run the bath in semi-darkness. I don't think I've ever been this cold before. My skin feels like marble as I pull off my icy underwear and wrap my bathrobe around myself, before heading back to the main room to check my phone.

I didn't get much at KLV Construction, but at least I got some photos. I'm going to email them to Jackson and tell him everything I know so far - which isn't all that much. I wish I'd managed to download those medical records. Something doesn't add up, and I know it has something to do with the workers' blood.

I pad silently across the dark living room. My windows are glowing as outside the snow has settled, making everything shine like cake covered in fondant. Moscow is definitely prettier in white. The only light shining into the room is yellow and sickly from the streetlight outside, casting eerie shadows on the ceiling.

Then I see him, a shadowy figure leaning against my wall.

"There you are," he says, stepping into the light of the streetlamp.

It's Konstantin.

He's wearing an expensive-looking dark blue suit with a starched white collar, as always, every bit the gentleman...save for the hard glint in his eye, and the breaking and entering.

"How the fuck did you get inside my apartment?" I say, wrapping my bathrobe around me and somehow managing to keep my voice steady.

Konstantin raises his eyebrows and gives me a look as if to say *'I'm a Vampire. What a stupid question.'*

He steps closer. "Did you never wonder how I discovered your real name? You really should change your luggage labels so they match your fake passport."

My first impulse is to run again. I turn to the front door, but he moves with incredible speed, a blur shooting past me. Next thing he's leaning over me, his hand resting on the wall above my left shoulder. I'm trapped.

"You were at my construction site this afternoon," he says. Not a question.

It was him. He was the one who followed me earlier as the sun was setting. But how? I didn't think Vamps could go out until it was properly dark? I try and duck under his arm but he's too fast, pushing me against the wall.

"It wasn't me," I say.

"Don't lie, Saskia. I told you on your first day at the club to behave yourself." His mouth is so close to my ear I can smell his cologne, his cheek smooth against mine. I open my mouth then shut it again. Konstantin isn't stupid, I won't get away with some bullshit lie - I will have to settle with a variation of the truth.

"I was trying to find my friend's brother," I mutter. "He works there."

"What friend?" His arm is still resting on the wall behind me, and I'm keenly aware that all I'm wearing is a bathrobe tied loosely around the middle.

"Ansel," I say. "One of your dancers. She's my friend and she hasn't seen her boyfriend in ages. She wondered if her brother had seen him, but she's been too busy working, so I offered to talk to him."

It's so close to the truth even I'm forgetting the real reason I was there.

"You work for *me*," he says, his breath warming my freezing neck. "Not my dancers. The site is off bounds. I need to trust you, Saskia." He adds the last part with a growl, and I feel the tension in his body pressing against mine. My heart is racing. His body is blocking me and I'm beginning to feel claustrophobic. I have to get him off me, I have to say something to keep him on-side.

"You said you wanted me to look into the disappearances of your workers and... I wanted to look for clues. I just wanted to impress you."

He steps back, pondering on my words, and that's when I make a run for it. I don't know where I think I'm going, or how I'll get away from him, but I run through the dark as fast as I can towards the door - and straight into a coffee table.

"Fuck!" I cry out, falling in a heap at his feet.

Konstantin looks down at me, shaking his head pityingly.

"Let me help you," he says, holding out his hand.

I bat it away. "Leave me alone!"

I cradle my ankle as the pain sweeps in, engulfing me in waves. I'm going to be sick. What the hell have I done to my foot? I can feel a lump already growing beneath my hand. I take a peek and groan. My ankle is a dark blue-green and my vision is beginning to blur.

Konstantin crouches beside me and I shuffle away. He's looking at me intently, his eyes as black as his brother's are white.

"I can help you," he says gently. "I'm a dancer. I have seen many a foot injury in my time. I have treated many a ballerina."

I think back to him dancing the first time we met. The way his shoulders rippled and his back arched, his face set like stone. So much beauty compressed into one cold psycho. He tentatively touches my ankle and I cry out in pain.

"I don't want your help," I spit. Who the fuck does he think he is, breaking into my apartment and scaring me, then intimidating me like this? I've gone through enough shit for this mission. I should at least feel safe in my own apartment.

There's a rushing sound and I realize my bath is still running and it's about to overflow. All I need is to flood my crappy apartment on top of all this shit. Leaving Konstantin crouching on the floor I go to stand, but as soon as I put pressure on my foot the pain shoots up my leg and I collapse. He catches me, gathering me closer to where he's kneeling on the ground and pulling my robe tighter around me. He keeps his hands at my collar, his thumb stroking the side of my neck.

"I'm sorry I scared you," he says. No ping. He's telling the truth. "Thank you for trying to help at the construction company. Did you find anything?"

I breathe deeply, trying to focus on his words and not the searing pain shooting up my leg.

"Nothing, except that your employees like working for you. They say you really look after them."

In a flash, he turns off the bathwater and crouches beside me again.

"I look after those I care about," he says. Gently he takes my chin between his finger and thumb and tips up my face so I'm looking up into his dark eyes again, his other hand resting on my throbbing ankle. "Let me look after you, Saskia."

"Do strip club owners get first aid training? Where's your certificate?"

A light smile flickers at his lips, then he opens his mouth a little. At first, I think he's going to say something, but I quickly realize he's making room for his fangs to grow. My heart flutters. I've never seen Vamp teeth up close like this before, and I'm transfixed. It's not like the scary movies where they spring out like sharp daggers. Konstantin's fangs are only about an inch longer than normal canines and just as wide. The only difference is that they are sharp. Sharp and thick enough to puncture flesh and leave two gaping holes large enough to feed from.

My breath quickens. Konstantin knows I'm a Witch. He's not going to bite me, so what the hell is he doing?

He lets go of my chin and plunges his teeth into his wrist, ripping at it violently. Then he holds his bleeding arm out to me.

"Drink," he says. He traces my lips with his finger, blood dripping down his arm and onto my white bathrobe. "It will heal you," he adds, giving me a crooked smile.

Hesitantly I do as I'm told and part my lips, letting him

bring his wrist to my mouth. I've never tasted Vampire blood before. I'm not going to pretend I'm not curious, even though the Blood Web is full of stories of vampires tricking humans into drinking their blood and then turning them without consent. I think twice and go to pull away, but the pain in my ankle has my entire body trembling and as soon as his blood touches my lips I know I have no choice.

Holding his arm in both of my hands I run my tongue against the gash at his wrist. I'm not sure if it's me who groans or him.

Oh! Vampire blood tastes nothing like human or Witch blood. There's no iron-like taste, instead, Konstantin's blood is sweet and oaky like a mature dry sherry. I suck hungrily. I know I'm being obscene but suddenly I'm unable to stop.

"Easy now, sweetheart. That's more than enough," he purrs.

No. I need more, just a little drop more.

Konstantin is laughing as he pulls his arm away, the first time I've heard him laugh, and I wipe my mouth with the back of my hand.

I'm buzzing, every inch of me feels alive. Not only does my ankle no longer hurt but I feel like I've enjoyed a week in the Maldives then sniffed a line of Columbia's finest. My bones are liquid and my head is floating, yet I'm also aching in places I shouldn't be - all too aware that beneath my bathrobe I'm naked and my nipples are hard.

The way Konstantin is looking at me it's clear he knows exactly what Vamp blood does to a Witch.

"A little bit of blood goes a long way," he says with a wink, sending a bolt of electricity shooting right between my legs. "Better now?"

He's so close that when he speaks it blows my hair out of my eyes. I've never noticed how full his lips are or how sharp his jaw. Even though his eyes are like blots of ink I can still see his pupils widen as they drink me in.

His teeth shrink back to normal and he straightens his tie. I want him to go. I want to have my bath. Except I can still feel his blood running through my veins, like hot water working its way through a block of ice. I'm burning up, and all I can think of is the touch of his skin against my lips and his blood sliding down my throat.

I shake my head, trying to clear my thoughts, and pull my bathrobe tighter at my throat.

"Get dressed," he says, walking over to my bed and throwing a pair of jeans and a sweatshirt at me. "We're going."

I catch the clothes he's thrown at me. Am I in trouble? "Where are we going?"

"Home," he says. "You live with me now."

⬤

When Konstantin mentioned going back home with him, I presumed he lived in an apartment. He doesn't. The car, driven by a thick-necked man who hasn't uttered a single word the entire journey, makes an abrupt stop outside a pair of wrought iron gates that swing effortlessly open.

Konstantin is sitting in the back of the car and he's watching me as we follow a winding drive flanked by tall trees like a tunnel. I can tell he wants me to be impressed, and I am. Because his house is a mansion. I had no idea there were homes this grand just outside Moscow in a suburb called Rublyovka. We pass an ornate fountain and lush lawns surrounded by blue spruces and marble statues before reaching the house itself.

"You live here?" I breathe.

"I built it," he says. "Lukka has the west wing and I have

the east. There's an apartment on the top floor you can stay in. We need to know where you are at all times. From now on you will leave for work with us and you will stay close to us. We have lots of enemies. I don't want you going anywhere alone."

They don't want others getting to me? Or they don't want me snooping into their business any further? I steal a glance at the silhouette of Konstantin's face against the car window. He's always so still. I wish I knew what he was thinking.

I sink into the leather seat and take a deep breath. Agreeing to live with the brothers is either the single most stupid thing I have ever done or proof that I take my job so seriously I'm prepared to climb into the beehive to get to the honey. We pull up outside an impressive winding staircase leading up to the house and he opens the car door for me. Without a word he takes my hand and I follow him up the stairs, across a large empty foyer sporting a sparkling chandelier similar to the one in the club, and up another flight of white marble stairs.

His hand is cool in mine, strong, but I have no idea where he's taking me. Or, come to think of it, why the fuck he's holding my hand. Is the bloodsucking thing like Vamp foreplay? Are we dating now or something?

I bite my lips together to stop myself from laughing nervously. This whole thing is freaking me out...and I'm not sure if even in a bad way.

Eventually, we come to a stop at the end of a plush hallway and he pushes open a set of heavy mahogany doors. We're in a large room decorated in tones of duck-egg blue, cream, and gold. Everything is in the baroque style, mixed with modern amenities. A four-poster bed and a huge TV screen set into the wall, more double doors leading to what looks like a huge changing area, and at the far end of the room a round, sunken bath big enough for an entire football team. It's overflowing with bubbles and there's a bottle of champagne and strawberries beside it.

"Too much?" he asks, nodding at the bath. "I called ahead."

When? He must have done it back at the other apartment while I was getting dressed.

"Is this my room?" I ask. It's bigger than most apartments I've lived in.

He nods.

"Thank you," I say, meaning it. I want to hug him. I want to do more than hug him.

What the hell is this freaky Stockholm syndrome shit? I'm thanking a violent, unpredictable Vampire who owns a strip joint and kills business associates. Maybe this is one of the weird side effects of Vamp blood consumption. That and the continuous ache between my legs.

I expect him to walk out of the room without another word. His usual cold unreadable self. Instead he's looking at me as if I'm a tiny kitten that's just turned up on his doorstep.

"Take tonight off," he says.

He turns to leave and I don't know what makes me do it, but I reach out for his arm and grab on to his sleeve. Maybe it's because I can still taste the sweetness of his blood on my lips, but I want…I don't know what I want.

He looks at me and I can't breathe. His pupils are so big that his eyes are blacker than ever. I can practically feel the heat coming off him.

"Is there something you need?" he says huskily.

I shake my head and let go of his sleeve.

"What the fuck is going on?" says a voice from the doorway.

Lukka is standing there bare-chested in baggy white trousers that fall halfway down his ass, with at least five thick chains around his neck. He's also wearing sunglasses – probably because of the glare of his gold jewelry.

"Nothing at all," Konstantin replies. "Saskia lives here now. And you're going to shut your troublesome mouth and leave her alone."

Lukka frowns and Konstantin gives me a slow smile, but the hard glint is back in his eyes.

"Rest. I'll see you tomorrow."

I can hear the brothers arguing all the way to the other side of their ostentatious home. And I just stand there, in the gold-trimmed bathroom of a pair of Russian Vampire brothers, wondering how the fuck I ended up here.

CHAPTER FIFTEEN

Konstantin's hands are iron cuffs around my wrists. He pins me down, angling my hands backward into his expensive silken sheets. My chest is bare and I arch my back to meet him. He likes it. Running his fangs over the side of my ribs, he ends the motion with a kiss above my navel. I groan, arching further so my hot core is closer to him. He's wearing nothing but ballet pants which do little to hide his desire. I wrap my legs around him, bringing him closer, wanting to feel that same hardness between my legs. With a firm palm, he pushes me back down.

"Not yet," he says.

He sits up, back on his knees and stares at me. That infernal dark stare. I want him inside of me, I realize. I climb on top, clamping my thighs around his waist. The sweet ecstasy of him beneath me makes my eyes close with pleasure. His hands are on my shoulders, pulling me down harder as I slowly begin to ride him. Up and down. Up and down.

He kisses my neck.

"Would you like some more blood?" he says, looking up at me suddenly. He dips his fingers in a large cut-glass fruit bowl beside him, letting the blood drip off them and back into the receptacle.

My breathing is ragged. "Yes. Please."

Konstantin smiles and splatters the blood across my chest, painting my breasts crimson as I gasp in delight.

With a jolt, I sit up and I'm wide awake.

WHAT THE ACTUAL FUCK?!

It's not exactly strange for me to have the odd horny dream, but nothing *that* intense. And it's common Para knowledge that blood feeders can sometimes have dreams about the Vamps the blood belongs to - but *sex* dreams? Maybe that's some Witchy side effect.

Well, I don't want Konstantin in my nightmares and I sure as hell don't want him in my dreams. *And* I *definitely* don't want him Jackson Pollocking my chest with his blood.

I throw my head back against the pillow and groan. I nearly broke my ankle because of Konstantin, and I've seen him snap a man's neck just as easily, yet now all I can think about is the taste of his fucking delicious blood.

Ugh! Get a grip Saskia! Both Volkov's need to stay the hell away from my nocturnal habits.

Plus, I also have a banging migraine. I've read that Vamp blood can do that to a Witch too. I groan again from the weight of my horny hangover headache.

I have no idea what time it is because I can't see out of the window. At dawn, the whir of metallic shutters jolted me awake as all the windows in the room were clamped shut. I knew Vampires didn't sleep in coffins during the day, I just didn't realize they make their homes one giant dark coffin instead. But then again, few Vamps are as rich as Konstantin.

Looking on the bright side, if the shutters are still down it means it's still daytime. Which means I don't have to get up for work right now.

I stretch out in my luxurious king-size bed and run my fingers against the fine sheets. I can hear Jackson's voice in my head, like I do every day, scolding me.

"Reporters are observers, Saskia. WHY THE FUCK WOULD YOU MOVE IN WITH GANGSTER VAMPS?"

Because of the thread count, Jackson. Duh.

In all seriousness, my disregard for my safety scares me sometimes. My mother has called me reckless since I was little, whereas she called my sister prudent and wise. Which is pretty ironic considering the prudent sister has disappeared and not the disappointing younger one.

Something between hunger pangs, the residue of last night's inappropriate dreams, and slumbering grief for my sister stirs in my stomach. It's a weird mix and it's making my headache worse.

I check my private phone which at least I've successfully kept hidden all this time. There are two emails from Jackson and three text messages. The last one asks if I'm dead.

Alive and kicking ass, I reply, keeping it both vague and positive.

That's all the big cat is getting this morning. My head is thumping enough without having to consider how crap I am at my job and imagining my impending dismissal as soon as I return to New York without a story.

I find a silk robe in the marble bathroom and set off in search of food. The halls echo with grandeur and the sound of my footsteps. I feel like Belle in Beast's castle which, after the creepy 'threaten you then rescue you' way Konstantin treated me last night, is unfortunately very apt. The suave bastard is definitely the kind of Vamp who would build a girl a library. Whereas Lukka, on the other hand, is the kind of

Vamp who would pull out all the pages from a good book just to make a few joints.

As if summoned from my sleepy thoughts, I find Lukka in the kitchen. He's bent over the sink brushing his fangs with one hand, holding a bottle of Veuve Clicquot champagne in the other.

He takes a swig, gurgles with it, and spits it into the sink.

I lean back, arms crossed. "Are you fucking kidding me?"

He glances over his shoulder, though with his Vamp hearing I'm sure he heard me coming.

"Good morning, little Witch." He flashes me a smile full of toothpaste. It comes across as half comedic, half demonic. I'm still not sure if he's evil or a fool…or both. If there's one thing I've learned investigating for The Blood Web Chronicle it's that the foolish demons are the most dangerous.

"Why would you gargle with champagne?" I roll my eyes to make it obvious I find his antics lame.

He observes me for a long time, a trickle of white saliva snaking its way down his chin.

"You must understand, us Russians," he says, "we live inside snow globes. Yesterday we had nothing, today we have more than we could ever need or spend. Tomorrow we might be dead." He takes a swig and swallows it this time. I watch his tattooed Adam's apple bob up and down.

"So…" He rounds the island toward me. "When you ask me why I rinse my mouth with champagne, I can only answer - why not?"

I look up into his strange milky eyes and think back to the metallic shutters at the window and the way he slashed the throats of all those guys in the restaurant as if it were nothing. As if he lives one night at a time.

"You really think you might be dead tomorrow?" I ask.

He cocks his head. "Always. I died once. I can die again."

There's an eerie absence of *pings*.

"You don't lie much," I say.

"Why would I lie?" A big fang-lined smile lights up his face. "When the truth is so much scarier."

I frown. He likes talking in riddles. It's more than a little irritating.

"I don't lie, little Witch. But I can't say the same for my brother."

Lukka puts the bottle in the sink and saunters out, cackling to himself and leaving me wondering what the hell he meant by that.

I grab the near-empty bottle and drain it. I should be having breakfast, or dinner, but living with Vamps has already rubbed off on me and I'm not about to waste good champagne.

●

I'm sitting in the back of Konstantin's fancy town car sandwiched between him and Lukka. There's enough room in the spacious back seat for none of us to touch but Lukka's shoulder borders on mine nonetheless. Konstantin has been talking on the phone to some guy called Vassily since we left the house. I'm doing my best to listen in, but all I'm getting is something about samples and results. He could be talking about anything. Lukka, on the other hand, is wearing the largest pair of headphones I've ever seen, bobbing his head at music so loud I can hear every word. He shows me his iPhone and I see an album cover of a musician with nearly as many tattoos as him. Lukka flashes me a champagne-clean smile and somehow detaches one headphone and hands it over to me. Music fills my right ear. OK, this is good. Apparently, I like Russian rap a lot more than I thought I would. The lyrics talk about bathing a girl in cranberry juice and my cheeks burn as I think back to my sex dream.

Snow flows down lightly and Lukka squeezes my hand to show me we are passing Saint Basil's Cathedral. I gawk at the sight of the Red Square and the most famous of Russian cathedrals, looking every inch the storybook concoction of primary colors and gold-dipped peaks. The entire Kremlin looks like it's made of gingerbread. It's a glorious sight, and for a second, I allow myself to get wrapped up in the beauty of Moscow.

Half an hour later we arrive at the strip club together and I'm now clad in what looks like a PVC nurse's uniform courtesy of Lukka and his little gift awaiting me. Needless to say, I prefer Konstantin's taste in clothes. If *he'd* dressed me today I wouldn't look like I'm about to administer a 500mg prescription of blow jobs.

Konstantin stops me as I exit the changing room.

"We have special guests tonight. My biggest rival, Rada, and his team. You will be working their table," he says. "Keep track of their lies, sweetheart. We think they might be involved with the disappearance of our cargo. Varlam, the man we disposed of at the Sakhalin restaurant, was a former associate of his. I had no choice but to connect the dots, so I've invited them here. Rada is the one who would benefit most from my loss of shipments *and* employees."

I nod, like I give a shit about his missing cargo. Konstantin's workers are still disappearing and he cares more about boxes than bodies. This whole time I've been focusing on the Black Rabbit and their KLV construction company, but I haven't thought about Konstantin's shipping company connections and all the crooked men tied up with that.

I merge into the crowded club, and an hour later I hear Konstantin's special guests before I see them. Like any other pack of powerful rich men, they are making enough noise for the entire club to notice them.

I saunter over to the entrance, and give the two men my biggest smile. Is this it? Just two of them?

"Good evening, gentleman. Welcome to the Black Rabbit," I say in Russian. "Follow me. We've reserved a special table at the front for you. Champagne on tap, compliments of the house."

They both have identical cheekbones and eyes clearer than water. Father and son. I'm guessing the older one is Rada – although he looks the same age as Konstantin. Vampires don't age, so it's rare to see a really old one. His son, dressed casually in a hoodie and jeans, looks around him eyes wide like it's his first time in a strip club. He looks my age, maybe a bit younger. According to what I've read on the Blood Web most Vamps who already have children when they're turned wait until their sons and daughters are at least twenty-five before converting them into Vamps. Most refuse to outlive their next of kin, but equally refuse to turn unpredictable teens into monsters.

Rada, dressed in a tailored suit complete with a white handkerchief in his breast pocket, isn't looking at the dancers though. His gaze is fixed on me.

"Where's Konstantin?"

I wasn't expecting that.

"He's out," I lie. "But he said I was to take special care of you."

The man nods, his lip curling in the corner. He then turns to his son and tells him to keep his voice down when talking business, because the Black Rabbit has long ears. Except he says it in Chechnian, so I won't understand him. How cultured they are. And how wrong.

"I'm expecting two more colleagues," Rada says to me in Russian as I bring them champagne.

A few minutes later a man and a woman appear, and I can see why Konstantin was worried about them. The second man is tall and bald with a tiger tattoo climbing up the side of his neck. He looks like he's been made from wooden blocks. The woman is slight and compact, and dressed in a pants suit. I thought no female clients were allowed in the club. I notice Rada's son edge away from her as she sits down beside him.

"Vodka," she shouts at me. "Two bottles."

As I set the vodkas before her I feel the touch of a cold hand traveling up the back of my thigh. I don't react though, being touched is not unusual in this place, but it's rare for the creep to be a woman. I glance at her and she runs the tip of her tongue between her teeth suggestively.

"Why are you not working the pole?" she asks.

"Not tonight," I reply as genially as possible. "Can I get you anything else?"

She loses interest quickly and turns to the two men who are talking in hushed tones, but Rada's son is on the periphery of the group and remains staring at me. It's not easy to hear what they're saying without looking like I'm listening, but maybe there's another way to get information.

I unzip the front of my dress a little until my cleavage is on full display and lean closer to Rada's son.

"What's your name?" I ask.

He glances at his father, as if asking for permission, but Rada is in deep conversation. This guy is no boy, but it's still clear who's in charge.

"Stepan," he says, squaring his shoulders.

Stepan has a cocky smile playing on his lips, but his pretty eyes tell me he's not used to being surrounded by Paranormal strippers. They are darting around the room, taking in the dancers, Shifter barman, and the loud groups of Vamps drinking blood from fancy decanters.

"Are you nervous?" I whisper in Russian.

"Not at all."

Ping.

"Your colleagues look a bit scary."

His gaze flickers over to the woman and the man made of bricks.

"They don't scare me," he says.

Ping.

I sit beside him, straining to hear what the others are saying. A few words float over to me, "Cargo…good price…they murdered them…find a buyer."

What cargo? Who are they talking about? I need to know - and I think I know who will tell me.

"You look younger than most of the Vamps in here," I say, running my finger along his arm. I feel him flex at my touch. "How old are you?"

"Twenty-three. Today's my birthday."

Bingo!

I whisper happy birthday in his ear and watch as his face clouds with nerves. With eyes and cheekbones like his I'm surprised he's not surrounded by girls every minute, but perhaps with a father like Rada he's not let off his leash very often. I decide Stepan's my key to finding out everything I need to know, I just need to get him away from this mob.

An icy claw grips my hand. The pierced woman is leaning over Stepan to get my attention. I jump up and plaster a smile to my face.

"Can I help you?"

She sneers. "We're getting thirsty."

I look at the undrunk bottles of champagne and vodka on the table. It's not alcohol they want to drink, and it's too early for the Blood Bunnies.

Rada and the other man have stopped talking and watch their female colleague with a look of amusement on their faces.

"What would you like to drink?" I ask.

"You," she replies.

The men laugh but I notice Stepan doesn't.

"Two more hours and they will bring the girls," I say quietly. "I can get you a bottle of... I can get you something else in the meantime."

She gives me a smile sharp as a dagger, then with lightning speed pulls me towards them until I topple over, landing on the lap of the bald man. His laugh is low in my ear.

"Special delivery," he says, making Rada laugh. He inches my skirt up and slaps my butt. "It's much more fun to get our drinks freshly squeezed."

I scramble to my feet and straighten out my ridiculous dress, much to their amusement. I'd like nothing more than to let them choke on my blood, but I can't go around poisoning *all* of Konstantin's business contacts.

On the way back to the bar I mull it over. So, these special guests like their blood fresh, do they? But do they hate the Volkov brothers enough to murder their employees for it?

I place a cut-glass decanter of god-knows-who's blood on the table and turn my attention to Stepan.

"Follow me," I say. The others have their backs to us, paying no attention to the only non-Vamp. "I have a birthday treat for you."

I've never given a private dance before – but Stepan doesn't strike me as someone who would know the difference between a good dance or a bad one. His hand's warm in mine, a rarity in these parts, as I lead him through the club to the rooms where I first had my audition with Lukka. If you could call it that.

I notice most of the rooms are occupied and I bite back a smile as Stepan's eyes widen, taking in the girls through each round window in the doors.

"First time in a Para bar?" I ask.

"Of course not," he replies.

He's lying. He reaches out and slowly unzips the front of my dress making my cleavage spill out. I curse Lukka and his stupid choice of outfit.

"You don't feel like a Vampire," he says. "You're too warm."

How far am I prepared to go? I thought maybe the human would be more intimidated by me, that we could talk and flirt and I'd get some info out of him, but perhaps I underestimated him.

He sits down on the burgundy couch wrapped around a small stage with a pole.

"I'm not a Vampire," I reply, swaying to the music that's funneled into each room.

He pulls the zip of my dress further down. "Well, you're definitely not a nurse."

"No. But how's your blood pressure right now?"

Stepan's misty stare switches off suddenly and he bends over laughing. Shit. What did I do?

"Oh, sweetie. This is never going to work. But I tried." I stop swaying to the music and zip up my dress. I don't know what face I'm making but I know my cheeks are burning and I'm clearly amusing him. "It's not you," he says hurriedly. "I'm just more interested in that sexy monkey boy behind the bar than any of you girls twirling your pretty asses around poles."

Oh. I sit down beside him with a thump and he gives me a grin.

"Cool outfit, though. Maybe I could borrow it sometime."

I playfully slap his arm and he laughs.

"So why let me lead you here?" I say, trying to keep the disappointment out of my voice.

"Did you see the people I was sitting with? I'd do anything not to spend an evening with them."

"Yeah, they didn't look very cuddly. How come you're not celebrating your big day in a Para gay bar?"

He gives a sad laugh. "Yeah, my father is from Chechnya, not exactly rainbow friendly. He would never approve."

"Who cares, fuck him!"

He laughs. "I already like you."

Oh well, so my seduction technique was wasted on him. But maybe I can still use my Verity Witch skills to get some intel on his father's activities and what they think of the Volkov's. There's a bottle of champagne on ice already waiting for us in the room and I pop it open, rolling my eyes at him as he grins over at me.

"We may as well have a drink," I say, passing him a glass. "Are you looking forward to being turned into a Vamp?"

"Yeah. Kind of. At least when I'm a Vampire I'll be able to be myself without the risk of being killed," he replies.

I instantly feel bad for asking. He knocks back the glass of champagne in one gulp and I pour him another.

"What's it like working for your father?" I ask.

He shrugs. "I've been part of his shit all my life. My mother died when I was a baby. I don't know. Work is work."

Well, that doesn't sound very gangster-like to me. And Stepan definitely doesn't come across like a cold-blooded body drainer.

"What's your job exactly?" I ask.

"Shipping. My father's company moves cargo. I have no idea what we're doing in this club, to be honest. We're not half as shady as most of the people who come here. I wanted to stay home and watch reruns of *Glee*."

We laugh together and I pour him a third glass. He's not noticed that I haven't drunk a drop yet. Plus, he's telling the truth. About everything.

"The way Konstantin talks about you all, I figured you were all tough guys. His main competitors."

Stepan makes a face. "You think we'd mess with the Volkov brothers? You've got to be kidding me. My father is good at what he does, even though the company he keeps is questionable, but fucking with the Volkovs is a death sentence - no matter how cute Konstantin's butt is in those tight suits he wears. Don't tell him I said that. But we work *with* them, not against them."

Even a human would know he's telling the truth. And yeah, he's not the only one to have noticed the ballerina butt on Konstantin.

"I like you, Stepan," I say, meaning it. "I bet if we went out we'd have more fun than you'd have hanging out with those scary friends of your dad's."

"They aren't anyone's friends. They're double-crossing pieces of shit. I have no idea why my father trusts them with our business. It pains me to know that my father being a Vamp means I'll never be able to take over his business. That we're all stuck together like this forever." He swigs the dregs of champagne from his glass and frowns as he pours the last drop out of the bottle. "All those thugs care about is money and getting their hands on the highest quality blood."

Quality blood? I think back to the employee blood test results on Konstantin's emails, to his Shifter Blood Bunnies and the results he was inquiring about in the car earlier this evening. What the fuck is Konstantin's obsession with super blood? Beyond the normal 'need to drink blood to survive' thing, of course?

"What makes blood premium then?" I ask.

"It's not *what*," Stepan says. "It's *how*. My father doesn't get involved in any of that, but his cronies are always talking about it."

He's drunk an entire bottle of Crystal on his own and is starting to sway a bit. I lean over to prop him up and he hugs me. He squeezes me so tight I feel the zip of my dress slide all the way down.

"It's so nice to speak to someone normal," he slurs.

I'm about to ask him what he knows about the drained bodies, when a resounding smash of the door flying open pulls us apart. Silhouetted in the frame is Rada…and Konstantin.

Stepan jumps up, his features instantly hardening as if he were the tough Vamp-to-be his father knows him as. I stand beside him, my breasts spilling out of my nurse's costume. The heat from Konstantin's glare has me quickly zipping my dress back up.

"I bring you to a business meeting and I find you fucking cheap whores?" Rada snarls at his son.

"It's my birthday," Stepan deadpans with a shrug.

"If you're really interested in that slut, I'll bring you back in two years when you're a *real* man. Then you can drain every last drop from her."

I look over at Konstantin but he says nothing. Rada nods curtly at him then marches away, Stepan following behind without giving me a backward glance.

Konstantin closes the door quietly behind him and leans against it, arms crossed and face stony.

"So, you give lap dances now."

It's not a question.

"Talk to me," he says.

"They're not involved in any missing cargo," I reply, keeping my eyes fixed on the ground. "In fact, Rada's son said everyone is too scared of you and Lukka to mess you around."

Konstantin's lip twitches as if this pleases him. I keep Stepan's comment about his tight-ass to myself, and neither do I tell him about Rada's gang's obsession with blood. That's something Jackson needs to hear more about. I finally have a lead and I'm not passing it over to Konstantin - not until I get to the bottom of it myself.

Konstantin is staring at me, but I can't decipher the look on his face. He pulls up the strap of my bra that has slipped down my shoulder and I suppress a shudder. His finger is cold against my skin and I remember the sweet taste of his blood sliding down my throat last night, and the way my core pulsed with want after.

"I don't have anything to worry about?" he says, tracing my lips with his finger.

I shake my head. He takes a step forward, closing the gap between us. Flashes of my dream materialize before my eyes every time I blink. Konstantin's blood on my chest, his body between my thighs, his mouth against mine.

I look away from his ink-dark eyes and clear my throat.

"You look nervous," he says. "Did you sleep badly?"

"No, I slept wonderfully," I said.

He smiles. "Of course, you did."

CHAPTER SIXTEEN

There are still a few hours until closing time but I've had enough for one night. Konstantin has avoided me since the episode with Stepan and I've spent my time pretending to work but really mulling over the intel I got from my failed seduction. I need to look further into Rada's cronies and why they may possibly want to steal blood from construction workers when it's so easy to walk into a bar like this one and get your fill. And why would construction worker blood taste better anyway?

I'm starving and the club is emptying. I head to the changing rooms where I know there will be cake. I can't remember the last thing I ate, and my headache still hasn't gone since I woke up.

At first it looks like the room is empty, then I hear a gentle snuffle. Ansel, the dancer from Kazakhstan, is in the corner huddled in a ball on the bench and Lukka is standing over her so I can only see his back.

What the hell is he doing to her? Why is she whimpering?

With all my might I shove him to the side and grab Ansel by the shoulders.

"Are you ok? Did he hurt you?"

She doesn't answer right away.

I swivel around to face Lukka. "If you hurt her, I will use that stupid gun holster you're always wearing to choke you in your sleep."

Lukka looks briefly taken aback, and I feel fear at the edges of my vision like a cold fog. Maybe threatening a murderous Vamp in his own club isn't the smartest thing to do.

Then he laughs, hooking his hands through his gun holster.

"This is Supreme limited edition, little Witch. It's not stupid."

That's what he got out of that?

Lukka continues laughing as he walks out of the changing room, the door quietly clicking shut behind him.

I turn back to Ansel and examine her for neck wounds or bruises.

"I'm going to kill him," I whisper.

"He didn't hurt me," she says, her voice small. She's crumpled on the bench like a wounded bird trying and failing to take flight. "He offered to help me."

"Help you? With what?"

"With finding out who hurt Maxim."

"You found him?"

She nods and her thin body starts to shake. I have the urge to cover her with a blanket, but that's the last thing you'll find in a strip club.

She closes her eyes and for a moment I think she's praying. Then she speaks.

"His body was discovered this morning. It was completely drained of blood."

Words fail me. I stare down at Ansel, the pain in her eyes is heart-wrenching.

The faces of that evil female Vamp and the guy with the tiger tattoo flash in my mind. Stepan didn't trust them and neither do I.

I envelop Ansel in a hug and let her sob on my shoulder. I can't say I'm that upset about the news, he didn't sound like the nicest of boyfriends, but I also know what it feels like to lose someone. I squeeze her tighter to me, the entire time itching to find out whether Konstantin already knows.

I knock on the office door. When there's no answer I walk in anyway.

"I didn't say come in," Konstantin says. A man wearing a white lab coat is beside him and they are bent low over some documents.

He signals for the man to leave his office then sighs, looking back down at his paperwork.

"What do you want? Looking for more people to practice your lap dancing with?"

I ignore his barbed comment.

"Thought you should know I sent one of your dancers home."

His head snaps up inhumanly fast.

"You did *what*?"

I knew this was coming – but what was I meant to do? Give Ansel a hug and tell her to get back on her pole and forget about her dead boyfriend? The girl is heartbroken and I'm so close to getting to the bottom of this. I need to quiz Ansel about all she knows, and to do that I need to be a true friend. Which is why I told her to go home and said I'd deal with the boss.

Konstantin's on his feet, teeth bared like he wants to rip me apart. He strides over, but I stand my ground.

"*You* don't manage my staff, darling," he growls, making

the last word sound like it has ten syllables. "Why did you do it?"

"Ansel's boyfriend was found murdered this morning. I figured even your rich client freaks would struggle to get it up for a girl getting tears all over her sparkling panties."

Konstantin's body relaxes and he rubs his temples. His teeth go back to normal.

"Who was her boyfriend?"

"A guy called Maxim. He worked at your construction site. Did you know him?"

He doesn't even have the decency to look sad or shocked.

"You think I know the name of every person that works for me? I did hear there was another murder onsite, but I didn't know he was linked to one of my dancers."

"Do you think one of your rivals is behind these murders?" I ask.

"Whoever it is they are being very sloppy," he replies. He turns around and walks back to his desk. "I like your work, Saskia. You did well earlier with Rada and his gang tonight. But that's the last time you do anything in my club without asking first. No more private dancing and no sending staff home. Understand?"

I nod. Realizing that he didn't answer my question properly.

"You owe me," he adds.

I think of all the different ways he might punish me, the dangerous jobs he might have lined up for me, but the last thing I'm expecting is what he says next. "Tomorrow. I have a box at the Bolshoi Theatre to see Swan Lake."

Ballet? Tomorrow? I wanted to talk to Ansel tomorrow, but maybe I should give her a day or two to grieve before I start quizzing her. I'll text her later. I've never been to the ballet and I'm not missing out on a trip to the Bolshoi. I must look like a kid at Christmas because Konstantin looks pleased with himself.

"Will you be dancing?" I ask.

"Not this time. My days as a leading man are behind me. You will be my date."

My heart stutters. "Business or pleasure?"

He smiles. "I'll let you decide."

CHAPTER SEVENTEEN

When I got back to the Volkov house this morning, just before dawn, a floor-length gown was waiting for me on my bed. Konstantin. The smooth motherfucker. Tucked inside the dress is a note telling me what time to meet him at the theatre that evening.

I'm trying, but it's hard to hate a guy who gives you the *Pretty Woman* treatment.

The driver pulls up outside the Bolshoi theatre and I climb out of the car Konstantin organized for me, gathering the folds of my dress so they don't touch the mounds of snow lining the streets like fondant. The gown is the color of fresh blood and fits like a second skin. The red full sleeves fall off-shoulder, halfway down to the cinched waist, and the train splits, red and black, and fanning out like the wings of a butterfly. Konstantin even included ruby earrings that look like droplets of blood.

I'm sensing a theme here.

"You look...exquisite."

Konstantin appears out of nowhere at the theatre entrance. He's in a black smoking jacket with a shawl lapel. He offers me the crook of his arm and I take it.

"Your hair looks very beautiful like that."

It's in waves cascading down my back. "Well you did send a hairdresser to the house this afternoon," I say. "I found it a little controlling at the time, but the day I say no to a free blow-dry is the day I've finally lost it."

He shrugs. "Devil's in the detail."

I gaze up at the statue of Apollo that presides over the columned back-lit entrance, as Konstantin leads me up the steps of the theatre and into the bustling foyer. We visit the coat check and I'm relieved to see I'm not the only one dressed like a princess tonight. We turn heads as we waltz past the red silk tapestries that adorn the white-walled Imperial hall. With a start, I realize people recognize Konstantin. He must have danced in this very theatre – the famous leading man.

"Did your original date stand you up, then?" I whisper as he steers me beneath the endless crystal chandeliers and ceilings painted in *grisaille*. We reach a wide set of red-velvet carpeted stairs.

"I was going to come alone. I do most things alone."

Doesn't your wrist get tired? I bite the joke back, it's too beautiful here. For once I'm not in the mood for my own sarcasm.

On the next landing, people are mingling and drinking flutes of champagne. Konstantin heads for the bar and orders one for me, as well as a single of eighteen-year-old Macallan scotch that probably costs as much as my dress.

Some members of the crowd nod at him, but most seem to be avoiding his eye. A thrill runs up my spine as I realize no one here but me knows what Konstantin is. Or what he's capable of.

He places his cool hand on the small of my back and I jump.

"Sweetheart, I have a little job for you. I'm going to introduce you to some people and make small talk. Squeeze my hand if they lie, just like you did in the restaurant the other night."

I think back to the bloodbath in Sakhalin. Is that why he has me wearing red? So that when he massacres some poor bastard it won't leave a stain?

He takes my hand, his lips flickering into a half-smile like he can read my mind. "Don't worry. I promise to be every bit the gentleman tonight."

"Mr. Volkov, I'm glad you could make it," says a deep voice beside us.

Konstantin turns and smiles at the old man.

"Boris, so nice to see you again," Konstantin says.

Ping!

"Are you with your beautiful wife this evening?" he adds.

"Unfortunately, my wife was feeling a little unwell," the old man replies, snaking his arm around the waist of a young blonde woman. "So, I'm here with my niece instead."

Ping. Ping.

It's like a cash register in my head. If this goes on any longer, I'm going to need an Ibuprofen.

"Let me introduce you to Saskia," Konstantin says. "She works with me. She's also one of the most remarkable women I've ever met."

I wait for the ping. There isn't one. I take a deep breath and shake the man's hand.

"Boris is one of my business partners," Konstantin explains, stroking his thumb along the inside of my wrist. I swallow and try to focus, but I can taste his Vamp blood on the tip of my tongue again. "Our latest venture is proving a little more complicated than first estimated though. Isn't that right, my friend?"

Boris looks surprised that Konstantin is talking shop at the ballet, but he quickly covers up his discomfort.

"Business is never straight forward, you know that. I too am very upset by the delay we've encountered. And the reasons behind it."

I squeeze Konstantin's hand. His face doesn't move a muscle.

"Of course," Konstantin drawls, all white teeth and flinty eyes. I notice the blonde woman is looking at my date more than her own. To be honest I don't blame her. "A man like you would never double-cross me, would you, Boris?"

The old man laughs. "Never."

I squeeze Konstantin's hand again and pray to god he waits until the last act before getting his revenge.

They say their goodbyes and Konstantin leads me to the back of the room. He's still holding my hand.

"Thank you for your assistance," he says. "There's just one more person I need your help with, then we can go to our box."

Our very own box? Even I know that's unheard of at the Bolshoi!

A tall slim woman is gliding towards us. She's wearing a white dress that falls in ruffles to the floor like freshly fallen snow, her dark hair gathered in a tight bun, and her eyes feline and smoky.

I feel Konstantin stiffen beside me. There's history here. *Ooh, interesting.*

"Katarina," he says. "You look radiant."

The woman doesn't smile. She's looking at me like I just spat in her champagne.

"You look wonderful too, Kostya," she says in a French accent. "It's nice to see you."

"Likewise."

"You never should have left us, you know," she says. "You belong in the ballet. There is no other place for you."

"I didn't leave, Katarina. I retired. Moved on to greater things."

"Silly boy," she coos affectionately. "Nothing is grander than the ballet."

A wave of something passes over Konstantin's features. I'm starting to feel like part of the decor when he finally introduces me.

"This is Saskia," he says. "My girlfriend."

Oh, so that's what this is about. The woman nods in my direction but ignores the hand I'm holding out for her to shake. *Rude!*

"I'm so pleased to meet you," she says. "I hope you're both very happy together. Konstantin is a wonderful man." *Lies.* "I must go, my boyfriend is waiting for me."

Five pings in a row. Wow, not one word of truth.

I don't squeeze Konstantin's hand though. Fuck him and his ego. If he wants to know if his ex still has feelings for him, he can go stalk her Instagram account like a normal person.

She leaves in a cloud of expensive perfume and he turns to me expectantly. I widen my eyes in mock pity and try not to laugh at the look on his face.

"I'm sorry things didn't work out between you both," I say. "For what's it's worth, she'd still be happy to plié on your face."

He frowns, watching the ballerina glide across the room.

"You are insufferable," he says, without looking at me. "Has anyone ever told you that?"

"The list of people who have called me *that* is under lock and key in my therapist's office."

"Insufferable," he repeats. "Yet enchanting."

Again, there are no pings, just the touch of his hand against the small of my back as he leads us through gilded pink hallways and towards the box. I take a deep breath as Konstantin's finger strokes my waist, his face watching mine expectantly.

When we enter the box, I gasp. It's like I'm standing inside a giant Fabergé egg. I've never seen so much gold and red velvet in one place, and I've definitely never been in a private box. There are four seats awaiting us, but the box is all ours. Konstantin doesn't strike me as the sharing type.

"The show is about to start," he whispers, pulling me down onto the chair beside him.

I gaze out at the theatre tiered with golden rows and endless red velvet. The ceiling is adorned with paintings of Apollo and his muses, and presiding over us is the largest chandelier I've ever seen, weighed heavily at its center with giant glass jewels.

The orchestra swells, the theatre goes dark, and I sit forward in my seat as the red and gold curtain parts.

For the next half an hour I forget who I am and what I'm doing in Russia as I get lost in the music and the story of Swan Lake. I watch the swans launch gracefully into the air, like a flurry of snowflakes floating across the stage to music I've heard all my life but never known how to place. Curved elegant arms, dipped heads, pointed toes - all perfectly in time as if the cast is just one person. I can't tear my eyes away.

After a while, I feel Konstantin's hot breath close to my ear.

"Are you following the story?" he asks, without making it sound condescending.

"No," I say. "But it's beautiful."

My stomach gives a traitorous flip as his gaze locks on

mine. I turn my attention back to the stage as dozens of dancers leap up in the air, their white tutus jutting out like petals around their waists. I always wanted to take ballet classes as a child but my mother wouldn't let me. She said ballet wasn't for Witches, that there were plenty of other things I needed to practice before I wasted time standing on tiptoes.

"Ballet," he ventures quietly, his hand landing gently on my thigh. "Is all about control."

I'm thankful we're sitting in the dark and he can't see my cheeks flush. I'm thinking about the dream I had about him, far too conscious of his hand on my skin to focus on his words.

I glance sideways at the dark silhouette of Konstantin's face. He's watching the swans pirouette on stage, their arms perfectly arched above their heads.

Just when I think he won't move again his finger edges further along the silk of my dress.

"The swans can only return to human form at night," he explains. "By the lake made from the tears of Odette's mother."

He's very chatty for the ballet but I don't mind. I nod and watch, conscious of his hand heavy on my thigh, his fingers performing a lazy sort of dance across the fabric. As the music rises his hold on me tightens, then he releases me altogether.

"*That* move there," he points as the male lead spins into the air. I lean forward to watch the drama unfold when I feel Konstantin's hand return, his fingers brushing against my dress where it splits at the thigh. Slowly he hooks and pulls the fabric up, parting the dress as he strokes across the creamy flesh of my thigh.

He's still not looking at me.

"*That* move takes years to perfect," he continues. "Dancers will try it again, and *again...*" His fingers take a stride with each word, each time climbing higher up my leg. "...and *again,*" he whispers, reaching my underwear and tugging it gently to the side.

OK. We're really doing this. At the Bolshoi.

Jackson's reminder of the word decorum flashes before me, but it's not like I haven't done things in public before. I mean, red velvet and Tchaikovsky sure beats the back row of a movie theatre.

I wait. He doesn't move his hand.

Konstantin continues watching the dancers while I watch him. Slowly, a ghost of a smile plays at his lips and I part my legs. An invitation.

"They will practice the leap endlessly," he says quietly. "Until one day they get it just right." As he says the word *right* his thumb tightly traces over the lace of my underwear, proving he knows exactly where to find my clit.

I bite back a moan. He waits.

"Yeah?" I whisper, encouraging him further. It's all I can say. I have no more words left.

"Ballet is a masterclass in control. Every move is calculated, *repeated*, practiced, until the dancer can't take it anymore…" With each wicked verb his thumb does another entitled stroke across the lacy fabric.

A searing heat is building between my legs, like a coil being wound tighter and tighter. I part my legs further and watch his chest rise and fall, his gaze still trained on the stage.

"Focus," he whispers. I obey and watch the ballerinas, arms crisscrossed and feet pointed, tip-toe along the stage and I wonder how many of them he's fucked. I've lost all sense of the story. He doesn't take his eyes off them, his face solemn and still.

"Ballet is about knowing the limits of your body and always stopping before you've gone too far…"

The music starts building as he gently pulls my lacy underwear aside and places his thumb directly on my clit. I want to keep talking but I can't. All I can do is stare at the dancers, their white costumes blurring like snowflakes. A male ballerina has just leapt onto the stage dressed in black feathers. He's the bad guy, Von Rothbart, tricking the princess. He's dark and evil, we're meant to hate him. But as he glides across the stage, his muscles flex and all I can think about is the way Konstantin looked in the dance studio. So much controlled strength.

I feel his breath against my neck. "Did I do this to you in your dream?" he whispers, sliding two fingers inside me.

How does he know about my dream? Of course, he knew the effect his blood would have on me. *Dick!*

I don't have the strength to express my indignation as his fingers move deeper inside me.

"When you were dreaming of me, is this how I touched you?"

I close my eyes, remembering the visions I'd had of us together in his bed. The music swells and Konstantin moves faster inside me. All I can hear is the sound of violins and piano and a deep oboe, and above it all, Konstantin's breathing getting deeper.

My dress has risen around my waist and when I open my eyes again the sight of his hand buried between my legs, moving up and down, has me building higher. With every stroke my vision blurs and the sensation mounts.

Konstantin leans closer to me, his lips grazing my collarbone.

"Did I make you come in your dream?" He drawls. "Or did I stop just shy…"

He lingers there. Letting me float on the edge. I move my hips forward, unable to resist sliding onto his hand.

"Control yourself, Saskia," he reprimands. "Hold back."

I try and do as I'm told, but it's getting harder to control myself with each whispered caress. I bite down a scream.

His mouth is in my ear and he licks the side of it, but his hand doesn't stop what it's doing. His furiously calculated movements turn from teasing to greedy, from gentle to hungry, with every stroke. God, he's good.

"Now," he whispers.

I don't want to obey him. I want to be a brat about it and make it last.

But I can't.

I let go and my entire body convulses, my thighs holding his hand in place as wave after wave crashes over me. Everything goes bright and I snap open my eyes as the lights switch on for the second interval.

Konstantin is looking at me intently, his smile smug and erect fangs glinting in the golden light. The intermission is announced.

"Let's go get some champagne," he says.

"You're very lucky to get access," Konstantin says, holding the door open for me. Swan Lake is long over and Konstantin had offered me a tour of the Bolshoi backstage.

"I'm looking forward to meeting the cast," I reply, my chest tight and thighs still throbbing. I place the back of my hand against the heat of my flushed cheeks. Oh my god, I really need to gather myself before meeting these prima ballerinas.

Between the swan princess realizing she'd lost her prince, and stars of the show drowning in the lake at the end, I don't even remember who played who. Konstantin is acting like nothing happened between us and I'm trying not to think about the fact that I live under the same roof as this Russian mafia Vampire and I just crossed the world's biggest line. A very dangerous but delicious line.

I also have no idea why he's bringing me backstage. Although the more time I have to cool off before we head back to his house, the better. The idea of Lukka picking up the scent of tonight's arousal is mortifying.

We enter a room lined with mirrors full of bone-thin people in different stages of undress. It's a lot fancier in here than the changing room at the club.

Konstantin takes my hand and squeezes it. Here we go again.

A cheer goes up as soon as we enter the room and Konstantin gives the cast the most genuine smile I've seen all night. He hugs each person one by one and congratulates them, and something aches in the pit of my stomach. This was his life before he was turned. This is who he was before he became a powerful monster feared by everyone.

"Ah, the leading man of all leading men has come backstage to tell us what we did wrong," shouts out a guy who I recognize as the jester in the show. He claps Konstantin on the back and grins. "Although at least you weren't showing us up out there tonight. We all look better when you stay in the audience."

The cast laugh and a light blush tints Konstantin's cheek.

"You were all stupendous," he says. "Flowers and champagne are on their way."

Another cheer. I'm relieved to see his ex and her tight white dress aren't in the crowd.

"Will you be coming back?" a young woman shouts out.

"Maybe. One day. I don't know," Konstantin replies. "But I doubt you've missed me."

They all shout out that they have, and that they want him

back, and he looks at me. He's waiting for me to squeeze his hand, but I don't need to. They're telling the truth.

I wink and he grins.

That's all he wanted, to come back to the ballet and feel loved. To return to the one place where he would be missed the most.

I swallow down the lump in my throat.

CHAPTER EIGHTEEN

There's a resounding silence in the back of the shiny tinted Mercedes. The hat-clad driver at the front is silent too. Konstantin stares out of the window, the lights of Moscow flashing across his face. I bought a little nutcracker at the gift shop for Mikayla. I do that sometimes, buy travel souvenirs for my sister as if to convince myself she will come back from wherever she went. Lucky for her they were all out of *'My sister got finger-banged at the Bolshoi and all I got was this lousy t-shirt'* options.

Tonight was an assault on the senses. I can still feel Konstantin's touch on my thigh and my stomach aches with a strange hollow sadness after having witnessed the intimacy between him and his friends. I suddenly realize I don't know how it feels to kiss Konstantin. I want to know. Oh god, now I'm thinking of the taste of his blood again and my heart starts beating loudly. Can he hear it?

I can't believe I'm wearing a couture dress, earlobes throbbing from the weight of heavy rubies, still reeling from the beauty of Swan Lake. I'm buzzing on bubbles. I can't sit still, and I keep fidgeting in my seat. Konstantin reaches out and stills my hand.

"Your life is really glamourous," I say lamely.

But it's the truth. The whole evening, even now sitting in the back of this car, imposter syndrome is making my hands clench. I know I'm a reporter playing a role, so I *am* quite literally an imposter, but it's not that. I can't shake the feeling that a girl like me shouldn't wear dresses like this. She shouldn't be in Bolshoi boxes. I can hear the sneer in my mother's voice, saying luxury like that is wasted on me. I can imagine my sister Mikayla wearing this dress instead. She'd look prettier than me, more sophisticated than me, and certainly better behaved.

"What's *your* life like?" Konstantin asks.

It snaps me out of my pity trip. It's the first time he's ever wanted to know anything about me.

"There's a lot less velvet," I reply. "More grime. My bedsheets are not as luxurious as you're used to. You wouldn't last a day in my apartment."

Something indecipherable crosses his features. "You think you know me. Most people do."

I think of his businesses, his mansion, the ballet, the sports cars lined up outside his home. I know exactly what he is.

"I want to show you something," he says.

Konstantin barks an address to the driver, and we change course.

We drive for over an hour down a giant freeway dotted with massive banners, twenty-four-hour supermarkets, and gas stations that boast having fresh *ponchiki*. My stomach rumbles at the thought of the little sugar-dusted donuts. The canapes at the fancy Bolshoi did little to tie me over, and orgasms make me hungrier than long-distance hiking.

We keep driving until there's nothing but mega markets and sparse birch wood forest. It's past midnight and the moon is high in the sky. With a jerk, we turn down an unlit road lined with wooden houses shining silver and frosted with lights now.

"These are *dachas*," Konstantin explains. "In the Soviet Union, many people had these weekend houses in the countryside. The tradition has continued."

Are we heading to his country house?

I start to imagine how grand Konstantin's second home must be. My mind briefly wanders to the thread count potential, quickly gravitating to images of sweaty limbs and his mouth on my neck.

The Mercedes rocks up and down over the bumpy road and I shake away the graphic fantasy. The houses we're passing are far from luxurious. They're dilapidated. Some of them have patchy makeshift roofs with rusty gates, covered in scraggly vines.

Where the fuck is he taking me?

"You have a country house *here*?"

The car stops by one of the most neglected wooden houses on the block.

Konstantin stares up at it as he answers me. "In a manner of speaking."

He steps out of the car and walks to the gate and the driver lets me out then returns immediately to the car to wait. I follow Konstantin, taking care not to let my dress drag on the tire-indented mud. Our outfits look so out of place here.

Konstantin unlocks the gate and we follow the path to the house. The property is overgrown and splashed in shades of orange and green from the rotting lichen. Even the trees surrounding the house are broken and decaying. A green mossy hole that may have once been a pond reflects a distorted version of us as we walk past.

My skin starts to creep. No one has lived here in ages, so why the hell are we here? Then it dawns on me. *This is where I'm going to die!* Us reporters think this at least five times a day, every time we find ourselves in the wrong place at the wrong time. Which is basically our job description.

"If you were going to drain me of my blood and dump me, you could have done me the courtesy of doing it back at the mansion. Or better yet at the Bolshoi. Now *that's* a classy way to die."

I'm talking fast because I'm nervous. But also, because I don't want to die. What if the theatre was just a big cover-up to put me at ease and in reality, he's discovered who I am and luring me to my death? If he were to kill me, a place like this would be perfect. A place where no one goes, where you can't tell the blood from the dirt.

"Quiet," he says, although his voice is laced with kindness.

I fidget again and he reaches for me, his cold hand closing around mine. He's looking up at the house with a type of fascination, like all he had to do was blink and it would be gone.

"This is where I grew up," he says. "This is what I came from."

"What? Here?"

Mouth agape I glance around as if I missed something. This isn't a *home* - this is a long-abandoned hole.

He's not surprised by my reaction. "Lukka and I were raised in this very house by our mother."

The dead mother I remember him saying he doesn't miss.

"And your father?"

He takes his time answering, staring at the building like it's a riddle he hasn't cracked yet. Then he pushes open the old door and walks in.

I follow eagerly, I need to know more, even though the house looks like it could collapse at any point. It's also... burned from the inside? Scorch marks cover the curling wallpaper. There's a modest living room that leads into a tiny kitchen with an archaic stove.

Some things are scorched, other parts are left intact. It's as if someone wanted to incinerate the house but gave up and left it half destroyed.

I once saw pictures of Chernobyl after it was abandoned, and this is what Konstantin's childhood home reminds of. There are ballet awards on the shelves collecting dust, a teddy bear in the corner, a cup of blossoming mold on the table.

The brothers must have left it exactly as it was, taking nothing of their old childhood into their new lives. But why?

Konstantin catches me observing his countless ballet awards.

"My father left when I was seven years old." He looks around the destroyed room with cold indifference. "I was a child prodigy. A ballet star. I practiced every single day and on weekends without fail. My father didn't want to deal with a demanding child, one who was costing him money – so he left. But my mother struggled to remain strong for us. She took me to all my classes and recitals at first, but soon gave up and turned to drink."

I wait for the *pings*, just in case this is some bullshit story he's trying to sell me. But the *pings* don't come.

Konstantin walks into another room. The only other room. In the center are a double bed and two cots. The entire family slept crammed together in here? Suddenly I feel bad laughing about his thread count.

"My mother wasn't a strong woman – she needed a man to look after her. Anyone would have done. She moved my stepfather into our home weeks after my father left. My stepfather was also a drunk. He didn't want to take on another man's son, and when she got pregnant with Lukka straight away he wasn't happy about that either. He was an angry man, impatient, cruel, and violent."

His use of the past tense does not escape me. Are both these people dead? And did Konstantin have something to do with their deaths? I realize I'm holding my breath as he continues his story.

"I understood early on that ballet was mine and Lukka's only way out of here. By the age of eleven, I'd secured myself a scholarship, walked miles into town every morning and took the train to the city, returning late at night. Lukka was three years old by then, a skinny weak child, but in order to pursue my career I had to leave my young brother behind. *With them*. I found fresh bruises on his body every night and he would beg me to take him with me, but I couldn't."

Tears sting my eyes as I imagine a young Lukka in this room. The squalor, the fear, the pain. I blink and look away.

"When Lukka became a teenager he no longer waited for me to come home, he would travel into the city and stay away as much as he could. He got into drugs and partying. After my performances I would look for him, sometimes it would take all night. This went on for years, and got harder as my job took me around the world. Then one night when Lukka was in his early twenties, about seven years ago, I found him at a rave. He'd pissed the wrong gang off, and he was covered in blood. We were both turned that night."

I pause, not daring to breathe. I can't believe it was Lukka's fault that his brother got turned. It shouldn't surprise me though. Konstantin isn't a man that things just happen to. Images of him at the ballet make my stomach drop again - he lost all of that for the love of his brother.

"When we returned home our stepfather was stinking drunk. We'd been away for days. We were still confused, scared and so hungry. He punched Lukka in the face then he used an iron bar to attempt to smash my legs. He wanted to cripple me, the dream I'd worked so hard for, and my mother just stood there. But Lukka was no longer a skinny weak little boy, no longer the bruised child I was forced to leave behind every day. My brother tore him apart and I didn't stop him."

Tore him apart. Konstantin and his wild dog.

"What happened to your mother?"

Konstantin looks away.

"She died not long after that."

I stay quiet. It's clear Konstantin isn't finished telling me his story. Although what I don't understand is why he's telling me in the first place. This will make a great exposé for The Blood Web Chronicle, yet I already know I won't be telling a soul about this.

"How did you adapt to being a Vampire?" I ask.

Konstantin stares into the distance, as if he's watching his life projected onto the decaying walls of his childhood home.

"Not being able to go out in daylight tore my heart out because it meant I was no longer able to dance. At first, I wanted to die, I couldn't see what life held for me anymore, but then I began to pursue other avenues. Being a Vampire is a powerful thing, sweetheart. It gets you places faster than being human ever could. It didn't take long until we could afford to leave our memories behind, and we never looked back."

And just as he did seven years ago he walks straight out of the house. I keep behind him, blinking back tears. I don't want to show him any weakness, and crying at someone else's sad childhood is selfish. But it's guilt I'm feeling. Guilt that I'm always complaining about my own mother but have never suffered this badly. Guilt that I've completely misunderstood the Volkov brothers. Guilt that I came to Moscow to take them down.

I think about my sister Mikayla. How last time I saw her eighteen months ago I suspected she was pregnant, then she disappeared. I've been searching for her ever since, hoping my job as a reporter will somehow provide a clue. It hasn't so far. What if she ended up living a life like this? Her and her secret child, poor and scared? I want to open up to Konstantin, swap one pain for another, but I can't run the risk of exposing myself...in more ways than one.

Snow crunches beneath my heels as we reach the dilapidated gate.

"Thank you for confiding in me," I say. "But why did you tell me?"

"Because it's time we got to know one another better."

Does he mean romantically? Or...

He lets me through the gate. "And Saskia..."

I turn, blinking furiously at the tears still threatening to fall.

"You should know I'd never feed on you."

He's telling the truth.

"Because I'm a Witch?" I reply.

Konstantin smiles, all signs of melancholy wiped from his razor-sharp features.

"No. You wouldn't be the first Witch I've fed on," he replies.

What? How? He must have his own antidote. I make a mental note to be more careful. The fact that he *could* feed on me, even though he says he wouldn't, changes the playing field.

He walks past me, and I realize he never answered my question.

"Wait. So why wouldn't you feed on me then?"

He gives me a crooked smile. "You're not my type."

I stand outside the car, startled. Surprised to find myself waiting for a ping that never comes.

CHAPTER NINETEEN

We arrive back at Konstantin's mansion at four in the morning and I'm exhausted. The ballet feels like it happened days ago. The house's columns and fountain shine under the full moon. Everything feels eerier when it's covered in silver like this, but I remind myself the moon makes no difference to Vampires – they're dangerous beasts every night of the month. Yet, I don't know, the Volkov's are feeling less dangerous every day that passes.

I think back to Ansel and her dead boyfriend. I forgot to text her. Earlier tonight I asked Konstantin how he kept the human police away from the crime scenes at his sites and he rubbed his fingers together. Money. Of course. But now that he suspects Boris, and Stepan mentioned his father's cronies and their blood-lust, perhaps Ansel can help me with the missing pieces to this story.

We walk through to the foyer and Konstantin stops at the bottom of the sweeping staircase. On the journey home something changed in him, like a shutter had gone up between us. He was silent, almost angry, as if by showing me a sliver of who he once was he's handed me some of his power. I don't know how to undo that. Was I meant to have shared parts of my past with him too? Do I need to be more vulnerable around him? Because there's no way I'm telling him anything true about me!

I take his hand and he lets me, but he won't look at me.

"I had a wonderful evening," I say.

The touch of his skin sends me straight back to the Bolshoi again and the feel of his fingers between my thighs. Then I think of the taste of his blood, my tongue coated with his power. Oh my god. I press my legs together and shoo away the images from my mind. This isn't helping anyone.

"Thank you for your assistance with the truth tonight," he says, pulling his hand away. "I have some things to arrange before I go to bed. I'll see you at work this evening."

Then he turns around and walks up the stairs without a backward glance. Not even a goodnight, much less a second act to what we started.

Well, what did I expect? It's not like we've officially been on a date!

I head to my room. I go to retrieve my burner phone to text Ansel when I see there are already four missed calls from her. *Fuck*! She's my only lead and I haven't had a chance to talk to her properly yet. I dial back but it goes to voicemail. Of course, it does, she's already back at work. And instead of comforting her like a true friend, or interviewing her like the journalist I'm meant to be - I was getting ballet finger banged by a Vamp who no longer wishes to speak to me.

I listen to Ansel's message, but all she says is thanks for getting her a night off work yesterday and that we should have a drink together one evening before her shift. She sounds awful. I really need to get back into reporter mode and keep away from Konstantin.

My stomach is rumbling so I head down to the kitchen.

Mealtimes don't exist for me anymore, but luckily the brothers keep their kitchen well stocked.

"Hello, little Witch."

I let out a small yelp and Lukka laughs.

"Why the fuck are you lurking in the dark?" I exclaim, switching on the light.

"Vampires see better in the dark."

He's on the floor, his back to the fridge, eating cake in his underwear. The way he's sitting I can see the expensive brand of his tight boxer shorts, and the shape of its generous contents. Damn you, Konstantin! There's nothing worse than getting a taste of pleasure, then being left wanting more.

Lukka licks one of his fingers and I can't help laughing. He has chocolate on his hands and down to his tattooed wrists. There's also a huge smear on his chest and the side of his mouth.

My grin fades as I imagine him as a child in that shithole he grew up in. Bruises instead of chocolate smears. A tiny kid on a dirty kitchen floor, eating whatever he could find, waiting for his big brother to come home and rescue him.

"What are you doing?" I ask.

"Waiting for you. Eating cake."

I sit down next to him, my red dress pooling around me, and take a slice from the plate beside him. It mushes in my hand and I laugh as I try to eat it without making a mess. I fail. But oh my god, this cake is delicious.

"I thought Vampires only ate blood," I mumble.

Lukka fixes his milky eyes on mine.

"You think hot metal-tasting blood is better than chocolate? Only one thing better than chocolate, little Witch. Sex."

At the mention of sex my stomach contracts again and now it's all I can think about. I sigh heavily. The last twenty-four hours have been surreal – a failed lap dance for a lead, Ansel's murdered boyfriend, sex dreams, ballet, foreplay, and a devastating glimpse into the horrors of the Volkov brothers' childhood. Too many feelings to bundle up into one evening.

I look at Lukka, so different from his restrained older brother. His chiseled chest is covered in gold chains, his teeth not quite fangs but not entirely human either, and his crazy hair all mussed up.

"You want it?" he asks.

I swallow. *I do want it. I really do.*

"The last piece of cake," he says. "If you don't want it, I'll eat it."

Oh.

He stuffs the slice into his mouth in one bite and smiles.

"You're an animal," I laugh.

"You like animals. They're cute. Where have you been tonight? You look very beautiful."

"Your brother took me to the Bolshoi."

A shadow passes over his face but he gives me another sticky grin. I'm not going to mention having seen where they both grew up, or that I know Lukka killed his stepfather. It's hard to imagine this big clown baby causing such carnage – but I saw him at the restaurant. I know exactly what he's capable of. Although now I've witnessed a glimpse of his past, everything makes much more sense.

"Ballet is boring. Cake's better," he says with a wink. He reaches out for something behind him. It's a bottle of champagne, the same expensive label he was using to brush his teeth with yesterday.

He offers it to me, and I take a swig. Foam bubbles out of my mouth and dribbles onto my chest. I go to wipe it off but in a blur he's there, at my neck, licking at the rivers of champagne dribbling towards my cleavage.

I don't say anything, and he doesn't stop. His hungry licks turn to sucking kisses, his mouth moving slowly over my bare collarbone, up my neck and to the side of my lips. I close my eyes, noting the chocolatey scent of his hands clasping my face.

"When we were children, Konstantin used to give me all his toys," he says, his lips moving against my cheek. I have no idea how he's done it, how he positioned himself kneeling between my parted legs without me noticing. His gold chains are cold against shoulder and I shiver. "My brother shares everything with me," he says.

No ping. There never is with Lukka.

My eyes are still closed and all I can think about is Konstantin's hands on me in the Bolshoi box. The way he looked at me when he told me about his cruel mother and wanting to look after Lukka. These brothers aren't monsters, they were just raised by them.

"Konstantin can't share me," I say. "Because I don't belong to him. And I'm not a fucking toy."

Lukka makes the same sound he did when he was eating the cake. A hungry sound, like he can never get enough of whatever he wants. He works his way to my mouth, and I let him. I let him kiss me and I kiss him back. Konstantin doesn't want me, he said so himself - I'm not his type. Everything is a power game with him. He just wants to know I'll do what he wants, and I will...while it gets me to where *I* need to be.

But this? I need this. Because with Lukka, life is all the fun without the games.

"Not like this," he says, pulling away and leaving me with a chin smeared with sweet champagne and chocolate.

I open my eyes, his face coming into focus. I feel queasy. The sugar and alcohol and everything that's happened in the last few days.

"Not like what?"

He sits back beside me and takes another swig of champagne.

"If we fuck, it won't be on the kitchen floor with you wearing that frilly dress. I want to take you out. Show you the *real* Russia - not the pretty golden lies we show tourists. Me and you and a good time. You want a good time, little Witch?"

I need to update Jackson. It's ten o'clock in the evening in New York, and I know he won't be able to settle for the night until he knows his intrepid undercover reporter is on to something. Except I don't have the answers yet. I need more time...but I also need this. A night out with Lukka might be the last fun I get before my boss catches up with me and fires my ass.

CHAPTER TWENTY

Light fluffy snow is falling in slow motion like silver glitter as I walk out of the Volkov mansion, the cold numbing my lips the moment I'm outside.

Lukka, leaning against his yellow Lamborghini in the bright white courtyard, is a sight to behold. His eyes, the same color as the snow, follow me as I walk down the grand steps. He grins his metal-lined madman grin and my stomach flips. His bleached hair is sticking up messily as usual, but the sides are now freshly shaved. Did he make a special effort for me?

He's sporting a white v-neck t-shirt and a white letterman jacket. He's not cold, because Vamps don't get cold, but it's a weird outfit choice for this weather, nonetheless.

He opens the passenger door of his crazy sports car.

"Where are we going?" I ask.

"I told you yesterday. I'm showing you my favorite places."

"Shouldn't I be at work tonight?"

"We only get the night time together," he says. "We can't work *and* play. So, I choose play."

He plops himself in the front seat and I wonder why he would even bother showing me his favorite places. Is he trying to impress me? Or is this some kind of competition against his brother?

I barely get time to put my seatbelt on before I'm tossed backward with the g-force of his car. Lukka blasts his techno as loud as it will go and swerves onto the freeway.

Konstantin was wrong about his younger brother. Lukka is an expert driver. Even if his driving scares the living shit out of me.

Half an hour, and innumerable broken traffic laws later, we arrive in the center of town. The Kremlin flashes by me, epic and cartoon-like, and pull up by a large department store called *Detsky Mir*. Children's world? Why are we going shopping in a toy store at night?

Lukka surrenders his keys to a very eager valet and a moment later his hand is on my waist guiding me into the shop. It's more like a mall, all-white linoleum and spotless shop windows, but we avoid the designer stores and head straight for the giant toy shop.

I trail him as he heads to the Lego aisle.

"Why are we in a toy shop?" I ask.

Surely this is not what he meant by showing me the 'real Russia.'

"Toys are like champagne," he says, "The question is not *why*...but why not?"

I can't help but laugh as Lukka grabs a cart and starts filling it liberally.

"But we're adults," I point out.

Lukka grins at me as he examines a My Little Pony set and flings it in the cart. "Would you rather I take you to a toy shop for adults, little Witch?"

I feel my cheeks heating and turn my attention to a

packet of sparkly slime. My head is a mess. Thoughts of Konstantin and the ballet rush through my mind, swiftly followed by Lukka building Lego while naked, or perhaps both of them together while we... *Get it together, Saskia!*

He snatches the slime from my hand and adds it to the cart that's already full to the brim. What the hell's he going to do with all these items? Surely buying half a toy store is a little indulgent, even for him.

"I think you have Peter Pan syndrome," I say. "You know like Michael Jackson or Mariah Carey."

"I love Michael Jackson," he replies, entirely missing my point. "Relax," he continues. "Just pick the toys that you as a little Witch would have liked."

I think about this briefly. I'm on assignment. I should be letting him lead and stop being so difficult. I look around the sparkly aisles. My mother wasn't into toys. No matter how much I begged, the only presents I received were linked to the occult. Crystals, Tarot cards, little bottles of herbs. Each gift would be given in the vain hope of unlocking magical powers I didn't possess. And with each present that didn't work my mother would get angrier with me. It took years to convince her that I didn't have any skills in any mystical fields - except being able to tell that my mother was lying when she said it didn't matter that I was so useless.

I pick up a scientist Barbie. I would have liked this as a kid. I would have liked to believe I could have saved the world, that I could have been something more important than a disappointing minor Witch.

Sheepishly, I set it in the cart. I can't believe I'm participating in this madness. I'm rewarded with a smile from Lukka. He calls over a shopkeeper and asks her to recommend toys for younger children. She leads us to a display table.

"These are our Christmas recommendations," she beams.

I can tell she's judging us, trying to crack us like a retail riddle. Is Lukka as rich as he looks? Is he as mad? Her gaze sweeps over me, clearly wondering why he would choose someone as normal looking as me.

She makes doe-eyes at him and bends seductively over a set of building blocks. *Seriously?* I give her the side-eye.

"What will you choose?" she says, ignoring me while giving him a look that says that she's the best toy on offer.

He smiles widely at her and I bite back a laugh as she spots his pointy teeth and recoils.

"I'll take one of everything," he says.

Every inch of the car is occupied with toys. Lukka piles two giant plastic bags on top of me and I can barely see any of the snowy freeway. I can still tell he's speeding though.

I have no idea where we're going. Probably to find a bouncy castle or one of those large pits full of colorful balls.

"Did you really need to buy this many toys?" I groan.

Lukka cackles and turns up the music without answering me.

Half an hour later we pull up to a large iron gate. A security guard is sitting inside a wooden booth, gloved hands clasped around a mug of something hot. He sees Lukka and his eyes fill with recognition as he hurries out of the booth, nearly tripping over himself.

"Nice to see you again, Sir Volkov," he stutters. "They will be so happy you're here."

Sir? I look at Lukka but his face isn't giving anything away. On the other side of the gates is a four-story building. It looks more like a school than a home. I don't feel comfortable about this. Who the hell lives here? And why are we bringing them toys?

The guard closes the gate behind us and jogs up to the car. He opens my door and takes the bags from me.

"Sir Volkov!" comes a cry from the building.

A middle-aged woman is hurrying down the steps from the front door, closing her fur coat mid-stride. She must have seen us pull up from the window as she was getting ready for bed.

"Sir Volkov," she says again, beaming. "We were not expecting you."

Although her demeanor is friendly, she has the look of a woman who commands respect. A teacher or an official of sorts. Although with Lukka she's pure docile and coquettish. She's no Vamp.

"No problem, Tatiana Vasieliva," he says with a wink. "This is a spontaneous visit."

I like that he uses her second name, a sign of respect. I'm even more surprised when he shows the same respect to the guard.

"Evgeniy Alexandrovich, there are more bags on the back seat and a little something for you to ward off the cold."

The guard throws Tatiana a guilty look, but her smile doesn't falter and he happily fishes out the bags full of toys from the Lamborghini, along with a bottle of vodka for himself.

Nodding his thanks to Lukka the old man trails up the stairs behind us, three bags in each hand, as we follow Tatiana inside the building carrying two boxes each. Once inside the warmth of the shabby hall the guard leaves the bags at our feet and Lukka puts his arm around my shoulder.

"This is my friend, Saskia," he says.

Tatiana shakes my hand. "I'm sure the children will be glad to meet her," she says.

Children? Lukka has children?

"Katya!" Tatiana screams into the depths of the hall. A pretty girl emerges and blanches as she sees us.

"Tea! Bring the cookies and tea. Put them out. Call the children," Tatiana barks. The girl nods and runs off.

"You spoil them, Lukka Volkov," Tatiana cries, nodding at the bags on the floor. "You already brought us early Christmas gifts weeks ago."

"It is nothing," he replies. "You can never have too many presents."

I'm still puzzling over what the hell is going on when Tatiana leads us to an adjacent room where a fire is burning in a large hearth. We pass a small moon-faced boy and Lukka ruffles his hair. Then I see more eyes settle on me. Children of all ages are filing past us to the room next door. Dozens of them with badly cut hair and serious expressions on their faces. Is this a school?

As we enter the room all the children begin to crowd around us. They know Lukka. More than that, they *love* Lukka. Some of them hug him excitedly, others cling to the wall giving him a shy hesitant smile. But most of them are watching me, eyes cold with mistrust.

"They're orphans," he whispers to me in English, so the children don't understand him. "I'm the...what is the word? Patron? Yes, the patron of this orphanage."

My breath hitches and my cold cheeks heat up with shame. I'd assumed the worst of him, when the truth was staring me right in the face. Lukka bought toys for the orphans he helps, because he knows what it is to be young, scared, and alone.

Some Verity Witch I am.

I can't imagine what face I'm making, but Lukka kisses me gently on the forehead then jumps up and shouts, "I have toys for everyone! Who loves toys?"

Over forty children start to squeal and shout and wave

their hands out as Lukka crouches on the floor and hands out toy after toy to beaming children. I watch him give the scientist Barbie doll I chose to a small girl with thick black hair.

"I want to be a doctor when I grow up," she says with a lisp, her big eyes staring up at Lukka. "Then I can fix diseases like the one my Mama had. I can save people."

"And what a great doctor you will make, Masha!" Lukka exclaims. She beams at him, cradling her new doll.

I blink away tears as Lukka sits cross-legged on the floor. The little girl scrambles onto his lap and settles there like he's Santa, asking him to open the packaging and chattering away about all the things her new doll can do.

I can't stop staring. This isn't the same monster who I saw tear out the windpipe of three men with a blunt fish knife. This isn't the dangerous clown I took him for.

He notices me staring and gives me a sad smile that says *'I told you I'd show you the real Moscow.'*

Lukka and I spend an hour handing out gifts and playing with the children, while Tatiana clucks around him offering tea and biscuits and thanking him profusely. The guilt of lying to both brothers about who I am eats away at my conscience after they've both shared so much of their true selves with me.

Eventually, Tatiana announces the children must get back to bed and she ushers them out of the room, each child clutching a new toy to their chest.

"You did a good thing," I whisper in Russian.

"I know what it is to not have parents," Lukka replies. He doesn't know I've seen his childhood home. That I know he murdered his abusive father.

"My mother was a good woman but a bad mother. When Konstantin and I were turned we went back home and I flipped and attacked my father. He was bad to the core. A few days later I heard our mother was dead. Konstantin says she killed herself because of what we became. It was my fault we got turned, and my fault she died. My stupidity killed us all." He sighs and looks down at his empty hands. I'm stunned into silence. "It's too late to save her...but at least I can help these children."

I take a deep breath. Konstantin had said his mother was dead but he didn't mention how. The way he talked about the woman it was as if neither of them cared about her anymore. But Lukka did. Still does. He's still a boy who needs love...just like these children.

I blink away tears and reach for my coat, but his hand shoots out and rests on mine.

"Not so fast," he says in a quiet voice. "I have a little job for you. Please."

The Volkov's and their 'little jobs'. I nod and he grins, leading us to the large sofa by the fireplace. We sit in silence and I have a strange desire to rest my head on his shoulder and tell him I know about his childhood, about his pain, and that he's not the beast his brother has trained him to be. Then I think about the blood he needs to feed on to survive. Lukka isn't a man, he's a Vampire. He can cuddle all the kids he wants – but he's still a killer.

"What do you need from me?" I ask him.

He takes my hand and shrugs with one shoulder. It's not like him to be hesitant. He looks worried.

"I think Tatiana is in trouble. Financially. I need you to tell me if she's telling me the truth when we speak shortly. I don't trust the owners of this place."

"Why?"

"I do more than bring toys. I have programs in place for education, clothing, food...but I'm not seeing many improvements."

"You want me to squeeze your hand if she lies?" I ask, holding up his hand in mine.

"You can, if you want," he says quietly. "Or you can just tell me in the car." I go to extricate my hand from his, but he holds it tighter. And that's how Tatiana finds us a few minutes later, sitting on her couch hand in hand like a normal couple.

"Oh, you're still here?" she exclaims from the hallway. "Did I forget something? Do you need anything?"

Lukka and I stand as she enters the room and he gestures for her to sit down.

"We just wanted to thank you," he says.

"Me?" she cries, both hands fluttering to her chest. "It is *you*, Sir Volkov, and your wonderful lady friend we should be thanking. So kind. So very kind."

She dabs at her eyes and more guilt surges through every pore of my body. I'm pretending to like this man. This Vamp. I'm pretending to be close to the brothers. When the only reason I'm in this country is to investigate murders and get to the bottom of their corrupt businesses. Then I'm going to spread their private lives anonymously across the global Para Blood Web. And there's me thinking *they* are the parasites.

"Tatiana Vasieliva," Lukka says gently. "I wanted to talk to you about finances."

Her face drops and I notice her hands shake a little in her lap.

"You want to cease supporting us?"

"No! Not at all. I just want to know that my money is reaching you. Are the children being looked after?"

She nods. I feel him tensing beside me.

"Everything is as it should be," she says.

"So, you are all treated well? By the owners?"

She nods again, her smile shaky on her lips. She must be wondering why the hell we're sitting there interrogating her.

"Good," he says. "That's good. But if you ever feel like something is wrong, or you have any problems, you come to me. OK?"

She nods, then with some effort gets to her feet and throws her arms around Lukka.

"You are our saint," she says, tears rolling down her cheeks.

"I'm far from a saint," he mumbles into her shoulder.

He's never said a truer word.

Back in the car it's my turn to be interrogated.

"Was she lying?" His gaze is level as he stares at the orphanage through the windscreen. Murder lingers in his pale eyes, waiting to be unleashed like a Siberian tiger. No more benevolent Santa.

"No," I whisper. "Everything she said was true."

And just like that his mood shifts. He gives me a wild grin and pulls out of the parking lot, waiving to the guard as he goes.

"I wish I ran that place myself. There is so much corruption, it's nearly impossible to control where the money goes," he shouts over the hum of the engine as he floors the gas. "I worry my money doesn't reach the kids. Or worse, once those kids are released at sixteen I worry that something will happen to them. I'd offer them work at the club or the work sites, but neither are safe places for young people."

He's speaking all the truths tonight.

"What would you have done if the owners had been pocketing your contributions?" I ask.

He smiles at me, a smile as sharp as barbed wire.

"Sometimes things can be solved with cash, and other times…" He opens his mouth a little and I swallow as his fangs slowly begin to grow. "Sometimes you need to use something a little more effective."

I suppress a shiver as he runs his tongue over one incisor, then shrinks them back again and turns the volume of the radio to full.

I sit quietly, surprised at my disappointment that this ended up being a night out with a goal. It's nice to be nice, but when he promised me a good time it wasn't this I had in mind.

I mentally slap myself. I need to stop looking at my time with the brothers in that way. I'm on an assignment. I should be happy I'm learning more about Lukka. Learning so I can get the dirt on him, on Konstantin and on their potentially murderous rivals.

But the problem is, everything I learn about Lukka just makes me like him more.

"That's my good deed done for tonight," he shouts over the music. "Now it's time we had some *real* fun. You ready, little Witch?"

My stomach flutters and I can't tell if it's full of butterflies or winged fear.

CHAPTER TWENTY-ONE

Lukka drives us out of the city towards an industrial part of town that I've never seen before. There's nothing here but empty lots and a dark ominous warehouse. Its cracked windows glisten in the light of the full moon like broken teeth, and dark vines strangle its exterior.

There's definitely no *fun* to be had here.

Lukka grabs me by the hand – his own so much colder and stronger than his brother's – and leads me to the side of the building. There's a door there, but it's been cleverly hidden. Doors that are hard to see rarely have anything good behind them.

Lukka knocks three times and a metal slit slides open, black eyes fixing on us. Completely black eyes. I've read about eyes like this on the Blood Web, but I've never seen them myself. Whoever is behind that door is a Werewolf. A mature one.

My breath hitches with a light yelp as I take a panicked stumble backward. A Werewolf bite can't kill a Witch like they can a human, but they *can* turn us. They also kill the biter and send us mad, just like the bite my father received that led to his suicide. I realize with horror that Lukka and I have that in common.

In a second his hand is on my back, cold, heavy and reassuring.

If Lukka knew who my mother was, he'd also know who my father was and how he'd died. Which would explain why I'm terrified of Werewolves. But I can't tell him any of that, so I'll just have to tough this one out.

"Don't worry, little Witch," Lukka says, his lips close to my ear. "If anyone tries to touch you tonight, they will die."

My tough act is clearly not that convincing. I take a deep breath as the door swings open and we step inside. It's a comfort to know that whoever is behind this door can never be scarier than the man protecting me. The Werewolf bouncer melts into the shadows and we descend a twisting flight of stairs leading to the underground belly of the warehouse.

"It's nice," I say shyly, his hand still in mine. "What you do for the orphans."

Lukka gives my hand a squeeze. "Everyone needs someone to look out for them. A protector."

That's what Konstantin has always been for him. His protector. The toy bringer.

We reach the bottom of the stairs, round a corner, and suddenly the air around us starts to shimmer and music explodes like it's been trapped in an invisible bubble. This warehouse must have been bewitched; holding in the sound to avoid unwelcome humans who would never make it out of here in one piece.

I must look shocked because Lukka is laughing at me over his shoulder. A wide smile is plastered over his flawless face as he guides me deeper into the club and past throngs of people dancing. Tiny fairy lights twinkle above us and at first

I presume they're strung up Christmas lights, then I realize they're bewitched fireflies flying in formation. These kinds of Witch party tricks are expensive. The only time I've witnessed such decadence was at an MA ball Mikayla once dragged me to in Spain. I've never seen anything like this with the Para community in New York, or anywhere else to be honest.

God, I seriously hope I don't recognize any Witches here that might know my mother, because explaining what I'm doing in Russia hand-in-hand with a millionaire Vamp would have my mom coming on the next plane quicker than a Werewolf at a full moon orgy.

A girl is dancing on a podium, gyrating her lithe body to the music. Her face flickers and twists from human to fox to human again. She reminds me of the girls at the Black Rabbit. Her eyes glow green, and her ears extend and turn red before going back to normal again, but her body never fully shifts. She spots Lukka pushing us through the crowd and winks at him with familiarity. Something stirs in my stomach. Is this where he finds his dancers?

The nightclub is a large dark space filled with strobe lighting, fairy lights and small stages. Along one end is a bar, manned by men with dry green skin and huge ears like Gremlins having a bad day – *Goblins*. They love the cold. I've had a few experiences with these creatures, but none of them good. I'd certainly not choose them to serve drinks when most can't even see over the bar. I'm relieved to see a couple of hot women walking around with trays of drinks too. Much nicer to look at, plus it means I won't have to go near the bar.

There are no humans here. Even those who appear human are something else, something Para and bad, pressed together tightly like one big bowl of trouble. I spot a group of men dressed head to toe in leather, bald heads tattooed with strange symbols. On another podium is a girl in a floaty skirt, her bare breasts covered in diamantes. She's hovering half a meter from the ground thanks to her fluttering wings. I catch her eye and she smiles at me. Her Vampire teeth are stained pink with blood. *Fuck!* I look away quickly.

She must be a Para-Cross. You can get them either through birth or turned. I've only read about mixed-blood Paras, I've never seen one up close. Fae Vamps. Shifter Elves. And my father – the Witch who was bitten and turned into a wolf every full moon. A curse that killed him. I can't help but think of my sister, Mikayla, and the baby she was carrying when I last saw her. Who in Para hell was the father?

I suppress a shiver as Lukka nods at someone behind me and a tray of shots is thrust between us. The waitress is dressed in white like an angel. I notice her neck, collarbone and wrists are covered in double-dotted puncture wounds. She's walking fast, a cat-like tail flicking beneath the folds of her skirt - this club's very own Blood Bunny. I wonder how much she gets paid to serve drinks to Paras before she herself becomes the last beverage of the day.

Lukka toasts us with a shot of blood and knocks it back in one go. My chest contracts at the wink he gives me, then I copy him with my own clear drink, shivering as it pools hot in my belly. Vodka.

"So? What do you think?" he shouts over the music, his cheek grazing mine. "My fun is better than my brother's, no?"

Konstantin's idea of fun is being admired and in control, whereas Lukka just wants to be surrounded by freaks who don't give a fuck. These are *his* kind of people, and in all honesty, I don't know *what* to think. I've been to plenty of clubs before, and I've even been to a few Para parties, but nothing like this.

"It's amazing," I shout back. "This music is strange, though. What is it?"

"Magic," he replies, threading his arm around my waist and pushing my body against his. "Can you feel it?"

I can feel a lot of things, but he's talking about the visible wisps of music winding their way through the dancers. Yeah, I can feel it now. An enchantment spell of the highest order - a complicated trick that only the grand Witches can perform. The enrichment of music with magic is no easy feat, but it's powerful. Some tunes can stop a man in his tracks, or seduce a woman, or even kill. This one is making everyone on the dancefloor euphoric.

I rest my arms around Lukka's neck and let the magic soak into me. Witchcraft doesn't affect Witches as strongly as it does other Paras and humans, but I'm not a very powerful Witch so I'm buzzing like a wasp in a jam jar. It's like tiny champagne bubbles washing over my skin, a whisper in my ear saying *'Do it, Saskia. Do whatever you want. You're young and alive and glorious. Now is the time.'* And I nearly believe it. I nearly do what I want. And what I want, with a Vamp in my arms and his lips so close to mine, is going to be a very *very* bad idea.

Lukka has his eyes closed, giving me a chance to take a long look at him. His pale skin and taut face. Thick lashes and crazy bleached hair. The tattoos climbing up his neck and temples, and a tiny speck of blood at the side of his mouth. Whose blood was he drinking? I'm partly revolted, yet I still have the sudden urge to lick it off his lips.

"Let go," he says.

What? I take my arms away from around his neck, but he shakes his head and places them back, pulling me closer until my body is flush with his.

"That's not what I meant, little Witch," he says into the side of my neck. I shiver as he runs the tip of his sharp incisor from my collarbone to behind my ear. "I mean let your body go. Sink into me."

The music is winding around us now, silver strands of magic loosening my limbs until I feel like I'm going to fall, but the magic is holding me up. I'm floating. My head flops forward on to Lukka's shoulder and we stay like that, swaying and moving to the hypnotic beat.

After a while I pull back to say something but Lukka is already staring down at me, giving me a twisted mischievous smile. Then he sticks out his tongue. Stark white against the tip of his tongue is a tiny pill. But not a normal pill. This one is pearlescent and shimmers as the lights bounce off it.

Drugs aren't really my thing. I haven't done anything too serious since my mother forced me to go to a mage party where we had to cut ourselves and put frog poison in our wounds. The goal was to ascend to a higher level of mystical power. Obviously, I didn't ascend. Instead, I rocked back and forth in a corner all night muttering theories about Charlie Sheen.

That vacation was not the precious mother-daughter bonding experience Mom had been hoping for. Why couldn't she have settled for a movie night of ice cream and *Love Actually* like a normal mother?

But this is nothing like that.

I don't know if it's seeing him in the orphanage earlier, this hypnotic magical music, or just Lukka being Lukka - but I trust him. He makes me feel untouchable. And inside this crazy club I feel wild yet safe. The outside world isn't real anymore. There are no consequences here. Lukka won't let anything bad happen to me.

I stand on my tiptoes and open my mouth, and he runs his tongue against mine, passing me the pill. It tastes like watermelon and straight away starts to fizzle in my mouth. He goes to pull back, but I won't let him. My hands graze the shaved side of his head and I cup the back of his neck, pulling him down. Then his mouth crashes upon mine, lips bruised and teeth clashing. The taste of fizzy watermelon and blood mix with Lukka's ravenous hunger for me and my head starts swimming.

His hands get lost in my hair and his mouth explores mine, his feral growl vibrating on my lips. My want for him is growing hungrier with every beat of this music. I'm floating. I'm falling. I no longer know where he ends and I begin.

His tongue is on my collarbone and I realize I want to feel the delicious sting of his teeth puncturing my skin. I want my blood in his mouth. I want to drink his and get high. I want him to consume me. But he won't. I'm not his food.

What am I to him? Who am I really? It doesn't matter anymore. Right now, I'm nothing but light and love and this beat. The music swirls around us like birds dragging colored smoke across my vision.

Lukka. Milky eyes, lids half-closed, moves his body with mine while trailing icy fingertips down my spine as if he's counting each vertebra. My hands reach under his top and I find his v-lines. I trace them.

"What the hell is in these pills?" I mumble, my voice sounding far away.

Maybe it's not my voice. Maybe it's someone else's. Someone standing in a tunnel on the other side of the world.

"You like it, little Witch?" he says.

His tattooed thumb brushes across my lower lip and I moan, taking it into my mouth. I'm hungry. For him, for more, for all of it.

He laughs. "The pill was my brother's idea."

I shake my head a bit, trying to clear it. I know what Lukka's saying is important, I need to concentrate, but I don't understand. Konstantin makes pills?

"Drugs? That doesn't sound like something Konstantin

would get involved in," I say. As if I know what Konstantin would get involved in. Less than two weeks with these brothers and suddenly I *know* then? I *trust* them?

It's taking all my energy to form each word. My face feels like Jell-O and my mouth like rubber. I want to be kissed again. I want to feel Lukka's cold lips on mine and make me forget why I'm really in Russia. I want to be the girl he thinks I am.

"Kostya makes them. Normal pharmaceuticals don't work on us Paras, so he created something special." Lukka's face floods with something like pride. "This is a happy drug. He likes to make our people happy."

I think back to a few days ago when I walked into Konstantin's office and he was talking to a man in a lab coat.

"Konstantin is a chemist?" I say.

Lukka laughs. "My brother doesn't get his hands dirty. Dr. Vassily makes them for him. He's a pathetic excuse for a Vampire, too whiny. I don't like him...but he makes good drugs."

What?

"Where?" I say. "Where does this doctor make your brother's drugs?"

Lukka shrugs like it's no big deal. "Kostya has a lab beneath the Black Rabbit."

A lab? I blink once, twice. What is he saying? Is this linked to the blood results I saw on Konstantin's email?

The pill starts to work its magic and I feel it travel through my veins like liquid stardust. The club's strobe lights flash and the twinkling lights flickers and the colored beams blind me and I let go. All questions evaporate from my skin. I let the music wash them away.

Tomorrow I can be a reporter, but tonight I'm Lukka's.

CHAPTER TWENTY-TWO

Lukka is light on his feet as we tip-toe through the Volkov mansion. He supports my weight because my feet are killing me from dancing all night, and the drugs and magic are still thumping through me, slowing me down.

I knock into a statue of a naked nymph and lightning-fast Lukka catches it before it shatters on the marble floor.

He curses.

"What? Scared of waking big brother?" I tease. Then I giggle. Because everything seems supremely funny.

Must be the Witch music. He frowns at me, ushers me into my guest apartment, and closes the door quietly. There's a moment of silence between us, as we just stand there, staring at one another.

"It's late," he says.

Although what he means is that it's early. The sky was turning pink when we shut the front door and the shutters are already down in the house.

I grin. "Stayed out past your curfew?"

He smiles down at me. The smile of a madman. "It's you

who stayed up past your bedtime, little Witch." He leans close to my ear. "*Spokoinoi nochi.*"

Goodnight.

When he withdraws I feel like the air has been ripped from my lungs.

A full night of kissing. A full night of dancing. And now he's just going to leave me here with nothing? With no.... *satisfaction?*

"Maybe big brother Konstantin will ground you. That's what your boss does, right? Punishes you when you've been a bad dog," I say.

It works.

With impossible speed, Lukka whips around and crosses the distance between us. He pushes me and I fly backward onto the bed.

"You don't know what the fuck you're talking about," he growls.

It didn't hurt but I'm still shocked at his reaction. I wanted his attention, yes, but I didn't expect to hit a nerve *this* sensitive.

Then Lukka tilts his head to the ceiling and laughs.

"You should see your face," he says.

I breathe out a sigh of relief. "Still prettier than yours," I tease.

"I'm sorry for pushing you."

Laying back on the bed I playfully nudge him with the tip of my boot.

"Then make it up to me. Take off my boots. They are killing me."

Lukka rocks back and forth on his heels, as if considering this. Then he reaches forward and hooks his fingers beneath the suede of my right thigh-high boot and slowly pulls. I feel the suede slide past my knees, and calf and foot. Lukka takes his time. He drops the boot on the floor with a *thunk*. Then pulls the other one off, even slower this time, allowing the boot to slide along the fabric of my tights. He drops that one too then contemplates me.

The release of no longer being in tight high heels is like a mini orgasm in itself. I groan and flex my toes. He turns to leave.

"And my tights!" I call.

When Lukka turns to me his expression is wild. He strides over to the bed, shackles my ankles with his hands and yanks me forward, hard, so that he's between my legs. I swallow, looking up at him. I know I was taunting him, but it feels real now. Terrifyingly real. Perhaps I've gone too far - yet I don't want it to stop.

The enchanted music is still flowing through my blood, making every inch of me thrum. The cold from his hands grasping my ankles feels like someone is running a tongue along them. No, not someone. Lukka.

I suppress a moan. I don't want to be that girl, the one who groans just from someone touching her ankles. Plus, Lukka might think I have a foot fetish, and that's not sexy.

My internal monologue is interrupted as he reaches forward and slides his hands beneath my ass, lifting me and causing me to arch my back. I gasp as he hooks his fingers into the waistband of my tights and slowly, infuriatingly slowly, peels them off. As he does so his thumb glides along the inside of my thigh, goosebumps collecting in its wake.

He tosses my tights to the floor and stands. "Time to sleep, little Witch."

There are a million reasons I don't want to sleep - the Vamp between my legs being the highest on my list.

But also, I'm parched. I gulp painfully against the dryness of my throat.

"Tell me a bedtime story," I say, my throat constricting at the words.

Before I can even blink Lukka's left the room with that Vamp speed of his. He's gone. The door slamming shut behind him.

Did he...? Did he seriously just leave me here. LIKE THIS?

I curse angrily and sit up. *The prick! That arrogant, stupid, blonde...*

With a *whoosh* Lukka is in front of me again. This time he's shirtless beneath his purple gun holster, and he's grinning. In his tattooed hands, he's holding a bucket of ice and an open champagne bottle. He managed to change, go to the kitchen and fetch a bottle of champagne in under ten seconds. I close my mouth, not realizing it was gaping open.

"I don't know any good stories for good girls," he says playfully. "All I know are bad stories...for bad girls."

He sets the bucket next to me and climbs on to the bed beside me, sitting up on his knees.

"Tell me a bad story then," I whisper.

His expression shifts. He's no longer amused - he's hungry.

Lukka runs his hand through my hair and cups my head, then brings the champagne bottle to my mouth. I wrap my lips around its head and drink, eyes gazing up at him. He pushes the bottle a tiny bit deeper into my throat, then withdraws it quickly making the foam trickle out of my mouth and down my chin. Slowly, he pulls my chin up and licks the side of my mouth. Then he raises the bottle and tilts it so champagne flows down his pale muscular abdomen. The foamy liquid trickles down his tattoos and onto my sheets.

I quickly put my mouth against his abs to staunch the flow, licking and sucking my way down the V shape of his Adonis belt. Lukka squeezes my cheeks in his palm and waterfalls champagne into my open mouth.

I don't take my eyes off him, not for a second, as I drink

and slurp the cold champagne he is pouring all over me. It flows along my neck, over my breasts, perking my nipples against the wet fabric of my dress.

Lukka stands up again and I'm breathless. My core aches for him. I don't want him to leave.

"You've got me all wet now," I say, wiping my mouth with the back of my hand. "And sticky."

He gives me a demonic grin and reaches for me again. I lie back as his hands slip under my dress, his fingers hooking the straps of my thong. Then slowly he peels it away.

I arch to make it easier for him and the glimpse of my flesh makes him utter a low growl.

I feel the fabric of my underwear as he slides it down my hips, down my thighs, and the feather-light touch of them on my ankles before he flings them aside. I arch my back again to give him a second look for good measure.

Lukka's fangs are out, making indentations against his lips as he bites them.

"I'll tell you a story," he says, his voice low and husky. "A story about a naughty little Witch."

He leaves me on the bed and wanders around the room, lighting decorative candles as he goes. His silhouette is eerie against the flickering light. He returns to the bed and looks down at me. Then he takes a slow deliberate swig of champagne, before setting the empty bottle aside.

With a yank, he tugs the knotted curtain ropes from my four-poster bed free. The ropes flex over his tattooed knuckles, and suddenly he's tying my ankles to the bedposts, my legs spread wide. I gulp.

"What did she do, this little Witch in your story?" I ask breathlessly. I want his hands on me again. I can feel the heat between my legs aching and growing tighter by the second. The ropes dig into the soft skin of my ankles, and pressure builds in my core. I sit up and stare at him from under my lashes.

"The little Witch hunted the truth," he tells me. His milky gaze is haunting in the dim light. He smiles, trailing a lazy finger past my abdomen, over my left breast, and brushing it against my mouth. "But the little Witch that sought the truth was made of lies herself."

This line of the story jars me even though his finger is still making lazy circles over my body and I'm halfway to pleasure town. Does he know who I am? Does he know I'm a reporter? Is that why he's calling me a liar?

Maybe he doesn't know anything. Maybe this is just Lukka speaking in fucking riddles as usual.

I'm trying to make sense of it when suddenly he's tying my wrists to the bed, lacing the remaining curtain ropes around the bedpost. He's gentle as the flutter of a butterfly, then quickly tightens them with a hard tug.

That's what Lukka is, tenderness wrapped in violence.

He reaches behind me into the ice cube bucket and plops a cube in his mouth. Then he smiles. A mad, feral smile.

No. He doesn't know who I am - and neither do I anymore

With his soft half-open mouth, he uses the ice to trace up my calf and along my inside thighs. I shudder against the cold, then yelp when I feel his ice-cold tongue slip between my legs. The cold pressure mounts higher and higher, higher still, until I can barely take it anymore.

Then his mouth parts me and I groan as I arch for the third time, held in place by the restraints. One of his incisors scrape teasingly along my labia and I moan out loud. He does it again.

"Stop," I whisper, my breath ragged. But I mean the opposite. What I mean to say is *go on, go on, go on.*

"Want me to stop?" he asks, popping another ice cube in his mouth.

I shake my head. "Give me everything."

Quick as a flash Lukka cups my ass and slips an ice cube inside of me.

I cry out as a deep cold fills me. I glare up at him.

"Fuck! That's cold."

Lukka fetches one of the candles he lit earlier.

"I'm cold too, little Witch," he says over his shoulder. Then his mouth is at my ear. "And yet I think you want *me* inside of you too. No?"

All I'm wearing is my bra and dress now. And it's useless because it's hiked up to my waist. I would be lying if I said I didn't want Lukka right where that ice cube was moments ago, before my heat melted it. I want to reach for the sizable bulge in his pants - the only confirmation that this little game is doing it as much for him as it is for me.

Gently, Lukka slips a hand into my bra and frees my breasts, one by one. He bends low and kisses them, licking slowly across every inch, his cold tongue making my nipples strain. I'm near screaming but I'm not going to make any more noises. Not a sound. This is a power game and I'm not about to lose.

I arch my back so that my breast is fully in his mouth. He bites down lightly and I suppress a groan.

OK, I'm not going to win this game. I struggle to hold back the moans of pleasure building in my core, my breasts are cold and my nipples aching. I want him, yet he's just sitting there looking at me, knowing I can't do anything but strain against the ropes.

Lukka grins then tips the melted candle and pours hot wax over my breasts. I turn and moan loudly into the pillow, the heat between my legs rising.

I can't take this anymore. He's won.

"Take off my dress," I hiss through ragged panting breaths. He pours a few more drops of wax on me and licks one of his fangs.

I'm done with ropes and taunts, wax and ice. I want him now. Completely. Entirely.

"Even when tied up you give commands," Lukka smiles, then pulls something from his pocket in a flash of silver. A purple butterfly knife.

"Is this your favorite dress?" he asks.

"NO."

In a series of fluid movements, Lukka slices the spaghetti straps of my dress and bra, then cuts the remaining fabric along the middle. He pinches the fabric and drags it away from my body, as if he were unwrapping a present, making sure to drag the fabric slowly past by peaked nipples.

I'm finally, and completely, naked.

Lukka hovers over me, his body inches from mine, and I arch up to meet him, my wrists and ankles smarting at the bite of the ropes. I tilt my head to kiss every tattooed carved inch of him. He growls softly in response.

"You want this?" he asks.

But he's no longer taunting me. He's looking at me, his milky eyes locking on mine. His gaze is careful, genuine. He's asking my permission.

I writhe against him. "Yes. Now!"

Lukka takes off his sweats and his boxers. I bite my lip at his size, and at the sight of the tattoos winding down to his groin.

I'm done with words now. I'm done with everything except his body on mine.

He keeps the gun holster on as he climbs between my legs, and I arch my hips toward him. Then, with a soft chuckle against my neck, he slides into me.

Pleasure rocks through me like summer thunder. Lukka

starts slowly, growling softly into my ear. For what feels like the millionth time, I hoist my body upwards, as much as I can in the restraints. His mouth lands on mine and he kisses me, deeply, his fangs clashing against my teeth. He starts thrusting harder now, matching the rhythm of his rough kisses. And I move with him, stroke for stroke, moan for moan. I bite his lip as he pulls back from me. His hands are in my hair now, bringing my mouth to his neck as he drives himself deeper. Neither of us is disguising our moans anymore. We are being loud, and the bed is rocking like a docked boat on stormy waters.

"Untie me," I moan. I can't take this anymore. I want to run my hands across his body. Wrap them around his neck.

He slices through the restraints at my arms and feet with the knife, and flips me so that I'm on top. I'm startled by the sudden power of having him below me, and still inside me. I push him into the bed, palms against his chest and ride him. Bucking, writhing, grinding into him as hard and deep as I can take it. I hook my hands around the straps of his gun holster and use it to my advantage, riding him harder and faster. Lukka gives me that lopsided grin of his and pinches my nipples as he groans my name.

I forget he's a Vampire, a lead I'm investigating, someone I'm meant to be scared of. Right now, he's simply mine. I pin his arms down above his head, my breasts inches from his mouth. My prisoner. The pressure is mounting and I'm not sure I can keep it at bay much longer. Lukka sits up, driving himself deeper into me. Hands on my waist, he kisses my neck and I slow my movements.

Lukka's mouth brushes my ear. "Come for me, little Witch."

The phrase is nearly enough to set me off. But I'm not done.

I won't be told when to come, he'll be begging for it when I'm done with him.

"I wish you could bite me," I say. I make my movements much slower and more deliberate than before, teasing him. I tilt sideways to expose my neck to him. "But I don't want to kill you."

I think of the vials of antidote I have, but there's nothing sexy about having a naked man between your legs gasping for air.

He looks up at me, his gaze intent. "How about you bite *me*."

I slow down.

"What?"

"Drink from me. You might even like it."

I clench, pushing him deeper inside me. Oh, I *know* I will like it. That's if he tastes anything like his brother.

He tips his head to one side, exposing his neck and the assortment of ink he has climbing from his shoulder to behind his ear.

"You can't hurt me, little Witch," he says, placing his hands on my waist and pushing me harder against him. "I want to see you with my blood around your mouth."

I don't wait for him to ask again. I run my tongue up his neck and then bite him. He jerks against me, and I feel him swell inside me. He likes the pain.

I bite again, this time breaking his flesh. At the first taste of his blood every hair on my arm stands on end and I nearly climax. His blood isn't dry sherry, it's pure nectar.

I suck hungrily, my left hand at his throat while the other pulls at his hair. His hands are on my ass, pushing me into him as I drink.

His thrusts grow faster as I move along the full length of him, his neck crimson red and my mouth slippery with his blood.

He's moaning up at the ceiling and I kiss him, his cries of pleasure mixing with my own. His blood on both our lips.

"Saskia," he cries into my mouth.

His nails dig into my back as I swallow down his blood and ride him faster and faster until he's shuddering in my arms and waves rock through me. My entire body tightens before pure pleasure flashes through it. Again, and again, and again.

We collapse on the bed. A knot of blankets and limbs. Blood and champagne. Both of us panting.

Silence follows. Blissful silence.

"You never finished your story about the Witch." I say after a while.

Lukka runs a hand across my hip bone and I lick his blood off my hand like a cat. It's too soon to think about doing it again, but I am. I could do it twenty more times if it feels like that again.

He rolls over on his side and stares at me, eyes white like fog, before answering. "I can't finish my story," he says. "Because I don't know how it ends yet."

CHAPTER TWENTY-THREE

The shutters are still down and I stretch out in the bed. Lukka isn't beside me. Sometimes he stays in my bed, sometimes he goes back to his room. Lukka told Konstantin I was ill three days ago and I turned both my phones off. And all we've done since our night at the club is fuck. And even during the occasional snatched hours of sleep, I've dreamed of fucking him, which we then re-enact as soon as we wake. Vamp blood is one horny trip.

I don't care about work or the missed calls from Jackson and my mom, and as much as I've been meaning to talk to her I don't even care about Ansel. I should, but once I got a taste of Lukka's blood he's all I've been able to think about...and he's hardly left my side since.

I switch on my phone and note the time. 3.45 pm. Neither brother will be up and about yet. Sometimes Konstantin goes for a run after the sun sets, or hits the gym downstairs. Lukka, on the other hand, has to be pushed out of bed most evenings to get ready for work.

I've been awake for hours thinking. No, not thinking... worrying. I've been wondering whether I should be reporting on the drug information Lukka shared with me. Whether I should look into it more. Pill-popping Vamps would make an interesting story, as would the crazy nightclub Lukka took me to. But what Jackson sent me here for was to investigate murders. Are all these things connected?

Lukka mentioned his brother has a lab. I think back to the holding cells I spotted in the club's private parking lot the night Lukka took me to meet his brother, and the man in the white lab coat I'd seen talking to Konstantin in his office the night before the theatre. All these alarm bells have gotten louder since discovering Konstantin likes making fancy drugs for his Vamp friends.

It doesn't make sense; the pieces don't add up, yet they keep spinning around in my head like smashed-up houses in a typhoon. And in the center of it all is Lukka, and the feel of his lips on mine as I licked that pill off his tongue and what we did straight after that. And what we've not been able to stop doing since. Does Konstantin know what we've been up to? Does he care?

All this time in Russia and still no story.

My phone rings, Ansel's name is flashing eagerly. Guilt hammers straight into the pit of my stomach. I haven't been to work. I haven't seen her.

My finger hovers over the red circle on the screen, then I mentally slap myself.

What's the fucking matter with you, Saskia? She's young, and her boyfriend just got murdered, and you're an investigator. Speak to her.

"Hi, Ansel," I say, forcing a grin on my face. My mother always says to act happy when on the phone. She swears people can hear you smile. But before the MA my mother used to charge people six-hundred bucks an hour to tell them their future, or to hex their former lovers. With those exuberant phone rates, I'd be smiling too. "I've been meaning to call you but I've been a bit tied up lately." I grin at my lame joke, then feel guilty about that too. "How have you been?"

"Oh, thank god you answered," she says in one shaky breath. "I'm not great. I really need to speak to you."

I close my eyes. I'm a shitty friend. Probably because I have zero experience in being a friend. Ansel doesn't deserve my pathetic excuses.

"Do you want to meet up?" I ask.

I look at the time on my phone again. There's still a couple of hours before either brother will wonder where I am. It's not like I'm a prisoner here, I'm allowed to leave whenever I want.

"Good idea. I don't trust phones," she says, her voice thick with tears. "There's so much I have to tell you. Bad stuff."

Of course, it's 'bad' stuff. I know all about loss and the darkness that comes with it. There's nothing 'good' about your boyfriend being murdered and being so far from home.

"Can we meet at the café near the club?" she asks.

"Where we had breakfast last time?"

"Yes. I'm so scared, Saskia. Things are bad." Her voice starts to wobble, and I feel it like a rock in my lungs. She needed me and all I've been worried about is my next orgasm.

"Of course," I say. "Shall we meet at six? We can head on to the club together after our chat?"

"I would love that." My mother was right. I can hear the smile in her voice. "Thank you, Saskia. You're a true friend."

I'm not. But I should be.

I shower, apply some bright red lipstick and run my fingers through my hair. I'm meeting her in an hour – but first I need to satisfy that itch. The club is about forty minutes away, which will leave me plenty of time to see what the hell is going on in the Black Rabbit's creepy parking lot before meeting Ansel. My first chance to slip away without

Lukka pinning me down and doing amazingly bad things to me.

I head down the hallway towards the flight of stairs leading to the front door. I pass a side table. There are ornate bowls and vases dotted all over this house. Some look like Ming dynasty pieces, all look expensive. The bowl I pass is inexplicably full of expensive fruit no one is going to eat, and nestled beside an orange is a bunch of keys. Lukka is always forgetting his keys to the club and his brother is always cutting him new sets. I was planning on sneaking into the parking lot via the club, but this makes my life much easier. I swipe them and drop the garage keys into my purse where I already put my passport and paperwork.

I'm about to go a lot deeper into this investigation, and I'm not prepared to have to come back for anything if it goes wrong.

CHAPTER TWENTY-FOUR

There was traffic on the way to the Black Rabbit and now I'm stressed I won't meet Ansel in time. I squeeze the keys I stole from the Volkov mansion so hard they leave metal indents in my fingers. As instructed, the Uber driver drops me off at the back entrance.

As silently as possible I open the garage and pray that anyone watching the security cameras won't find it strange that Konstantin's new employee has let herself in. It's early evening and I could just be fetching something for the Volkov's who can't do so themselves during dusk hours.

I make my way across the garage. The two holding cells loom in front of me like the gaping mouths of a two-headed dragon, all metal bars and concrete. I take a deep breath but walk over anyway. Based on my journalism experience, the stuff my gut tells me to keep away from is normally the first place I find my answers.

It's dark in the underground parking lot. The space fits about ten cars, I imagine they all belong to the brothers. I spot the dank cells, poorly lit by one singular bulb, and between them, I locate another door. A heavy grey door that camouflages effortlessly against the concrete walls. *The lab is underneath the Black Rabbit,* Lukka told me, and I'm willing to bet it's behind this very door.

My burner phone buzzes in my pocket. It's Ansel. *Shit!* I'm meant to be at the café soon. I press the red button. She'll have to wait. It's not like me turning up late is going to make her feel any worse than she does already.

I turn the handle and enter a large room that looks like an underground security office. There are desks drowning in paperwork, coat hangers, a tea station, and a TV with flickering security feeds. Mercifully, none of the security staff is here. I imagine running into Dimitri the bouncer bear in these confined quarters and shudder. My sneakers stick lightly to the floor, as if I'm crossing an ice cream parlor. What the fuck? The room is dark too, lit only by a solitary lamp in the corner, but I can still see oil-like streaks by my feet. I bend down to touch them when a booming voice stops me cold in my tracks.

"Make it possible!"

My head whips around at the sound of a familiar deep male voice shouting in Russian. I scan the room, but there's no one there. Voices rise again behind me. Where the hell are they? They can't be upstairs in the club - I wouldn't be able to hear them from all the way down here. There are two more doors nearby, one has a keypad and the other doesn't. The man I'm hearing must be behind one of them. I place my ear against the first door and listen.

"I've told Konstantin, I need more time to perfect the product," says a second voice, more nasal and whinier than the first.

"Well, you're out of time, Vassily." I recognize that man's voice, but I can't place it. "It fucking stinks in here. Let's go. You can be the one to tell Konstantin you need two weeks instead of one. I'm not getting defanged over your lack of professionalism."

Wait! He's talking to Dr. Vassily? Wasn't that the doctor Lukka mentioned?

Footsteps follow, and they're heading straight at me. *Fuck. Fuck. Fuck.*

I skitter backward and cower behind a nearby desk as two men enter the office. From my vantage point, I can just make out the flash of a lab as they let the door shut behind them. I was right - that's where Konstantin makes his secret drugs.

I peek from behind the desk and finally get a look at the two men speaking. The first voice belonged to Rada, the homophobic shipping magnate that Konstantin thought was messing up his business. Well, he's clearly not so innocent as I (and his own son) thought. I guess Rada and Konstantin are working together now.

"He can't defang *you*," a man in a lab coat moans. He has to be Dr. Vassily. "You're his new business partner. But *me*? I'm about as disposable as a Blood Bunny. You could delay the shipment, or tell him we need more time for logistics. Lie. If the sun pill formula isn't perfect when we ship there could be Vampire casualties."

"Konstantin doesn't see business partners as his superiors, *Vasya*. And I'm not about to make the same mistakes Boris made and go behind his back. If I'm running the business side, I'm going to do this right. No bodies. No lies. *No late deliveries.*"

Rada's fangs grow menacingly, his face stern. He's decided. Rada is a man who gets things done.

Dr. Vassily looks away and pours them both a cup of tea.

"I can't cope with that volume or that time frame," he complains, each word shrill and petulant. I can see why Lukka hates him. "Can't we outsource to the Swiss?"

"The Swiss are planning to charge us triple. We have no choice, we will need to expand these facilities." He waves his hand around the office as if that's where the expansion will go. "We can use the rest of the parking lot, create a better line-up. Konstantin is having ten more buses full of workers commuted in from various sites. They've all been fed over the last six months and are ready for extraction."

Workers? Extraction? *What the fuck?* Has Konstantin been steroiding up his KLV workers and then extracting their blood to make drugs with? It makes no sense. Konstantin hasn't been acting that different lately. Not that I would know, I've not seen him since the Bolshoi. Although now I come to think of it, Konstantin *has* made it really easy for his brother and I to be together without demanding anything from either of us. That's not like him at all. What's the evil bastard been doing while Lukka has been in my room the last three days?

Dr. Vassily sighs wearily. "It will be hard to expand the laboratory down here. Lukka will not be happy to give up his beloved parking lot."

"Konstantin can handle his mad brother. He never involves him anyway."

I let out a silent sigh of relief. At least there's that.

"But why can't we have more *time?*" the doctor asks again.

"We have to shift the product quickly, or we risk another leak. Or another coup."

Dr. Vassily adds sugar cubes to his tea. "I thought Konstantin took care of the leak. That Kazakh boy from the site."

Ansel's boyfriend, Maxim, was the leak?!

"It's not just the boy. Turns out his girl, the bunny bitch, supplied information to The Blood Web Chronicle a few weeks ago. Konstantin's hacker found the correspondence on her Blood Web account. He thought it was the boy at first, but he was just nosey. It was his girl who did the snitching."

My phone starts vibrating again. It's Ansel, asking me where I am. I resist the urge to cry. How am I going to tell her the man she loved died because of her whistle-blowing?

"I never liked that rabbit Shifter anyway. She's not even hot," says Dr. Vassily.

I blink away the *ping* of his lie. *Creep.*

Rada drains his tea down to the bergamot dregs. "Pack up the latest samples. We're going to see Konstantin."

"Go to Konstantin? But it's sunlight hours!" Dr. Vassily exclaims.

Rada grabs him by the cuff and Dr. Vassily's fangs protrude defensively, but it's a pathetic sight. His canines are half Rada's size.

"Take a sun pill and shut the fuck up."

With this, he drags the doctor out of the security office and I'm left in silence.

Pop a pill? A pill that will help Dr. Vassily go to see Konstantin in broad daylight? *If the sun pill formula isn't perfect when we ship there could be Vampire casualties,* Dr. Vassily's earlier phrase plays through my mind.

The doctor is concerned about shipping out a faulty product before it's perfected, a product Konstantin is working on that helps Vamps withstand the sun. More pieces of the puzzle collide in my brain as one horrible realization comes after the next. Konstantin has been creating some kind of chemical in his underground lab, spiking the construction workers' food with it to make their blood better, then draining his victims like prize-winning friesians.

That's my story. I have it. *Fuck!*

Another thought slithers into my brain and it fills me with dread. Konstantin has found out that Ansel was the whistle-blower who contacted The Chronicle. He won't let her get away with that. I have to warn her!

And if Konstantin has been hacking Blood Web accounts he might have even found out that I work for The Chronicle. *I might be in danger too!*

FUCK!

I hurry forward, then freeze as I hear a noise. Someone is coming back, and judging by the heavy footsteps it's Rada. Maybe he's forgotten something - perhaps the product samples. Quickly I reach for the nearest door, fling myself inside and close it.

It's pitch-black in here. I hold my breath - both from fear and the putrid stench in whatever room I'm hiding in, and I wait. And wait. Will Rada's Vampire hearing be good enough to pick up the thunder of my heartbeat behind the door? There's the sound of him rifling through paperwork and banging drawers, searching for something, and then, finally, he leaves. Footsteps recede and the door shuts with a click. I finally breathe out.

Relieved, I slump against the wall and close my eyes. My heart is thundering and I attempt to steady myself, palms flat against the wall behind me. I need to calm down before I call Ansel. I take a deep breath of the thick tangy air, stifling a cough from the stench, but as I straighten up my hands come away wet and sticky. *What the hell?* My chest tightens with panic again as I pat the walls, tracing my way back to the door frame until I find a light switch and flick it on. I blink, look at my hands, then blink again. They are bright red and glistening.

Oh no. I turn around, slowly, and survey the room.

Everything is white. White walls, white benches and a white tiled floor. It reminds me of the Blood Bunny room. I squint at the bright strip lighting and blink a few more times, trying to customize myself to the glare. So much white, the perfect canvas for the crimson splashes of blood dripping down the walls. Blood. Blood everywhere. I clamp my hand over my mouth to stifle a squeak of a scream trying to escape, my lips now covered in the cold blood from my palms.

Something is dripping. *Drip. Drip.* Like the slow tick of a clock. I step forward and nearly slip on a black puddle at my feet. *What the hell is going on?* I look up, and finally find the source of the blood. Two bodies. Boris and his Bolshoi theatre date are hanging above me by hooks embedded at the back of their heads, swaying limply like mutilated scarecrows.

Now I know where Konstantin has been the past three days.

CHAPTER TWENTY-FIVE

I cover my mouth as I dry heave in the back of yet another Uber as it whizzes through the grey streets. I washed my hands and face using kettle water, before getting the fuck out of there as fast as I could, but I can still see blood beneath my nails.

I can't believe the whole time Lukka and I were wrapped up in tangled sheets, Konstantin was torturing work associates and their loved ones. Boris, the same man whose lies I alerted Konstantin to at the theatre. I let out another whimper. *Oh my god, this is all my fault! First the men in the restaurant and now Boris and his innocent girlfriend - all because of my lie detecting.*

Not only is Konstantin a megalomaniac trying to make super blood pills that help Vamps go out in the sun, but he's the worst monster I've ever known.

And Ansel is about to be his next victim.

The acrid smell of death still lingers in my nostrils, my stomach spasming in shock. I put down my phone and vomit in the footwell of the Uber. The driver screams at me, but I don't care. Every time I blink all I see is haunting flashes of the white room, signs of the struggle Boris and his girl must have put up, and their slow torture. They were both still dressed in their ballet finery. Konstantin must have gone back for them right after he showed me his childhood home. I gag again at the thought that I let the bastard touch me with the very same hands he used hours afterward to do *that.*

As soon as I got in the Uber I texted Ansel to find somewhere safe and wait for me. A few minutes later she sent me the location of where to meet her. I don't trust my phone isn't hacked, or hers, so I can't text her everything I've discovered. I need to explain it all face to face.

I've also let Jackson know, via my other phone, that I need immediate removal. The Chronicle has procedures in place for that. He didn't even waste time asking me the details, he just told me to get back immediately.

My hands are shaking as I look in my purse and double-check I have everything. My fake passport, my paperwork, and money. I don't care about my clothes. Then my heart sinks. What about Lukka? I want to call him, but I have to get to Ansel first.

The address Ansel gave me leads me to a courtyard between a large group of soviet blocks. I look around but can't see her. I'm about to keep walking when a shadow moves in a nearby arch. I flinch, but it's her. Thank god!

She's wearing a heavy teddy bear-looking coat, her arms wrapped tightly around herself. The pink bobble on her hat nods back and forth as she runs over to me.

Melting snow sloshes beneath my feet as I cross the distance between us. "Did anyone follow you?" I ask, my breath forming foggy clouds between us.

Ansel's honey eyes dart behind me, her gaze crawling up the building, before wrapping her arms around me tightly.

"No, why?" she says. She's shaking, and I hold her closer. "Why would I be followed?"

"Konstantin knows you're the one who leaked KLV info to The Blood Web Chronicle."

She stiffens in my arms and withdraws.

"I don't know what you're talking about," she stutters.

Ping.

"Don't worry," I say, rubbing her arm. "I'm an undercover reporter for The Chronicle. I'm the one they sent to investigate this. We have to get away now, you're in danger."

Ansel doesn't look convinced, but then she doesn't have many options either.

"I got suspicious a few weeks ago," she cries, as I lead her away from the glare of the streetlamp to a dark corner. "That's why I voiced my concerns - but now I *know* I was right about these murders not being accidental. Maxim called me last week, before our argument, and told me he'd been to see the site doctor because he was feeling unwell. They told him he was fine...then he was killed. I went to collect Maxim's things from his bunk a couple of days ago and I found something in his clothes. Look." She holds out a piece of crumpled paper with numbers printed all over it. It looks similar to the test results I saw on Konstantin's laptop. "I guess he went to get a second opinion, but they don't make sense. These bloodwork results are strange, it says he was taking something similar to steroids. My boyfriend would never have taken steroids, Saskia. *Never.*"

I steady her with my arms, forcing her to focus on me.

"Ansel, you need to get out of here. Do you have anyone that can hide you? Anyone that you trust?"

"She has me," a gruff voice announces from over my shoulder.

I know that voice, and it covers every inch of my body in goosebumps. I turn slowly to find Dimitri standing in the archway behind me. I've not heard him speak much beyond the word 'no'. The club bouncer is wearing a light blue Adidas tracksuit, a different variation of his usual attire, the top zipped up tight over his barrel chest. It's bitterly cold but he's not wearing a coat, as if he's too tough to be scared by something as trivial as a Russian winter. His gold chains shine in the moonlight, but his face is partly in shadow thanks to the black bucket hat he's wearing like a bad Baltic imitation of a 90s Liam Gallagher.

My body pivots and I shield Ansel with it.

"What are you doing here?" I shout.

"I called him," Ansel says, sidestepping me and standing by his side. "Dimitri is going to help me leave the city."

She looks up at him, her gaze warm and trusting. He returns it and my heart releases some of the tension it's been holding. Dimitri may never have liked me, but I've seen the way he looks at Ansel. He adores her. Plus, he's strong, he can protect her. But does he care enough to turn against his boss? Right now, he's all we've got.

"Take her far from here," I say. As if I could tell this giant bear what to do.

Dimitri nods. "You need a ride to the airport?"

"No," I reply. "I'm heading back to the club. There's something I need to do first."

I've decided I *do* need to talk to Lukka. I need to tell him what I've discovered about Rada and Boris, about the laced food and that his brother is behind it all.

"We'll drop you off," says Dimitri, and I nod.

The three of us make our way through the arches and courtyard to where I'm assuming Dimitri's car is parked. My phone buzzes and I glance at it. Jackson has texted me. He sounds more concerned than usual and confirms he's already booked me a ticket for tonight. If I didn't know any better I would think he was worried about me.

I text him back quickly as Ansel's footsteps pitter-patter beside me, accompanied by Dimitri's heavier tread. The Tetris motion continues in my head, pieces of information falling and fitting and not fitting at all. Then it hits me.

Dimitri doesn't know I'm a journalist – so why did he offer to take me to the airport? Why is he assuming I would run as well, just because Ansel told him she's in trouble? Unless Konstantin told him who and what I really am!

"How did you know I would be leaving the country?" I ask him.

"You just mentioned it."

I didn't. The *ping* of his lie is like a bucket of cold water on my frozen skin.

His smile is small and sharp, but through the shade of his hat I can still see his eyes growing smaller and narrowing - the predatory eyes of a bear.

My head flickers from side to side, calculating the best direction in which we could run, when suddenly a set of thick ivory claws morph from the bouncer's skin. I brace myself for impact, to feel the slice of them gauge through my abdomen, but instead his paws close around Ansel.

"No" I scream as she lets out a sound that is neither a yelp nor a whimper, her eyes wide with fright. I go to move, to shout, to reach out - but I'm too late. In one swift motion, Dimitri slices Ansel's neck open with a single claw and she falls with a faint *thump* to the slush beneath our feet. And all I can think is 'death should make a larger sound than that'.

At my feet lies a limp black rabbit, her fur moving in the bitter wind and flakes of snow clinging to her soft down. Like all dead Shifters, Ansel has morphed back.

"First the rabbit, then the rat," Dimitri growls.

My scream is drowned out by the bear's roar as he makes a lunge for me. I duck, a shadow looms in my peripheral, then everything goes black.

CHAPTER TWENTY-SIX

As I come to the first thing I'm aware of is the gentle hum of *Moonlight Sonata*. The classical song slithers through the darkness towards me, ebbing in and out of focus.

The second thing I notice is that I'm swinging, my body moving from side to side to the sweet gentle music. Am I dancing? I feel like I've taken one of Lukka's pills again, but I know I haven't, because the last thing I remember was a bear and a *thump* and...

Then it hits me. The third and strongest sensation. Pain. Intense and all-consuming pain crashing over me. My eyes snap open. The excruciating sensation has turned my world upside down.

I blink three times and slowly my eyes adjust to the dark space I'm in.

I *am* upside down. I stare at the floor as it rises and falls, rises and falls, trying to move my hands but failing. They are tied behind my back and my ankles are bound above my head. I recognize the room I'm in – it's the holding cells in the Black Rabbit's parking lot.

"Dobroye utro." Konstantin's lacy voice matches the melodic rise and fall of the piano.

"I wouldn't call this a *good* morning," I spit, mustering whatever bravado I can manage considering I'm swinging upside down.

Konstantin steps into my line of vision, his face contorted in mild surprise at my response. What? Did he think I was going to give him the whole *'Oh my god, I can't believe you're the villain!'* speech? I'm not. I wouldn't be hanging upside down if he wasn't. Ansel wouldn't be dead if he wasn't.

I swallow and ask the most important question.

"How does Lukka fit into all of this?"

Konstantin waves his hand as if he were swatting away a fly. "Lukka isn't involved in my other business."

"Which is?"

He reaches out and runs a finger along my cheek. He looks so sure of himself.

"I thought you would have figured it out, little Miss Reporter."

If he knows I'm a reporter, then why am I not dead? As if in answer to my question Konstantin goes to the door of the cage and calls out the name of Dr. Vassily.

The sniveling doctor doesn't spare me a glance. He's clearly used to watching people suffer in the Black Rabbit basement. He busies himself by a small table, which wasn't in the cage when I was in here this evening. What the fuck is he doing?

"Untie me, Konstantin. We can talk," I say, my breaths growing heavy, my headache near unbearable.

Konstantin ignores me as he watches the doctor layout a series of syringes. At the sight of their exchange, my entire body seizes up, causing the pain to double.

"You already know I own a pharmaceutical company,"

Konstantin examines one of the syringes. "I hear you enjoyed testing my creations."

How does he know about my night with Lukka? Does he know we slept together?

"You're a glorified drug dealer," I spit.

"It started with recreational drugs, but as you know, sweetheart, we have moved far beyond that now."

"Like your super-blood sun pills?"

"Sun pills, yes. A few years ago, I started trading in modified blood. Organic, clean, enhanced blood sourced from the strongest of subjects..."

"You're not describing free-range chicken," I interrupt him.

"Am I not?" Konstantin mimics a look of surprise, eyebrows arched, then smiles. "As you know I also deal in enhanced Shifter blood. Experimenting with various blood blends led me to the sun pills."

"You drug your workers with enhancement drugs through the food you provide, then drain them to death and put the blood in pills to sell on the Blood Web?"

Konstantin nods, looking a little impressed with my investigative skills. "Our super blood operation was flawless for years. Undocumented workers come and go and no one could trace their mass disappearances to us. We hid the bodies well." I try desperately to get out of the restraints smarting my bloody wrists, while Konstantin busies himself with the syringe. It's impossible. These brothers sure know how to tie a girl up.

"That is..." he continues. "Until Boris got greedy and started having his associates, like Varlam who you met at Sakhalin, steal entire shipments from me. Of course, once Boris's employees found out about the super blood they started attacking my workers, draining them out of greed - sloppily leaving their dead bodies dumped on my sites for anyone to find. That's when your friend went and ran her mouth to The Chronicle. So, you can imagine my luck when a little Verity Witch fell right into my lap and helped me weed out all the rats in my organization. Now all these problems have been taken care of. I should thank you, really."

He was playing me all along. He used me for his own investigative purposes, all the while I thought I was investigating him.

"How long have you known I'm a reporter?"

"I had my tech guys look into it shortly after you arrived. They struggled with the encryptions, I admit, but your mistake was not knowing Russia has the best hackers in the world. Your movements were suspicious too."

"My movements?"

Konstantin reaches out and pinches my Black Rabbit pendant between his fingers.

"The pendants are bewitched with tracker spells. It's how I saw you at the construction site. It's how I tracked Ansel's movements too."

"The map in your office," I say weakly, recalling the elaborate map of Moscow hanging in his office, flickering with bewitched moving lights. It's how he knows where all his little rabbits are. *I should have known.*

I let everything sink in as my body rocks slowly back and forth. Grief is heavy in my stomach and gravity is threatening to make it flood out of me in the form of vomit.

"You didn't have to kill Ansel," I choke out through a sob. "She didn't even know the whole truth."

"Yes. It *is* a shame. She was a sweet child," he drawls, "But when you build an innovative business such as mine, there will always be collateral damage."

"You know what? You're not some visionary, you're just a pathetic trafficker," I shout. "Nothing more."

His smile waivers a little.

"I'm not some backstreet dealer, sweetheart. My sun pills are going to change the world."

He's right. If this crap gets out, *no one* will be safe from Vampires.

"Why are you doing all of this?" I ask. I feel faint. So much blood has rushed to my head that I can only ask the simplest of questions. "You already have plenty of money."

Although I know it's more than that. Having enough wealth has never stopped someone from wanting more, but with Konstantin, his reasoning always runs deeper than that.

He doesn't answer me, so I goad him. "Your medical lapdog over there said your product wasn't ready, that it would cost Vamps their lives if it was released too soon."

Konstantin glances at Dr. Vassily with irritation. "Like I said, collateral damage."

"I don't understand why you're doing this!"

Konstantin sighs. "We Vampires have been cast out to the shadows for too long," he says, tapping the syringe. "But not anymore. We were created to rule this world. We belong in the light."

Konstantin is already so powerful in the night, why would daylight be so important to him? How much more will he gain? Then it hits me. *Ballet!* Being unable to walk in the sun cost him his life's dream. Finally, Konstantin's motives make sense.

"The moment I was turned," he says, "I could see that us Vampires were the *real* gods. I knew it the moment I took my mother's life. As I watched the weakness and humanity drain from her, I knew there was no other god in this world as powerful as me."

Konstantin killed their mother.

My heart already aches from all the blood pumping to it, but upon hearing Konstantin's confession my pain for Lukka crashes down on me like a thunderous wave. Poor Lukka, all these years thinking that his mother killed herself because of him.

"That's why I built us our own chapel," he gestures at the ceiling. He's talking about the Black Rabbit.

"So, this is about power?" I say.

"*Everything* is about power, sweetheart."

"There are other ways to power, Konstantin. One with a smaller body count."

"The road to power is paved with bodies," he answers coolly. "Especially in mother Russia."

Dr. Vassily has finished whatever he's been working on in the corner of the room and straightens up as Konstantin pulls something from his pocket. He holds the vial up to my face. Even upside down I recognize my bottle of Witch blood antidote.

"Imagine how delighted I was," he coos. "To hear the Vamp who attacked you talk of a Witch blood antidote. Your precious MA has certainly kept *that* new development quiet..." He shakes it in my face. "Useful stuff, this. No wonder you wouldn't want other Paras getting their hands on it. Oh well, too late."

The Mage Association are the only ones who can produce this. If Konstantin releases it across the whole Para community us Witches will become totally defenseless.

My heartbeat gallops wildly as Konstantin rolls up his shirt sleeve and injects himself with a groan. It must hurt as he shoots the doctor a vile look as if the unpleasantness of the drug were *his* fault. The fact that the shot was meant for him instead of me is somehow scarier because now I have absolutely no fucking clue what this monster is doing.

Konstantin crouches down until his face is inches from mine. I can't believe I once enjoyed staring into these eyes. I can't believe I let this piece of shit near me.

"Thanks to you delivering this handy little antidote

straight into my home, I had my doctor study it and make me another version. A special Vamp version which will allow us to finally get to feed on Witches properly." I'm shocked into silence, but Konstantin hasn't finished. "Imagine how many Vamps are going to enjoy the thrill of a Witch for dinner," he says.

I swallow again. He's developed a drug that allows all Vamps to feed on Witches? Not just an antidote. *This is huge.* If he can achieve that, he can achieve anything...and it's all my fault.

My voice is croaky as I attempt to reason with him. "Why go through the effort of devising a drug to feed on me, when you can literally feed on anybody else?" I shout, my voice wavering. "Is power over me that important to you?"

He laughs. "Don't be silly, sweetheart. Your blood means nothing to me, in fact, it tastes like shit. Through this medicine, my latest design, I'll get to do more than just drink. I'll also get to absorb your abilities."

I close my mouth quickly and Konstantin's smile widens. It's terrifying. Out of the corner of my eye, I see the doctor leave us, and although I know he's not on my side all I can hear is my heartbeat hammering against my tight chest knowing I'm being left alone with Konstantin.

I want to scream. To call out. To beg. But it won't make any difference. It's too late.

Konstantin slowly lowers down his shirt sleeve, then with unnatural speed he plunges his teeth into my neck. His fangs, buried deep into my soft flesh, burn like a brand. Each suck at my neck making me sway from side to side. I can hear the rush of blood leaving me, feel myself losing consciousness as my body grows weaker. Konstantin drinks deeply, his hands moving to either side of my face to keep me steady as he lets out soft moans of pleasure.

"This medicine makes you taste delicious," he groans. "That's an added bonus."

Eventually, he releases me and leaves me swinging like a piece of meat in an abattoir as I drift in and out of consciousness

"Tell me a lie, sweetheart," he coos, his mouth smeared with my blood. "I want to see what Verity magic I can do."

"A lot of people love you," I say weakly.

I can tell when the *ping* of my lie hits him, because he looks both angry and pleased with himself. His face twists into a snarl and he throws himself at me again, this time sinking his teeth into the other side of my neck. Pain pulses from my chest to the crown of my head, sharp and relentless. Then he lets go.

"Just finish me already," I growl.

"Oh, no, no, no, Saskia," Konstantin tuts, his eyes hooded in post-feed ecstasy. "There's an art in feeding. It's like an orgasm. It's all about control and drawing it out, savoring the moment. But I've already taught you that lesson. Haven't I?" He gives me a look and I know he's thinking of the Bolshoi. Thinking of the way he had me teetering on the edge of a climax until *he* decided when I'd come. I fucking hate him.

He places his face close to mine, whispering in my ear. "I'm going to *nearly* drain you, sweetheart, over and over again, keeping you on the verge of death. But I won't let you fall. Where's the fun in that?"

He's taking pleasure from my suffering. I feel the bile slipping down my throat.

"Think about it, Saskia. Why would I *ever* kill you?" he coos. "The abilities I've just sucked out of you will only last as long as the blood is in my system, so I need to keep taking it. Although it won't be long until I find a way to synthesize it. Truth pills - what do you think? It has a certain ring to it, don't you agree?"

His words are taking shape in my hazy head. He's going to leave me hanging here indefinitely like his personal lab rat. For how long? Terror rocks through me and I start to shake.

"You're broken," I say quietly. I need him to know that beneath the layers of my terror, beneath the layers of hate, I pity him. "It's no surprise though. I mean, your father left you, your mother didn't care about you, and when your brother finds out that you're as evil as your parents were, he'll hate you more than anyone."

It works. His level gaze narrows and I'm almost grateful when his teeth plunge into me again and the whole world fades to black.

CHAPTER TWENTY-SEVEN

Konstantin fed on me so many times I eventually passed out. My eyes flicker open and I realize I'm still in the cage but at least this time I'm the right way up and no longer restrained. Someone has propped me up on a concrete bench and littered around me are empty syringes and little glass bottles.

What the fuck have they been pumping into me?

Or has Dr. Evil been extracting blood samples to get to work with on truth pills? My neck stings but the pain isn't too bad. I run my hand over what I expect to be a huge wound, but it's just two tiny dots like scabbed-over pinpricks. Have they been injecting me with fast-healing meds? Or making my blood stronger by filling me with power-enhancing steroids? I'm no vegan, but for the first time in my life I know exactly how a farm cow feels and it's not cute.

I try and get to my feet, but my legs can't hold me up and I flop back down again. *Great.* Not only am I trapped in Vamp jail, in an underground private parking lot where no one is going to come until nightfall, but I can't even stand up.

I lean my head back against the concrete wall and shout. My throat is sore, but that's the least of my problems.

"Hello?"

Silence.

"Anybody there?"

What am I expecting? Batman to crash in?

I can hear movement next door. What if Konstantin is still there? Will he come back for more? I haven't eaten in ages, but I feel like I'm going to throw up.

The lab door behind me opens and the weaselly Dr. Vassily enters and places a full syringe on the small table by the door.

"Mr. Volkov has asked me to prepare more antidotes," he says, pointing to the injection. His face is deathly pale even for a Vamp, and his watery eyes are rimmed red. "He will be back soon, so stop shouting."

Looking him dead in the eye I let out a scream as loud as my sore throat will allow.

In a flash he's by my side, face inches from mine and Vamp teeth bared. Unlike Lukka's thick white fangs, Dr. Vassily's are yellowing and pathetically thin, I'm tempted to snap them out of his slack-jaw mouth.

"You think you can threaten me with those pin-dick fangs?" I say. "An office stapler would do more damage than what you're packing."

"Keep talking, you little bitch, and I'll kill you!"

"No, you won't," I say. "Konstantin needs me more than he needs you."

The doctor snarls and looks me up and down like I'm a piece of meat. Which, after what they've been doing to me, I guess I am.

"The world is not short of Witches," he spits. "Witches who are far more powerful than *you*. But there aren't many doctors like me. So, keep quiet and rest. Mr. Volkov will be back soon, and we need you to be compliant."

A smile creeps over his face and I want to wipe it off with a chair. But there's nothing left in the cage now except a concrete bench attached to the wall, a small table, and a floor full of trash.

The doctor slams the door loudly behind him and I do my best not to burst out crying. It's freezing down here. They haven't even given me a blanket.

Come on, Saskia, I say to myself. *You've got out of worse situations than this one. If you can burn down a Shifter mafia den and fight a Siren queen underwater, then you can get out of a cage.*

I have no idea what time it is, but it has to be morning by now, which is probably why Dr. Vamp is grumpy and my torturer is either in his mansion or upstairs in the club having a nap. There's only one car left in the garage and it's too ostentatious to belong to Konstantin. I squint at it and....wait. *No way.*

It hurts to smile but I do so anyway. That car belongs to Lukka. It's not his prized yellow Lamborghini, but another pink model from his collection. A sick feeling creeps over me at the thought that maybe he's in the club, that he's been in on this all along, but I push away my fear. I've just spent the last three nights (and plenty of day action too) with him and he's never once lied to me. He has no idea I'm in trouble. I'm sure of it.

What was it he said about his cars being his babies? About using something even better than a nanny cam to watch over them?

I pick up one of the empty syringes off the ground and weigh it in my hand. If I can hit the car, maybe Lukka's phone will alert him that someone is damaging his property?

I stumble over to the bars of my cage, my legs wobbling beneath me, and throw the empty syringe as hard as I can at his car. It drops a meter away. Nowhere close. This is why I never took part in athletics at school.

I grab a tiny glass bottle off the ground and throw that instead. It's heavier so it goes further, but I'm still a shit shot and it lands with a light crash on the ground nowhere near his car.

I try again, then again, hoping Dr. Vassily next door can't hear the noise I'm making. Nothing works and I'm left with no more options, all the trash from my cell now littering the parking lot instead.

I look around the sparse room, contemplating taking off my boots and throwing them next, when I spot a full syringe behind me. I don't want that fucking thing anywhere near me anyway - not if it means Konstantin gets another go at draining me dry.

This is my only chance. If I miss his car Lukka will never know what happened to me and the world is going to be overrun with Vamps who can also do Witch magic...in the sunlight. *Fuck that!*

I weigh up the syringe in my hand. It's heavier than the other items were. I can do this. I *have* to do this. Taking a deep breath, I channel my inner Katniss and take aim. *Bam!* The syringe hits the wing mirror of the fancy car with a satisfying crack - disappointingly the syringe remains full and unbroken.

With a loud slam, the door to the lab flies open again and the doctor steps out, this time looking more exhausted than angry. Someone needs a coffin nap.

"What was that noise?" he asks, his voice dripping with weariness.

Shit, he's noticed I've tidied up my cell. Fast as a flash he grabs my face and edges closer.

"No one is coming to save you, Witch bitch," he hisses. "Only the Volkovs have the key to this garage during the day and they are both sleeping. One more word out of you and I'll wake Konstantin so that he can deal with you himself."

He can say what he likes, but I know Lukka doesn't sleep much.

After ten minutes I'm convinced either Lukka's phone hasn't alerted him or he's not heard it. After twenty minutes I start telling myself that maybe he's in on this after all. Then, after thirty minutes, a side door at the back of the garage slowly opens and I see Lukka's bleary and concerned face.

I've never been so happy to see anyone in my life.

Except he doesn't look in the direction of the cages, he only has eyes for his car baby. He jogs over to the car and runs his hand tenderly over the wing mirror, picking up the glass on the floor and looking around.

I want to shout but I daren't. I can't let the doctor know I've summoned help. I wave my arms around and Lukka finally notices me. He goes to speak but I hold my finger up to my lips.

"Help me," I whisper. "Get me out of here."

He lets out a confused laugh and runs his fingers through his messy hair. He looks half asleep. He's bare-chested and wearing baggy white trousers, his usual array of gold chains around his neck, and a pair of plastic Adidas sliders. Was he sleeping upstairs? He must have been because he couldn't have driven over from the house in daylight. Unless he has sun pills. Has his brother told him about them already?

"There you are!" he says, his face lighting up. "I've been calling you. I came to the club last night looking for you and I've been there all day waiting." He frowns and walks over to me. "What are you doing down here? Did you get trapped, little Witch?" He gives me his demonic sexy grin. "Or have you been waiting for me to join your cage?" He raises his eyebrows suggestively and a feeling of both relief and sadness washes over me. Lukka has no idea what his brother has been up to.

"This is serious, Lukka," I say. "Konstantin is involved in something bad, *really* bad. He's creating some crazy new drugs! You have to get me out of here."

Lukka laughs again and leans his head against the bar. He blinks lazily.

"I know about the pills, little Witch. We tried one together, remember? Let's go back to bed."

I grab his hands through the bars, snapping him out of his tired daze. "Your brother did this, Lukka." I show him the marks on my neck. My lip starts to tremble and I swallow down the onset of tears. "He's developed something that not only means he can drink Witch blood, but he absorbs our powers, *my* powers. Konstantin hurt me, Lukka, and even Dimitri's in on it. They killed Ansel."

A shadow passes over Lukka's face, his features setting like stone.

"You're saying my brother fed on you?" He strokes the side of my neck and I can't help a tear from falling down my cheek. "And killed Ansel?"

He's still holding my hand, his cold fingers interlaced with mine. I squeeze them. "Please," I plead. "Get me out of here. Quietly. Dr. Vassily is inside the lab and he says he's going to kill me."

"No," Lukka says, shaking his head slowly. "Kostya makes *happy* drugs. He would never bite a Witch. He would never bite you. I don't understand."

"Your brother made that medicine over there," I whisper, pointing at the full syringe on the floor by his car. "It's derived from an antidote I had. It helps Vamps feed on Witches and absorb our powers."

Lukka makes a face, his fingers slipping from mine.

"Please!" I cry. "Take it, if you don't believe me. Take it and then feed on me. It will give you Verity powers and then you will know I'm not lying."

"You want me to inject myself with something from a parking lot floor?" he says.

I look at the lab door behind me. *We don't have time for this!* I lean forward and hold his face in my hands. All I see before me is the broken boy who lived in squalor and idolized his big brother. An orphan who never wanted to grow up. The only man who has never lied to me.

"Lukka," I say, staring into his milky eyes. "I know the world is a bad place, and I know you don't want to see it, but this is your chance to save so many people. Innocent Paras, humans, and children like the ones you already care for. Please, inject yourself and drink from me, and you will know that I'm not lying to you."

Lukka swallows, tattoos jumping at his throat, and gives a light nod before walking over to the car and taking the syringe. He's a Vampire, he knows there's nothing he can inject into his body that will kill him, but he still looks hesitant as he plunges the needle into his arm.

"Now what?"

I push my arm further through the bars, my eyes begging him to trust me.

"Bite me," I say under my breath. He stares at me for a long time and I nod. "Please," I mouth.

I can see the shift in his gaze. No Vampire can hear those words without being aroused. His fangs grow quickly, thick and white, and he looks down at my hand now cradled in his. Then gently he leans down and plunges his fangs into my wrist. I gasp at the sting, but it's not unpleasant. Unlike his brother's attack, Lukka's bite is gentle, hesitant, and just as quickly he pulls away. He's waiting to see what effect my blood has on him. He looks up, a light frown flashing on his forehead. Nothing. I haven't poisoned him.

"I told you," I say. "I can't kill you now."

He smiles. "Little Witch, I've wanted to taste your blood since the first moment I saw you. You taste like strawberries in winter."

My stomach spasms with images of the last three nights we've spent together, but I don't have time for flirting. *We* don't have time for flirting.

"Drink," I say, but he's already there, my wrist pressed against his eager lips, my blood dripping in scarlet rivulets down his chin and dripping on to his bare chest.

"I hate your lips on my skin," I say.

Lukka jumps up like he's been shot, covering his ears with his bloody hands.

"What was that?" he cries.

I smile. "A lie. Us Verity Witches hear a strange ping in our heads when someone lies. Now you can too."

His shock turns to a grin. "So, you *do* like my lips on your skin?" he says.

I roll my eyes. "You disgust me, Lukka. The last three days have been awful. And that thing you do with your tongue? I hate it."

He screws up his face as the three *pings* of a lie ringing through his head have him wincing in discomfort. "So unpleasant! Do lies feel like that every time?"

I nod. "Unless I'm telling the truth. Watch. You're the only one I trust in this country," I say.

He waits, his face falling slack as no *ping* resonates through his mind. His hand darts through the bars and he strokes my cheeks now wet with tears.

"Your brother hurt me," I say again. Lukka's jaw tenses. Silence. "He is creating pharmaceuticals to sell to other Vamps. Super blood he's been draining from his workers, *your* staff, by spiking their food. Pills to help Vampires walk in the sunlight. He killed Ansel, her boyfriend, hundreds of illegal immigrants. He's dangerous."

Lukka's fangs have detracted and his demonic grin has been replaced with the face of a boy who has never known love. He goes to say something when the door behind me slowly creaks open.

Lukka disappears in a blur.

Has he gone? Has he left me? I quell the mounting panic climbing up my chest.

"Shut the fuck up!" the doctor shouts, striding over to me. "Have you been drained to insanity that you're now sitting here talking to yourself?" He looks at my bloody wrist. "Are you trying to kill yourself before we do? Mr. Volkov should have finished you off while he was bleeding you dry, you dirty…"

The doctor doesn't have the chance to finish his sentence before the bars of the cage are ripped out and Lukka is holding him up against the wall by his throat. He slams the back of the scientist's head against the concrete.

"Have you been hurting my little Witch?" Lukka shouts in his face.

Dr. Vassily's head shakes violently from side to side.

"No! Of course not! I would never hurt her."

I can only imagine how loud those *pings* in Lukka's mind are, because they are loud in mine too. Lukka's fangs grow again and he tightens his grip on the doctor's throat.

"Have you been killing innocent humans to sell their blood and create drugs?"

"No," Dr. Vassily croaks.

And that is the last words he'll ever utter as Lukka dives at him and takes a lump out of his jugular, spitting the fatty mass of blood and tissue onto the floor. He lets go of him and the doctor's body falls to the ground, his head hanging on by nothing but his exposed spine. Lightning-fast he grabs the side table by the door and smashes it against the wall, driving the splintered wooden leg into the doctor's chest. I've never seen a Vamp get staked before. I expected him to explode messily, or turn to smoke, but instead Vassily just collapses. Slowly, like a human.

Lukka turns, and I recoil. He looks like a demon; his handsome face smeared red and his white designer trousers soaked in the doctor's blood.

"I'm glad I wore plastic shoes," he says, licking his lips.

I throw my arms around his neck covering myself in sticky gore, but I don't care - my clothes are already encrusted with my own dry blood. Lukka holds me tight and I realize it's not just relief he's feeling. He's upset about his brother - I proved that I wasn't lying about the doctor, therefore Lukka also knows everything I said about Konstantin is true. I place my hand on the back of his head and he holds me to him tighter.

"Thank you for believing me," I say.

"You're bad at lying. I already told you that."

I look down at the Doctor beneath my feet.

"Sorry you had to kill him," I say.

He shrugs. "Never liked him anyway. Besides, killing is easier the more you do it."

I feel the *ping* of his lie and I embrace him harder. Who would Lukka have been had Konstantin not kept so much from him, while using him as his own personal guard dog?

"We have to get you out of here," he says, his voice shaking a little. "I can only protect you so far."

I nod. "I need to fly back home. My passport is in my bag. I will get a taxi."

"No! I will take you, my car has tinted windows so I'll be fine. The keys are in the office." I go to stand by his car but he pulls me to him again. "You are coming with me. I'm not letting you out of my sight until you're safe. Let's go."

"But won't Dimitri be in the club? He's there day and night." I imagine him racing back to Konstantin as soon as he killed Ansel. *Piece of shit!*

Lukka steps back and strokes the hair out of my face, leaving a line of blood in its wake.

"You think that teddy bear scares me?"

CHAPTER TWENTY-EIGHT

It's strange to be back in the club during the day. All the shutters are down but the cleaners haven't yet been. The place is a mess. Glasses are scattered all over the tabletops and floor, and one solitary stiletto sits on the small podium stage. I recognize it, it belongs to Ansel. *Belonged*. I swallow down the guilt. I could have saved her if only I'd met up with her sooner instead of spending three days in bed with Lukka. It's my fault she's dead.

We walk past the bar and stage and head towards the door marked *No Entry*. Just as Lukka goes to tap in his code a gruff shout echoes from the other side of the club.

"Where are you taking her?"

Dimitri is bounding over to us, his huge paw-like hands clenched into fists. He's still wearing the baby blue Adidas tracksuit, the jacket zipped tightly over his barrel-like middle, but he's taken off his stupid hat. I notice a dark mark on his sleeve and realize with a start it's Ansel's blood. Images flash through my mind of the bear slicing through my friend's neck. My head begins to swim and I blink, doing my best to focus.

Lukka turns to Dimitri, pushing me behind him, and gives the bouncer a slick-red smile.

"Fuck off and go back to your cave," he says.

Dimitri's eyes are black and perfectly round, like two pebbles pushed into a snowman's face. "Konstantin says no one is allowed in his office, and that includes *you*," he barks at Lukka. Dimitri's copious gold chains clink together as he stands before Lukka. He rubs a hand over his buzz-cut, his neck as wide as his boxy head, and tips his chin up to signal us to leave. "Take the Witch back to her cage or I'll gut her like I did her friend."

The two of them stare at one another, white eyes boring into bear eyes. Neither of them moves, watching, waiting.

"I don't take orders from you," Lukka growls, then he flies at the bouncer, teeth bared and eyes flashing with white-hot anger.

He aims for the jugular, knocking Dimitri down and plunging his fangs into his neck. With a roar, Dimitri rears up and pulls the Vamp off him as if he weighs nothing.

The bouncer is already tall, but now it's like he's standing on tiptoes towering over Lukka. Slowly at first, then all at once, Dimitri rises taller and taller, his legs thickening and shoulders rounding. The bouncer's tracksuit fades and in its place is white fur stained yellow by Moscow's smog, thick and matted like piss-stained snow. Dimitri's hands have turned to giant paws, his palms black and padded, and nicotine-stained claws spring out like daggers and swipe at Lukka's chest.

The bouncer is a polar bear? A huge motherfucking polar!

I'd guessed Dimitri was a bear from the first time I'd met him. I thought he was your average woodland bear or something, I don't know, but nothing this huge. As he rises on his back legs he's nearly double my height and I let out a yelp and I duck behind a column. He swipes out again and snarls, making Lukka stagger back.

I watch as they stare at each other, the bear on his hind legs and the Vampire with his fangs out ready to pounce. In a blur, Lukka flies at him again, and with impossible speed jumps up at the bear's throat and digs his fangs into Dimitri's neck once more, this time ripping at his flesh. Dimitri's bear fur is thick and coarse, but it's quickly turning pink as blood oozes down his neck. Lukka jumps down and spits out a lump of flesh, like a Russian Mike Tyson, his face smeared with blood and thin white hairs sticking to his bloodied lips.

"Get back," he shouts out at me, putting out a protective arm as I step behind the column again.

Dimitri sways then falls to all fours with a thump. His head is lagging but his eyes are still piercingly black and fierce. Lukka looks like he's ready to strike again but then, with an almighty cry, the bouncer lunges at him. With the strength of ten men he knocks Lukka over until Dimitri is looming over him, one giant paw pinning down his chest, the other clawed paw raised and ready to disembowel. Lukka looks at me fleetingly and my chest constricts. He can't move. Lukka is trapped.

"I will kill you, Dimitri," he growls, but we both know the bear has won.

I look around for something to throw at Dimitri who's roaring up at the ceiling with such force I can feel it vibrating through me. I consider throwing a barstool at him, or a side table, but after my pathetic aiming efforts with the glass bottles and Lukka's car earlier, that's not a risk worth taking. Putting down the chair I glance over at the small stage beside me and pick up the abandoned stiletto.

This is a stupid fucking idea. But, to be fair, my best ideas normally are.

Giving a ferocious cry of my own I run at Dimitri. He has

his giant paw in the air, and just as he's about to swipe at Lukka I jump up and stab the stiletto heel into the Shifter's temple. It makes a sickening squelching sound as I drive it deep into the bear's head, right up until the platform sole of the shoe, pushing as hard as I can.

"This is from Ansel to you, you ice-capped piece of shit!" I scream as blood sprays over my hands and up my arm.

The bear stops, closes his eyes, Lukka stills beneath him. Then, with a soft whine, Dimitri crashes down to the floor.

All is silent as I stand there, my arms warm and sticky with blood, staring down at a giant polar bear with a stripper's shoe sticking out of his head beside an injured Vamp who I've spent the last three nights having wild sex with.

What even is my life?

"You're OK," Lukka confirms, seeming more worried about me than he is about himself. He jumps to his feet and pulls me towards him with both hands on my behind. He kisses my neck, smearing Dimitri's blood all over my collarbone. After a minute my trembling body and shaky breaths return to normal but he continues to hold me. "You saved my life. That makes you my hero, little Witch," he whispers in my ear.

"Come on," I say, taking his hand. He's shaking too, but you wouldn't know it by the red-smeared smile he's giving me. "Let's get out of here before your brother finds us."

"Too late," comes Konstantin's voice behind us. "I'm already here."

CHAPTER TWENTY-NINE

I notice right away that Konstantin has changed his clothes since our last meeting in the cage. He's wearing a three-piece suit made of navy wool, complete with a faint print stripe and polished leather shoes. Unlike his brother, he clearly hasn't been sleeping while I suffered alone in my cell.

He looks down at the bouncer on the floor. Dimitri has remained in animal form. I wonder how Konstantin will explain to the cleaners what a huge polar bear is doing lying in the middle of a strip club with a sparkly stiletto sticking out of his head.

Ansel got her own back on the beast after all. I want to smile, but I don't.

"I'm surprised to see you here, little brother," Konstantin says, taking in the blood on his chest and clothes. Lukka's holding my hand, and it gives me a small thrill that Konstantin isn't liking it. "You don't normally get involved in my business ventures," he says.

"Saskia isn't a business venture," Lukka hisses. "She's a

person. You had her in a cage, Kostya, and you hurt her. I'm getting my car keys and I'm getting her out of here."

"You know she's a reporter, right?" Konstantin says. "She works for The Blood Web Chronicle."

Lukka isn't hearing any pings, and the pain in his eyes makes my stomach contract. He looks away from me and lets go of my hand.

"Release her go, brother," he says to Konstantin again.

"I can't. If I do then the first thing she'll do is expose what we've done."

"What *you've* done!"

Konstantin rounds upon his brother, his face inches from his.

"Everything I've ever done, I've done for *you*." He says it so quietly goosebumps rise all over my flesh. "Your expensive clothes, those ridiculous cars you drive, our *mansion* – who pays for that? I looked after you as a child and I'm still looking after you now. I give you everything, Lukka. I make you happy. I'm on the cusp of a great breakthrough, a chance for us to return to who we once were. Everything you love you will be able to do in the sunlight, you will have infinite power, and all for the sake of a feeble few who don't matter to anyone...like this one."

In a blur, Konstantin's hand shoots out and grabs me around the throat.

"Let her go!" Lukka shouts as his brother drags me over to one of the small stages and throws me against the dance pole. My head cracks against the metal and I stumble, landing on my backside. He produces some extra-long zip ties from his suit pocket and binds my wrists together around the pole.

"Who the fuck carries zip ties in their pocket?" I say, trying to keep the fear out of my voice.

"The kind of Vampire who needs to keep girls like you under control. I told you, we're not finished yet!"

"Look at what your brother is, Lukka," I shout. "He's *dangerous*. He killed your mother with his bare hands because he can't control himself."

Konstantin turns to Lukka, his face filled with derision like everything I say is exhausting.

"Brother," he says, walking over to Lukka with confident strides. "Of course, I didn't kill our mother. Saskia is deranged. I would never lie to you."

I hear a number of *pings* and I know Lukka can hear them too. Konstantin is lying and he's breaking his brother's heart right in front of me.

Slowly, eyes wide in horror, Lukka shakes his head from side to side and starts walking away. When he reaches the wall, he slides down it and lands in a heap, knees raised and head in his hands. Then he starts to rock.

Konstantin walks over to him and lays a hand on his shoulder.

"Go home, Lukka. I'll deal with the Witch. I won't hurt her. Go and have some champagne, play some music, relax. Everything is going to be fine."

My head rings with Konstantin's lies, and Lukka puts his hands over his ears making himself smaller and smaller on the ground, rocking and mumbling something under his breath.

"I thought you were good," he keeps saying. "I thought you were good."

When he looks up his face is streaked with tears.

"You said our mother killed herself!" he screams. "You said it was because of what *I* had done. That it was *my* fault we'd been turned, and she'd killed herself because I was an uncontrollable Vampire and she was scared of me." He's shaking on the ground, his body curled up tight as I imagine he sat all those years as a neglected child.

"You shouldn't mourn her," Konstantin says, his voice void of any emotion. "She was a bad person and she killed herself. So what? I'm the only one who has ever cared about you."

"Stop lying!" Lukka screams. "You killed her because she always stood in the way of your dreams. Because in having me she gave you something bigger to worry about than the ballet. But she was our *mother*, Kostya! A weak human who needed our help, but instead you murdered her. Because it made life easier for *you*! Just like the way you have manipulated Saskia."

I sit up straighter at the sound of my name. The binds on my wrists are stinging, but the more I struggle the more they cut into my skin.

Konstantin leans into his brother, cradling his head. He's speaking so softly I can hardly hear him.

"I promise to make all your pain go away," he says. "My new pills will give us the power we deserve. You are all I care about, little brother. You are safe."

No, he's not. Konstantin's lies are getting louder and louder and with every word he utters Lukka's face twists in agony. Tears are streaming down his face, turning his cheeks pink from the blood he's soaked in. He looks over at me and my chest feels like it's been stabbed a thousand times. He knows I can hear the truth too, and it's killing him.

"You will let Saskia live, won't you?" Lukka says quietly.

Konstantin's hands are still cupped around his brother's face. "Of course," he lies. "She's worthless anyway. I've heard her sister is the one I should *really* be working with. Power like hers is worth harvesting. Maybe I will track her down."

My head shoots up. What the fuck does he know about my sister? Does he know where she is?

"Tell me where Mikayla is!" I shout, trying to stand but only making the plastic dig deeper into my wrists. "Don't hurt my sister, please. Just tell me where she is."

Konstantin laughs, looking over at me like I'm something on the bottom of his Italian brogues.

"See, little brother? Sibling love is a hard bind to break. Go home and relax. Let me take care of this mess."

Lukka slowly looks up from his crumpled position on the floor. His lips are turned down at the edges like a sad clown.

"Except this isn't your mess," Lukka says. His skin is as pale as his eyes and his face glistens with tears. "*I* did this. This is all *my* fault. If you hadn't come looking for me all those years ago you wouldn't have been turned as well. You'd have stayed a famous dancer, people wouldn't have died and my mistakes would have remained my own. Because of me, we are both monsters."

Konstantin shakes his head. "We aren't monsters, Lukka. We are gods."

"We are fools."

Konstantin's grip on his brother's face tightens. "Listen to me, Lukka. I will always protect you. I love you."

I close my eyes. The ringing of that lie is the loudest yet.

Lukka's face sets hard, his pale eyes as empty and cold as a snow drift. "No, Kostya," he replies quietly. "You love no one. The merciless cannot love."

Suddenly Konstantin lets out a deafening scream – a sound I never imagined leaving his lips. His cry is followed by choking and a gurgling sound. Konstantin's back is to me and from where I'm standing all I can see is his body slumped forward over his brother. I can't see what's happening. But I *can* see Lukka's face and the expression on it chills me to the bone. His jaw is clenched, his face is still, and his eyes are glowing.

I jump as something makes a cracking sound followed by the tear of splitting fabric. Then Lukka's hand explodes out the back of his brother's suit.

And clenched in his fist, bloody and pulsating, is Konstantin's heart.

CHAPTER THIRTY

It's been snowing all day. And even though it's twilight now, the evening is lit up like day by the glare of everything coated white. After Konstantin's death the city gained inches of snow, turning everything from smog-kissed to silver. I've never seen the Volkov mansion look so beautiful. So calm. So empty.

Konstantin's elaborate funeral was two days after Lukka killed him, and was attended by every Paranormal of note in Moscow's underworld. Although Lukka kept the news of his death away from the human press, refusing to give his brother the adoration and ballet martyrdom he so craved.

The Para community believed Lukka when he blamed the death on Rada, whom he had framed and killed the next day. The entire Volkov fortune passed seamlessly to Lukka, who took the entire process in his stride. Perhaps he inherited some of his brother's control after all.

Lukka made a convincing mourner as he stood beside Konstantin's body, adorned with one thousand red roses, flawless in the Italian suit that perfectly disguised his lack of a heart.

Lukka and I spent every day since making love and playing in the snow, erasing our dark memories with pleasure.

But the silver snow is a lie, neither of us can forget what happened. I can't wait to leave this country – yet I'm not looking forward to saying goodbye. I've bought as much extra time from Jackson as I could, but his patience is wearing thin.

Lukka loads my suitcase into the trunk of a car I've never seen before. This one is gold.

"I could have gone to the airport by myself," I say to him. "I could have left hours ago when it was still day and not bothered you."

He turns to me, his ghostly eyes full of warmth.

"No. I told you, little Witch. I will stay by your side until I know you are safe."

I don't know how Lukka cleaned up the Black Rabbit, or killed Rada, or cleared up his tracks. What became of the pills? I presume he closed the club and has people to clear up the dead bodies he leaves behind. I don't even know what he did with his brother's pulsating heart after he ripped it out of his body. I suppress a shudder. I don't want to know.

"Will you be OK?" I ask him as I settle into the passenger's seat of his car.

He gives me a smile, his gold-capped teeth glinting the same shade as the interior of his hideous ride.

"You're asking if *I'll* be OK?"

I nod and he gives me a light peck on the cheek.

"What's that for?" I ask.

"For caring."

I swallow down the peach stone of a lump in my throat and stare out of the window so Lukka won't see my eyes fill with tears. I don't think he will be OK. I can't imagine what he will do without his brother. Can Vampires drink themselves to death? Can Vampires kill themselves?

We pull up outside the departures lounge of the airport.

"I don't think you're allowed to stop here," I say.

Lukka's lips twitch in amusement. All this time together and I'll never get used to how no law ever applies to him.

"Your plane leaves in two hours," he says.

I nod but stay in my seat, my head flopping back on to the headrest as I let out a deep sigh.

"What if I stay?" I say eventually.

Lukka snorts. More sad than amused. I never thought I'd find myself begging to stay with a Volkov brother. But as horrific as the last few weeks have been, my time with Lukka has also been some of the best moments I can remember since Mikayla's disappearance.

"My world is too dark for you, little Witch," he says.

He hasn't mentioned his brother's name since he murdered him. I wonder if he ever will.

"Just a little longer," I say. "I can keep you company until you're OK."

"I will never be OK," he says. "But I will dance and party and drink and fuck all the same."

He places a hand on the side of my face and the warmth of a solitary tear scalds my cold cheek. "And someday I will see you again."

I wait for the lie, it doesn't come. It never does with him. Lukka leans forward and slowly licks my tears away.

I laugh. His eyes bore into mine and I can't read what he's feeling.

"You don't belong in my world, little Witch," he says. "You're fire. I'm ice."

I take a shaky breath and turn for the door handle. Lukka

spins me by my shoulder, grasps my face with both hands and kisses me. He puts everything into that kiss. I can feel it pouring out of him. Regret, passion, fear and determination. And I kiss him back. Wordlessly, I let him know he matters, he's strong, and although I lied to him at first, he's seen more of the real me than anyone has for a very long time.

And in that moment, I know Lukka Volkov will be just fine.

He lets go of me so suddenly I fall back against the car window.

"Leave," he growls. "Write your story."

We step out of the car together and he hands me my suitcase. I turn to go but he pulls me back, pushing something into my hand.

"Thank you," he whispers.

I unfurl my fist. It's Ansel's Black Rabbit pendant, mine is already in my bag. I try and speak but no words come out. I close my eyes as I think of my friend – a girl who deserved better. All Ansel had tried to do was give her family a chance at living. She'd worked hard, so had her brother and boyfriend, and now two of them were dead and countless others. Fodder. Pawns. Nothing but cheap labor and free blood for the rich and powerful.

"Will you look after Ansel's brother?" I ask. "He has nothing now. He's lost everything."

Lukka nods and I believe him. He kisses my forehead lightly and I close my eyes. When I open them again Lukka has gone, and all that's left is the cold touch of his lips on my skin and the throaty rumble of his ridiculous car swallowed by the Russian night.

●

It's cold on the plane, but I'm used to the cold now. I pull my laptop out of my bag and take a deep breath. I have a long flight home, and I no longer sleep at night. I start to write.

Have you ever wondered what Vampires miss most? Their humanity? The loved ones they lost to time and age? The people they used to be?

Ballet dancer Konstantin Volkov (34) missed the sun. And he was willing to pay a hefty price to get it back. Even if that price was the blood of hundreds of Vampires and hundreds of humans...

I don't stop typing until I'm finished and proud of what I see on the page

For Lukka's benefit I've slightly tweaked the article and let Rada take the fall for Konstantin's death. For the benefit of humanity and all Witches I leave out Konstantin's ambitions with the Witch blood antidote and the scope of his developments. No one needs to know how close the sun pills were to being a reality lest a bunch of copycats emerge from their coffins and try their hand at big pharma. So, I paint his projects as being doomed from the start.

EPILOGUE

It's mid-March and I'm dressed for summer. After weeks in Moscow, an overcast spring day in New York feels like mid-August. The subway is crazy, as usual, but the bustle of people is somehow comforting. I don't want to see snow or another concrete block for the rest of my life.

Jackson called me into the office this morning and, like the good girl I am, I got out of my stale pajamas and threw on some make-up. I thought about getting a cab, but the truth is I want to be around people. I've been on my own for weeks now and it's not helping my mental state.

I squeeze on to the carriage and give a mom and her kid a tight smile as I shuffle past them. I normally hate packed trains, but this makes me feel safe. Because right now not a lot does. Every time I close my eyes all I see is Ansel's throat being torn open and Konstantin's beating heart in the hand of his brother.

It's been over a month since I got back from Moscow. Jackson said I wasn't to come into the office until all the fuss had died down – just in case people worked out it was me who wrote it and I was followed back to headquarters. The story broke three weeks ago, and I've had no contact with the outside world in all that time except for Jackson's updates. Apparently, Lukka has been very co-operative and assured my boss he'd dealt with all loose ends. Whatever that means. More dead Vamps? No more rivals? A destroyed lab? I hope so.

I get off at my train stop. I'm early. I can't believe, after all this time, that in just a few minutes I'm going to be back in front of Jackson finding out how I did. A few months ago, I was close to getting fired. My boss had told me this story would make or break me. Little did I know just how much it was going to *really* break me.

My phone vibrates in my pocket and I take it out. I never gave Lukka my real cell number, yet every time I get a message my stomach flips thinking it will be him. It never is. He was right about fire and ice not mixing, he belongs in my past. I glance at my phone. It's my mother. Of course, it is.

Why won't you pick up the phone? I need you in Barcelona. The MA is in trouble and you need to be here.

I sigh. Is she for real? No *hello, how are you*? Just a list of commands. We haven't spoken in a long time, not since Mikayla went missing in LA eighteen months ago. Sometimes Mom sends a cursory text, sometimes I ask her if she's any closer to tracking down my sister, but we generally keep it simple and formal. She's been calling me for the last two days and I've ignored her, deciding if it's that important or about Mikayla she'll text. And *this* is her big emergency - a summons to the Mage Association headquarters? I don't think so.

I head for the train station exit, lost in an aggressive internal monologue with my mom along the lines of *'why should I do you a favor when you do nothing for me?'*, and as I pull my rail ticket out of my pocket I stop. And blink. It can't be. On the other side of the train platform is Mikayla. My sister is on the other side of the platform!

I haven't been sleeping well and the work therapist I spoke to on the phone told me hallucinations can be part of PTSD. I look again but she's still there, her hair long and wavy over her shoulders, staring at me. She's wearing that felt hat I always hated. The one with the green trim.

"Mikayla," I scream.

I don't care who's looking at me, I need to get to her. But she doesn't reply or wave, she just stands there smiling, like she's been waiting for me forever.

I run along the platform towards the exit so I can reach the other side, so I can get to my sister, but then a train shoots by at full speed. I keep my eyes trained on here through the blur of the train windows rushing by, but it's impossible.

As soon as the train has gone, so has Mikayla.

●

"How are you feeling?" Jackson asks me. He's been doing that a lot lately, asking about my feelings in every email he sends me. It's not like him.

My hands are still shaking from the vision I saw on the subway, from running around for another fifteen minutes screaming out her name.

I place my trembling hands on my lap. My boss doesn't need to know that along with insomnia, night terrors (on the rare occasions when I *can* sleep) and the odd panic attack, I can now add hallucinations to my list.

"I'm fine," I reply.

"You did well." He gives me that famous look of his - like

he's both proud and disappointed, and like I'm sitting in front of him naked. Which just makes me think of *him* naked. Which is not helping the jumble of moods I'm dealing with right now.

"Your article was a great success. It's had a record-breaking number of hits," he says in his deep English accent.

"I'm glad my near-death experience has increased your advertising revenue," I hit back.

He laughs and I realize how much I've missed the jerk.

"Saskia, I wouldn't have sent you to Moscow had I known how rough things were going to get." He leans forward, touching the tips of his fingers together into a spire. His eyes flash yellow and I'm reminded that he's a Shifter like Dimitri. Except when I look at Jackson all I see is sleek panther muscles. He'd never hurt me.

"I can look after myself," I say.

"You certainly can. A stiletto? Did I read that correctly?" He looks down at my boots and makes a face. "Glad to see you're wearing flats today."

I can always rely on him to say the unsayable. There's no such thing as 'too soon' when it comes to Jackson and inappropriate jokes.

"Is Lukka OK?" I ask.

Jackson nods.

"You did the right thing," he says. "Mr. Volkov gave a statement. He got a team in to investigate how far Konstantin had got with the drugs. You know, had you infiltrated the lab one week later the daylight-protection drugs would have been available to Vampires all around the world. You've saved a lot of lives, Saskia."

"Not enough," I reply, thinking of Ansel and her boyfriend.

"For someone who was asked to just write a story, you

did well. Unfortunately, your death toll is rising, but you got the scoop."

I know he's joking, but he's right. Merpeople, Shifters, Vamps. Who else am I going to have to blow up or kill just to get to the bottom of a story? Then I think of Mikayla and what Konstantin said. He had heard of her. I saw her on the subway. She's out there somewhere!

My investigations take me to the darkest places in this shitty Paranormal sub-world of ours, but I know that's where I'll find my sister. It's why I need this job and why I'll never give up my search.

"I have a new job for you," he says. "If you're ready."

I nod and wait. Silence.

"You look worried," I say, looking at the lines forming on Jackson's forehead. "Tell me my next assignment is Fae tax evasion in New Jersey, or a missing Shifter kitten in Boston. I could do with an easy mission this time."

"You're not going to like it. It's a Witch one."

"No."

"You're the perfect person to get in there and check it out."

I sigh and lean back in my chair. He's not going to stop until I listen.

"Aren't there some Gnomes in the Maldives that would make a great story, or Nymphs in Bora Bora. Send me there."

He has the decency to smile at my joke. I'm not that lucky, Paras rarely settle in calm exotic locations.

"There's been some upheaval in the Gothic Quarter of Barcelona. An unknown sigil has appeared and there are rumors that the head of the MA has gone missing."

"Maribel?" I exclaim. Is that the 'trouble' my mom was referring to?

"You know her?" Jackson asks. "Of course, you know her, she must be friends with your mother."

I nod. "My mom has been trying to call me for the last couple of days, wants me to go out to her. She sounds worried."

Jackson leans back in his chair and gives a rare wide grin.

"No." I say. This shit has Catalan Bruixas written all over it. They love a bit of anarchy. "Why me? Send someone else."

"Your mother has asked you to go out anyway. The Mage Association won't suspect you. That way you can get to the bottom of the strange sigils and Maribel's disappearance and see if they are linked. Plus, you'll make your mother happy."

"I don't want to make my mother happy," I say, like a premenstrual petulant teen.

My mom has no idea I'm a reporter, so this could easily work, but the only thing worse than stepping foot anywhere near the MA is having to pretend to my mother that I actually want to see her and spend time with her. She still blames me for Mikayla's disappearance. I also heard she has a new lover – and I'm so not up for playing happy families.

"Don't make me call my mom," I beg Jackson.

"No need. You'll be seeing her face-to-face soon enough. You leave on Monday."

"What? But today's Friday!"

"*Nuquam vero.*"

The truth never waits - a slight deviation of The Chronicle's Latin slogan, *Veritas Nuquam Perit* - the truth never perishes.

"You know when Para chicks on Paramour say they're looking for a Latin lover? They don't mean a Latin speaking Shifter, right? In case you think you're impressing anyone."

He contemplates me, his teeth tugging at his bottom lip.

"So much sass," he says. "Yet so little work ethic."

"Fine, I'll take the assignment." I flick him the finger on my way out, accompanied by a wink. "But I want a promotion. Adios much*gato*!"

I giggle inwardly at my Spanish take on *bye bye pussy,* then speed up so I get the last word, but I fail when I hear his thundering voice trail behind me.

"*Hasta luego*, Witchling!"

ACKNOWLEDGMENTS

Oooof it's been a year!

This book is one-part quarantine, one-part deep female friendship, and one-part reader support. We both wanted to sit down and write something for fun - something R-rated, funny, and sexy, and we couldn't have picked a better year to do so. Thank you to the Blood Web Chronicles for serving as our refuge in these weird, messed up times. Reader, we hope Saskia's story gives you some much-needed escapism too.

It's a challenge dedicating a sexy book to someone, you don't want your aunt to feel like she helped you pen your wild sex scenes, but still, this book wouldn't exist without the help and support of a number of people. A deep thank you to author Anna Day for being an early reader and champion of our work. Thank you to wildly supportive and nourishing Facebook groups like 20BooksTo50K, MWHITL, and Writer's Café (special hugs to Emma and Wendy), as well as Jennie at Collab Writers who has supported us from the start – Hollywood, we're coming! Thank you to Jenn Faughnan for being so generous with your time and teaching Jacqueline Photoshop so that we could have such beautiful covers.

Thank you to our loyal and amazing street team the Verity Knights – especially beta reader extraordinaire Claire Knight and the super supportive Rachel Goodson-Hill. Thank you to the Sitting Room, and its fearless leader MMT for the world-class education on sex-positivity.

To our husbands Pete and David, thanks for being good sports during endless conversations about paranormal sex and what goes where (sorry, it's not going to end anytime soon!). Thank you to Jacqueline's ancestral home Moscow for inspiration on our first stop in the Blood Web journey. Thank you to Andrey for your insights into the Moscow strip club world, and to our immigrant parents for making it possible for us to have lived in so many places so we've been able to describe them with a degree of authenticity. And a cuddly thanks to our pets Laika, Bruce, and Buttercup for being our cozy fluffy apocalypse serotonin boosters. But the biggest thank you goes to one other - for the long non-writing conversations, patience, hard work and phone therapy sessions. Because sisterhood is as vital to humans as it is to our Witches - especially in hard times. Here's to many many more Blood Web adventures!

ALSO BY CAEDIS KNIGHT

Want to find out how Saskia's story began?
Discover the *Blood Web Chronicles* prequel novella
SIRENS OF LOS ANGELES.
Out now on Amazon!

VERITY KNIGHTS

Want to play an active role in shaping the *Blood Web Chronicles* and Saskia's story?

Visit the Caedis Knight website and apply to be a part of the elite *Blood Web Chronicles* street team- the Verity Knights now!

veritas numquam perit

ABOUT THE AUTHORS

Caedis Knight is the pen name of two established fantasy authors, Jacqueline Silvester and N J Simmonds. Silvester began her career in screenwriting and lived all over the world before going on to pen her highly successful YA series *Wunderkids*. Spanish Londoner Simmonds' background was originally in marketing before writing her fantasy series *The Indigo Chronicles*, along with various Manga stories and writing collaborations. Together they created *Blood Web Chronicles* - their first paranormal romance series set in Europe. Great friends and avid travellers, you can find them whizzing between one another's homes in Germany and the Netherlands, or having Zoom calls to excitedly plot Saskia's next humorous sexy adventure.

ABOUT THE AUTHORS

Did you enjoy the book? Say hi to Caedis and let her and your friends know!
Find Caedis on Facebook, Twitter and Instagram!

Printed in Great Britain
by Amazon